"I have a feeling my life will become quite dull once you go out of it."

She looked at him as openly and invitingly as she could, but he only turned quite cold again.

"I don't want to see that dress on you again."

Try as she might, Justi could not twist his statement to mean that he wanted to see her out of it. "Why ever not? It is not low cut."

"It reveals your arms too much."

"I did have a few qualms about that, but the armbands disguise my muscles."

"It's the fabric," he complained. "I can see every move you make in it."

"That is true of half the women in the room. Why are you so conscious of it with me?"

"Because I am responsible for you," Richard blustered.

"You do want to get rid of me?" Justi countered.

"Yes— No! Not like this . . . !"

Dear Reader,

June's *Unicorn Bride,* by Claire Delacroix, is truly a big book. This sweeping medieval tale tells the story of Lady Alienor, a young woman betrothed to a man veiled in secrets and legends.

Popular author Margaret Moore brings us the latest installment in her Warrior series, *A Warrior's Way.* Awarded an estate for his valor, knight Hu Morgan is doubly pleased to acquire a wealthy wife in the bargain. However, the lady in question is decidedly less enthused about the match.

Jonathan Harris and Polly O'Neil make an unusual pair of lovers in *Timeless,* by Western author DeLoras Scott. Jonathan has been given a second chance in life and love, thanks to Miss Polly, but she soon begins to wonder exactly who—or *what*—he really is.

Laurel Ames creates another romp set in the Regency era in *Homeplace.* Masquerading as a boy in order to keep her inheritance, Justine Mallory finds herself in trouble when her handsome guardian decides to make a man out of her.

And keep an eye out for the *Promised Brides* Historical short-story collection, with authors Mary Jo Putney, Kristin James and Julie Tetel.

Sincerely,

Tracy Farrell
Senior Editor

Please address questions and book requests to:
Harlequin Reader Service
U.S.: 3010 Walden Ave., P.O. Box 1325, Buffalo, NY 14269
Canadian: P.O. Box 609, Fort Erie, Ont. L2A 5X3

LAUREL AMES

Homeplace

Harlequin Books

TORONTO • NEW YORK • LONDON
AMSTERDAM • PARIS • SYDNEY • HAMBURG
STOCKHOLM • ATHENS • TOKYO • MILAN
MADRID • WARSAW • BUDAPEST • AUCKLAND

ISBN 0-373-28826-3

HOMEPLACE

Books by Laurel Ames

Harlequin Historicals

Teller of Tales #163
Castaway #197
Homeplace #226

LAUREL AMES

Although Laurel Ames likes to write stories set in the early nineteenth century, she writes from personal experience. She and her husband live on a farm, complete with five horses, a long spring house, a carriage house and a smokehouse made of bricks kilned on the farm. Of her characters, Laurel says, "With the exception of the horses, my characters, both male and female, good and evil, all are me and no one else."

Chapter One

Near Stowmarket, England
April 1809

The thin, boyish figure looked small on such a big black horse. The girl, dressed in leather breeches, top boots and a nankeen jacket, spoke softly to her mount and patted his neck. She and Bluedevil had been stepping along the trail through the oaks with as little noise as a deer might make. They surprised two owls courting on a limb. Justi's laughter echoed under the canopy of oak leaves as she drew disapproving stares from the birds before they parted and flew heavily off through the trees.

Justi had been running some errands in Brinley and had waited for the mail before coming home the back way past Squire Coates's lands. She seldom missed a chance to pass through her oak grove. It was a magical place to her. Even on the hottest day of summer it seemed but early morning under the shelter of the giant trees with their heavy cover of leaves.

She halted her horse, slid off and sat on a fallen trunk to open her mail. There was only one letter, enclosed in a package from a London printer. This time he wanted a novel translated from the French. She leafed through the book and thought it would not present much of a challenge. Even though the work consumed all her free time, she considered it easy money and was sure she would need it one day.

Bluedevil shook his bridle impatiently, since he found little grass to occupy him among the deep ferns in this part of the wood. Justi put the book away and stood on the dead log to remount. She rode Bluedevil out of the sanctuary of the oaks and looked down over the holding of Homeplace, seat of the earls of Mallory for over two hundred years. The stream she splashed across with her horse ran the length of the property, through the sheep pastures and past the sheep barns in the center to collect in a watering pond not far from the ivy-encrusted stone house. Beyond that the barns and paddocks of the stud farm were just visible through the trees.

Justi eased Bluedevil into a rocking canter through the last fields before home. There was only one gate in their way, and it was much too fine a spring day to stop and open it. She gripped with her thigh muscles as he jumped to clear the fence with easy grace. Bluedevil loved to jump as much as she did. The rhythmic thud of his hooves on firm ground, the way she rocked to match each of his smooth strides, made it all worthwhile—the great deception, the years of lying to hang on to Homeplace. Some day she might take one jump too many and end up with a broken leg. The thought that an accident might, at any time, reveal that she was a girl and not the true heir did not frighten her.

Born Justine Mallory, she had been christened Justin because her mother and nurse were too frightened of old Basil Mallory to break the news to him that the child born posthumously to his only son was a female.

"It's a son, m'lord," was what Nurse reported nervously to the anxious old man propped up in bed with his medicines and warm wine at hand. He had threatened to turn the young widow out of the house if the baby was not a boy. Initially Lady Miriam eased her qualms about Nurse's extraordinary lie with the knowledge that Basil Mallory was dying. Thinking he had a male heir would let him go peacefully. She didn't know him well enough to realize he had been dying off and on for ten years.

So it was a secret between Nurse and Miriam. No one else was allowed to attend to the child, and its first years were spent in happy ignorance of its confused status. Since Justi was a sturdy child who never required the attentions of a doctor, the deception was not discovered.

As the old earl teetered through his seventies between deathbed dramas and rollicking good health during the hunting season, Miriam's dread grew. The earl's discovery of the truth might carry him off with a fatal heart attack. She decided that was too much to hope for, and she placed no faith on his liking the child well enough not to turn them all out. Miriam might have confessed her extraordinary lie had it not been for Nurse.

Ever since Justi could remember, Nurse had bullied both of them into doing what she considered in their own best interests, and hers. She had pooh-poohed Miriam's fears and objections and instructed Justi in how to act her part. Justi thought it was a wonderful game. It was not until Justi was ten that her grandfather liberated her from the schoolroom to teach her to ride. In time she ceased to fear him as her mother did. She and the old man were constant companions, and Justi obeyed him now rather than Nurse, with whom he did not get along. Of course Lord Mallory did not get along with anyone.

Justi seldom dwelled on her predicament. She had accustomed herself to living hour by hour and to enjoying every ride, every stolen moment. Injuries from falls she carried home and nursed privately with a stoicism born of necessity. Even from the two who knew her secret she kept her hurts so as not to worry them.

She made herself bring Bluedevil to a trot as she came into the stable yard in case Mother was watching for her. But no one appeared at the corner window nestled in the ivy, which slowly consumed the old stone house. Justi's bedroom, too, was at the back of the house overlooking the stable and gardens, with a distant view of the woods. Grandfather preferred the front view of the drive down to the road.

"Better walk him a bit, Jim," she said to the stable lad with her tight-lipped smile. She wore her brown hair long, more for her mother's sake than anything, and tied in an untidy queue at the back. It often fell across her forehead in a charmingly boyish way that made her look younger than her sixteen years. It accentuated a squarish jaw and straight nose. Her straight dark eyebrows, when furrowed in thought over gray blue eyes, made her look like a lad who took himself much too seriously.

Justi had drilled herself not to laugh. Anything but a rueful smile revealed two impish dimples. And in her opinion a man, even a young one, should not have dimples. She certainly moved like a boy, taking the back stairs two at a time and bursting into her mother's bedroom unannounced.

"Justi, must you always clump around like that? It would not hurt for you to be quieter, if you can't be any more graceful."

"It might, in my case. Remember, I can't afford to look foppish." She looked around at Nurse, who chuckled as she sat knitting. "Everything depends on me never looking in any way feminine," Justi said in the rich low voice she cultivated.

The frail blonde who had once been such a beauty rose and brushed back her child's dark brown hair. "Where will this all end? We must have been mad. He is sure to find out now with you growing up."

"Not if I stay thin like you." Justi pulled away to go and lounge on the window seat looking out over the rose garden.

"Let the boy alone," Nurse said without looking up from her knitting.

Justi used to laugh when Nurse said this. The joke had ceased to be funny.

Well into her seventieth year, Nurse, who had no other name to Justi, had cared for Miriam as a child. Now she was a fixture at Homeplace, always to be found in some odd corner knitting when she was not interfering in the ancient kitchen.

Justi stared at the moving fingers with fascination. Justi had begun to wonder if reality was slipping away from the old woman, if she was not serious when she called her a boy. That is certainly what she had wished Justi to be all these years. It would have solved all their problems. Grandfather would have been happy, and "Justin" would have inherited Homeplace someday. Well, Grandfather was content, as much as he could be, and Justi would inherit, but only so long as no one discovered her secret. By rights the entailed part of the estate should pass to a distant cousin, Richard Mallory, from a branch of the family Grandfather hated.

Justi's imitation of a boy was so ingrained that even when alone with her mother and Nurse she did not drop the pose. She really only knew how to be a boy, and she felt sorry for women who had to ride sidesaddle and trip around in skirts that would not let them run without falling.

"He's rewriting his will," Miriam said ominously, interrupting her daughter's scrutiny of Nurse.

"Again? Every time he decides he's dying he sends for the lawyer and goes over that thing again. I think we are in a worse case than we were this time last year. We only sold two of last year's colts, and both wool and lamb prices have been down."

"Justi, how bad off are we?"

"Sorry, Mother, I didn't mean to worry you. It's nothing that can be mended by rearranging his will. If only I could use some of my money to put things right."

"How much have you got, dear?" Miriam turned from her dressing table expectantly.

"It's really our money. You helped me with the translations. After that last book of poetry, close on to four hundred pounds. Enough to keep us all for a little while if

Grandfather would ever turn us out. And then there's no reason we should not go on working for Meecham and Bates. I'm glad, now, you made me learn French, even though it wasn't much fun at the time."

"Oh, your lamentable education. You should have had a proper governess."

"Tutor, Mother, tutor, and I have nothing to complain of. You taught me how to read and that's the key to everything else. I do wish I understood accounts a little better, though."

"I was never good with numbers, but my watercolors were always much admired, and I was accounted to play the pianoforte very prettily." Justi's mother looked loveliest when reminiscing on her youth. The lines of worry seemed to relax, and the way she held her chin up was almost provocative. She had been a prisoner at Homeplace all of Justi's life.

"I suppose I do like to paint and play music, but they are not very useful skills for me, and Grandfather doesn't approve of either occupation."

"You must have some accomplishments in case you're ever found out. Else who would marry you? You aren't likely to have a dowry."

"I'd say being able to shoe a horse or deliver a lamb is an accomplishment. Besides, if I'm found out, there'll be such a scandal no one will dare marry me, ever."

"But dear, you sound almost like you don't ever wish to be married."

"I can't see that it would be much use to me. I'm pretty happy and I can do much as I please. Most of the married people I've seen don't look happy at all."

"Your father and I were happy."

"Yes, I'm sure you were the exception to the rule." Justi bent over her mother's shoulder to look at the two of them in the glass. "It's a good thing I'm not pretty like you. This never would have worked."

"Well, you are not ugly by any means. You just favor the Mallory side."

"Would you allow me to be handsome?" Justi teased, giving the mirror her sternest look.

"I would allow you make a very pretty boy," Miriam compromised.

"Pretty!" Justi said in disgust.

"What you do, you do well, if only it were a thing worth doing. I'm sorry, child, I let this happen. If only I had not been so weak."

"It wasn't your fault. It was Nurse who lied about me."

"I didn't tell him the truth when I found out."

"As sick as you were? I'm glad you didn't. I cannot picture myself as anything but what I am, though I had rather not be thought pretty. I shall have to work on my scowl more."

Justi's grimace made Miriam laugh.

"Come, we'd better go down for luncheon or we'll be late," Justi warned.

"Yes, it's terrible when he gets put out before a meal. I can't eat a thing."

For the first time it occurred to Justi that she was now the one who was running this rig. Left to her own devices, Miriam would have confessed the truth years before. Nurse had always dissuaded her. Now the old woman had no power over either of them. Justi was the one who kept the scheme going. She did know it was wrong and she did have a plan for them in case she was found out, but if it came to confessing the whole to her grandfather, she could not do it. She did love him in an odd sort of way and wanted him to be proud of her.

As they came down the front stairs, the butler was helping the lawyer on with his coat.

"Oh, Mr. Baird, aren't you staying for luncheon?" Miriam asked.

"No, no, I'm afraid I must get back to town. Always more work to do. Sir Mallory wants to appoint a guardian for Justin, so I must track down this cousin, Richard, the next in line for the title."

"But, surely, Mother is my guardian if I require one?"

"No, Sir Mallory was very explicit. He wants a man in charge of the estate until you come of age. Well, good day to you."

"Justi, he's never done anything like that before. You don't suppose he's really dying this time."

"I don't know, Mother. I'll try and find out tonight."

Justi's grandfather had been so ill this winter he had missed all the hunting, and Justi did not like to go without him. Homeplace had few visitors at any time but when it was known that the old earl was ailing, only Vicar Mayfair and Squire Coates dared brave his lacerating tongue. They had known him long enough to realize he didn't mean what he said when laid up with his numerous ailments.

The old earl usually slept in the afternoon and sent for Justi to keep him company in his room each evening. That this left Miriam alone with only Nurse for company in the loneliest part of the day did not even occur to him. That night he was being more than usually querulous over the cards, especially if Justi lost a hand to him on purpose. The chessboard went flying across the room after only a few moves, and even hearing about the new young crop of lambs did not please him.

Being ranted at and called an idiot no longer hurt like it used to, not since the revelation that it was the pain that was talking, not the grand old man who, in some sense, loved her. All the servants and Miriam came in for their share of abuse, but no one had as much patience with him as Justi.

"I took Bluedevil over that tall hedge by Squire's Lane today. I believe he's as surefooted as ever Old Blackwell was."

"Blackwell, now there was a horse for you. He didn't look like much, mind you, but God, could he jump! There was nothing he wouldn't try. I put him over a loaded hay wagon once that was blocking the crossroads."

"You never did!"

"Aye, and he didn't knock off more than half the load."
His chuckle and Justi's peal of laughter rang together as
they had for so many years. The further back her grandfather remembered, the more distance he seemed to be able to
put between himself and his present pain. Justi thrived on
the stories of famous hunts and narrow escapes. Her
grandfather took the most pride in the stories that revealed
what a mischievous scamp her father had been. If only he
could have broken his neck on the hunting field instead of
dying in bed of a fever. "I suppose that's what's in store for
me, too."

"You're just tired, Grandfather. You'll make a recover.
You always do. I shouldn't be keeping you up." She arranged his pillows, resisting, as always, the urge to kiss him
good-night, and she put out the candle.

Instead of feeling slightly better in the morning as he
usually did, her grandfather was worse. One look at him
sent Justi riding for the doctor. She found Dr. Trent at his
home in Brinley, and harnessed his cob for him while he
finished breakfast. "How bad is he?" Dr. Trent inquired as
he mounted into the gig.

"The worst I've ever seen him."

"He's seventy-five and he's lived a hard life. It's only a
matter of time. You do realize that, don't you?"

Justi's face told him of an unwillingness to accept that.
She paced the upper hall from front to back the whole time
the doctor was with her grandfather.

"Is he bad?" Miriam asked softly.

"Very bad, this time, I think. I should have realized it and
gone for the doctor last night. Mother, you don't really hate
him, do you?"

"No, of course not. At least, not for a long time, now. I
suppose I'm still a little afraid of him. But he has done right
by you, I'm sure. It's only that I don't know what we are to
do now. Do you see what I mean? When we had no choice

but to keep on pretending it was almost easy after a while.
But now what do we do?"

"I don't know. I can't think about that right now."

"He wants to see you, Justi." Dr. Trent looked grave.

It was obvious the doctor had given her grandfather
something for the pain. His eyes were no longer piercing, his
speech was thickened as it used to be when he'd been drinking.

"So you've been making a bit of a stir today, sir?" Justi
took hold of his hand and sat in the chair by the bed.

The old man's memory rambled through many years and
he told snatches of stories Justi remembered and many she
didn't. He rearranged facts to suit himself and finally
fetched up in the end talking to his long dead son, David.
"You'll take care of Homeplace? Keep it safe?"

"I will, I'll take care of it," Justi said. "I'll remember
everything you've taught me." The old man let go then of
the last things left to him, and Justi was sure he broke his
neck on some imaginary hunting field, over the only jump
Blackwell ever missed.

"There's one letter here you should read, sir." Richard
Mallory had just returned from an unpleasant task and was
in no mood to have another problem thrust upon him, even
by his hardworking secretary, Braden.

Braden was an apologetic, brown-haired young man.
Richard had never run counter to his advice on matters of
finance. Braden was also a workhorse when it came to doing the accounts and clearing away correspondence. Richard kept himself appraised of all doings but trusted to
Braden to carry out his orders unerringly.

"Can't I deal with this later?" Richard cast down his
driving gloves on the library table and reached for the offending document.

"It's from Baird and Weston in Stowmarket, sir, the so-
licitors for your great-uncle, Basil."

"Oh, no, he hasn't gone and died, has he?"

"I'm afraid so, sir."

Richard was dark-haired, a head taller than Braden, but was judged by many to be too severe to be called handsome. His straight brows and firm lower lip gave him a formidable, unbending appearance most of the time. He seldom smiled, and seldom had cause of late. His dark blue eyes were either bored and weary or alight with anger, never at Braden, but most often at his stepsister, Clara, or just lately over his half brother, Harry.

As he perused the extensive letter, his brows knit and his frown intensified. "Well, as threatened, he has left me sole guardian to his sixteen-year-old grandson, currently living with the boy's mother. I'll wager the estate is in a bad way, too."

"Will you be bringing them here to London or to Amberly?"

"Lord, that's all I need. I have enough on my hands trying to straighten out Harry's mess and Clara's affairs. Best that they stay where they are for now."

"You don't mean to go there, then?"

"Not at present. I've missed the funeral, at any rate," Richard said, folding the letter thoughtfully. "Write Baird to do as he thinks best until I can make the trip. Tell him I've been detained here by family matters."

"This Baird is of the opinion the boy should be shipped off to school," Braden informed him, "but his mother won't hear of it. Apparently, he's been taught at home by the local vicar."

"Bit old for school, I should think," mused Richard. "I suppose he could have a tutor to whip him into shape before we have to deal with him. When you write, ask what the boy's deficiencies are, then see if you can find someone willing to go to Stowmarket—not a scholar, strictly speaking. The boy probably knows nothing of the gentlemanly arts. Find someone who knows fencing and boxing and who might be able to supervise the boy. That's more to the point than Latin and Greek."

"Very good, sir. Baird will await your convenience on the settlement of the estate. Oh, and Harry has been waiting to see you."

"Send him in," Richard said with a fiendish grin. "This I'm going to enjoy. It cost me enough."

Harry entered the study quietly as Braden left, and remained standing by the door. Richard, who was leaning on the mantelpiece, continued to stare at the empty grate for some minutes after he was aware of his brother's presence.

Although he had come of age six months ago, there was still much of the boy about Harry. He had the dark good looks and height of their common father. It remained to be seen, Richard decided, if Harry had inherited that same unsteadiness of character. After eight years as his guardian, Richard expected some high-spirited pranks from Harry but was not prepared for serious trouble.

Harry nervously cleared his throat and began a prepared speech that Richard cut short with his piercing stare. "So, you want to know your fate, whether you will have to marry the fair Elsie or be sued for breach of promise? You realize they waited till you were no longer under my protection to entrap you?"

"Yes, I see that now."

"Too bad you couldn't see that then. Well, I have made Elsie's mother, if that's who she is, an offer of financial recompense, which she has accepted."

"I'll pay you back. I swear it."

"No! What with? That's an end to the matter. I do not want it spoken of again. Your mother has suffered enough between you and your sister, Clara."

Harry left silently, but before Richard had settled himself at his desk, his stepmother, Julia, sought him out.

"So, you didn't beat him."

"Five years ago I would have. Would you have preferred I did?"

"I'm sure Harry would have preferred it. You'll have to sell your hunting lodge, won't you?" Richard shrugged.

"That will be punishment enough for him. He does so enjoy the times you two spend together there." Although Julia was still attractive in a dignified way, it was obvious from the gray beginning to adorn her blond hair under its lace cap that she was some years Richard's senior, but only the unkindest of persons mistook her for his mother.

"Yes, I will have to part with it, but not entirely on Harry's account. If it's any comfort to him, our sister Clara is like to cost me far more than Harry."

"Richard, I'm so sorry. It's terrible that you are still taking care of all of us when you should be married with a family of your own."

"I don't think I've missed much." Her hurt look softened him. "Sorry, Julia, that was unkind."

"It's been five years since Evelyn died. You should think of yourself finally and find someone else."

"I was thinking of myself. That's the problem. She was too young to have a child, perhaps too delicate altogether. All I could think of was an heir. I shall never make that mistake again."

"You are still young. There is time for another family for you."

"Do you imagine I still grieve? I scarcely remember Evelyn's face." This was said with a certain grave bitterness that made Richard look older than his twenty-eight years. Thrown into his fortune at twenty, he had not lost his head as another young man might do. This was fortunate, since he became at that time responsible for Harry and his younger sister, Alicia, and, unfortunately, Clara, Julia's child by a previous marriage.

"Once we get everything settled here I want you to take Clara to Amberly and keep her there."

"I will if I have to tie her up. It's a good thing we didn't bring Alicia out this year. The scandal might have ruined her chances."

"And I'm not sure we'll be able to afford a season for her next year. Don't say anything to her yet. It all depends on how much of a mess our young cousin, the earl, is in."

"You have never been to this Homeplace, have you?" Julia asked.

"No, what's it like?"

"I remember your father took me there right after we were married. That was before your father and your great-uncle, Basil, had that falling out. Gloomy old house. It will be a wonder if it's still standing."

"Thanks for cheering me up, Julia."

The first Monday after the funeral Ned Thompson came up to the house at seven sharp for orders for the week. Justi was having early tea in the dining room, wandering about with her cup and saucer, looking out at the new spring day as one would look at a brand new baby lamb.

In a way she was surprised to see Ned. She had somehow assumed everything would be different without Grandfather. But, as Badger admitted Ned, hat in hand, she smiled her firm smile at him and realized that most likely everything would go on as before.

"Morning, young sir."

"Morning, Ned. Have a cup of tea?" The offer, as always, was respectfully declined. Justi thought of how often she had listened to Grandfather giving Ned instructions in this room and, when he was too ill to get up, how often she had conveyed Grandfather's orders to Ned here. Her mind raced. "I'm a bit on end here yet. What about cutting hay off the High Fields today?"

"I had a walk up there yesterday. It were a bit wet yet. May give it a try tomorrow or next day, though. First we need team shod."

"Masters been drinking again, has he?"

"I didn't check, but after he lamed Tess that last time, I don't hardly like to trust him with our horses."

"Let's tackle that right after lunch then. Any day work to be done?"

"There's plenty of wall to rebuild after the winter if there's money to pay for it."

"No worries there for a while. Now I can use my own money for what needs doing. Don't worry. I'll let you know if we are running short. What else?"

"Lads are busy with lambs, of course. Grandfather can take young lads to make a start coppicing hedgerows."

"Sounds fine."

Ned's visit impressed on Justi that she was now responsible for a much larger family than just her mother and the household servants. The tenant farmers mostly worked on shares, but extra work for which they were paid cash was an important part of their income and had a significant influence on the economy of Glenncross.

Justi's ride that day took her clear to Stowmarket to get money from the bank. She came back by way of Brinley to check for mail and make some purchases for the household. At each establishment she asked for an accounting and was amazed how friendly tradesmen became when an account they had given up on was paid in full. So, for a modest outlay, she received in return an enormous amount of goodwill.

There were few shops in Glenncross itself but on her way home Justi managed to call in at each of them to see if anything was owing.

Some folk began to talk that the old earl had left Justi a fortune after all, but those who knew better corrected them.

"The money's coming from somewhere," Caleb Swindon remarked at the Ram's Head. "He rode by yesterday asking what repairs were needed to my cottage, long overdue though they are. Next he's planning on adding a room to me son Tom's place."

"He told me he does a bit of translating for a printer in London," Ned informed the usual crowd. "He's been saving all that money since the old earl wouldn't let him spend it on the estate."

"Is that respectable work for him?" asked Caleb.

"If he doesn't get his hands dirty and it pays the bills, it's respectable enough for me," affirmed Ned.

"Justi ain't afraid to get his hands dirty. Mind how he helped get that hay in last year with the thunder and lightning rolling and the rain on the way. I couldn't have handled the team better myself in such conditions."

In the days and weeks that followed, the farm workers began to look on Justi with tolerance and some measure of approval. They had always thought him to be relaying orders from the old gent. But when his directions, humbly proffered, sensible and open to discussion, kept coming, it dawned on them that Justi had been taking care of things for some time.

"Justi—I mean, my lord, your mother's been looking for you." Justi dismounted and handed Bluedevil's reins over to Jim.

"Best call me by my name, Jim, or I won't know who you're talking to. Is that Mr. Baird's carriage?"

"Yes, he's been here a good hour."

Justi opened the door to the library and only half came in. "Perhaps I'd better change first."

"Oh, no, dear, come in. Mr. Baird has to leave soon. Justi! You're half covered in mud. You didn't fall?"

"No, there was a lamb fallen down the bank into the stream. I couldn't just let it drown."

"Never mind that now," said Baird. "I have news from London. Your cousin can't come to see to things just now, but he wants to send you a tutor and I'm to find out what your needs are."

"My needs right now are for a blacksmith who isn't drunk two days out of three and a cook who won't poison us, not a tutor."

"Now, we must comply with your cousin's wishes. He is, after all, your guardian."

"Very well. Since you ask, I need to learn German and mathematics."

"German, I don't quite see . . . well, never mind. Is that all?"

"That's it. Have you any idea what this tutor will cost us between his salary and what he'll eat?"

"Oh, your cousin intends to bear this cost himself. The estate is really not in a frame to handle such expenses yet. I'm sure I don't have to warn you not to run up any debts." Baird looked owlishly at Justi.

"On the contrary, I have been attempting to rid us of some of our debts, but it's a little hard to plan when you don't know the full amount owing."

"Time enough for that later when things are settled." Baird had consistently refused to give away any details or even read the will until cousin Richard was present. "Just be patient, my lord."

"Justi, what will you do when cousin Richard does come?" Miriam asked when Baird had left. Far from becoming more lighthearted, she had become even more fearful of the future.

"I'm not sure. Perhaps, if he sees things are running pretty smoothly and we don't need him, he'll go away again soon. I would think it would be pretty boring for him here. Besides, he probably has his own affairs to look after."

"But, are you going to tell him?"

"Tell him what? Oh, that. If I do, this all belongs to him, you know, except for the stud farm. I suppose it will depend on what sort of person he is and how I think he'll treat us. I'd have to be sure he'd not ruin Homeplace. Once the truth is told, there's no undoing it."

"Well, Braden, have you found a German math instructor yet? Why German, do you suppose?" Richard pondered, peering out the window at the tempting spring day. Even though he had sold his expensive bays, he had still his grays to drive and hoped to get through the morning's business in time to take them out before lunch.

"I have no idea, sir. Perhaps he thought it would be impossible to find one, so he wouldn't have to have a tutor at all. At any rate, there is only one applicant who comes close, a Gerard Dumont, a young Frenchman, stranded in London, not a teacher, really. But he's obviously traveled extensively on the Continent and claims a knowledge of German and Italian. As for mathematics, he will vouch for only what he retains from the university. He has recently made his living giving fencing lessons."

"Ah, that's something. Will he undertake to teach the boy fencing?"

"I'm sure he would, sir. He would take the post for a modest fee, plus his living. Do you wish to interview him yourself?"

"My dear fellow, that's what I pay you for. If he's willing to go, ship him up there. Damn!"

"What is it, sir?" Braden came to the street window.

"My sister Clara. She wasn't supposed to arrive until this afternoon."

"I suppose you'll want to see her alone," said Braden, gathering his papers.

"You coward! If you had any loyalty for me, you would help me beat a hasty retreat out the back door."

"No good, sir. They are taking her carriage round now. Her people would be sure to see you waiting for your team to be hitched. Besides, she would rout you out before you were well gone."

"Don't look so smug, my friend. It falls to you to tell her coachman and footman that they are being let go. All her servants, in fact, except her dresser. If the new owners of her house wish to litter it with all that uniformed livery, I'd be surprised."

"Yes, sir." Braden left to do his duty, just as Clara Redmond threw open the doors to the library with her own hands.

"How dare you sell my house and have my jewelry confiscated!" Richard grabbed her clenched fists before they could do any damage. Clara's hair was more auburn than brown, and she had, from time to time, had her hairdresser encourage it toward a more reddish tint. Just now, with her green eyes glinting in rage, she looked less than pretty.

"We have been through all this with the lawyers. You knew it was coming." He let her go.

"You could pay my debts if you would," she fumed.

"I might have contrived it a few months ago if I'd known what a case you were in. Once you went to the moneylenders you were ruined. If it's any consolation, the sale of your house, furnishings and jewelry scarcely pays half your debts. I have had to sell a good few things, and lease this house for the season, to cover the rest."

"You gave up this house? But where am I to live?"

"With the rest of us at Amberly. There really is no choice, my dear. At least there are no roulette tables there to tempt you."

"You beast! I hate you!" She flung out of the room, probably to have a good cry in the well-appointed bedchamber that had been prepared for her.

Julia entered in her wake, smiling tiredly at Richard. "She made a scene, didn't she, dear?"

"Oh, it wasn't half as bad as I feared. All the vases are still intact. When can we be ready to leave? The new tenants take possession next week. They will take on our house servants, except Braden, the valets and maids, so we won't lose them."

"I have our things half packed already and I won't let them unpack Clara's trunks. You know, this will be the first summer we have spent at Amberly since you were all children. Things were so simple then."

"No, they were not. Clara was spoiled even then."

"I remember her taunting you."

"She made me miserable."

"Still, that was no reason for your father to force her into that marriage with Redmond. What was he afraid you would do to her? I think if she had been allowed to choose her own husband she might be quite happy now."

"More likely the fellow would have been plagued to death no matter who he was."

"Surely you don't hold her accountable for that."

"I'd go pretty far to get away from her tongue, myself."

"Perhaps she will settle down now."

"I intend to give her no choice."

Chapter Two

Gerard Dumont arrived in Stowmarket the beginning of June, not looking forward to his internment, but glad at least to escape his London creditors. He had fair, straight hair and a lithe figure kept in shape by fencing. A young man was watching him as he descended from the stage, so he carried his valise over to the rather shabby gig.

"Are you from Homeplace?"

"Yes, I'm Justin Mallory." The boy shook his hand firmly.

"You came for me yourself?"

"I had business in town. Besides, if I'd sent Jim, he'd be half a day behind with the stable chores. We only keep one lad at the house stable. Of course, we have four grooms working down at the stud farm. We raise workhorses."

"We? Meaning your mother and you?"

"That's right. Here, let me help you get your trunk. I was wondering. This cousin of mine, Richard, what's he like?"

"I'm afraid I couldn't tell you." Gerard's French accent was very slight. "I never met him. I was hired by his secretary."

"So, you've no idea when he's coming?"

"I'm afraid not. I can only tell you that I have a six-month contract." Justi drove competently through the crowded town, neither wasting time nor taking chances.

"I was just curious," mused Gerard. "Why German?"

"What? Oh, I do a bit of translating for a printer in London, French to English mostly, sometimes English to French. But he's looking for someone to translate some German treatises."

"Really? Does it pay well?"

"Better than farming. Of course, in a bad year, throwing your money down a rat hole makes more sense than farming."

Gerard chuckled. "I should warn you, I'm not really a tutor. I just needed to get back on my feet. I've never taught anyone before, so I don't know if I'll be any good at it."

"We should be able to get somewhere in six months."

"Did they tell you I'm supposed to teach you fencing, as well?"

"No one tells me anything. I'm getting a little sick of it."

Miriam found Gerard charming. Gerard found the luncheon rather sparse and asked for some wine.

"What do you think of him, dear?" Miriam asked Justi that evening.

"I think he knows how to make himself agreeable, when he chooses. He is new here. Perhaps he's just worried about us liking him."

"So you don't think he meant it," Miriam pouted, "when he said I didn't look old enough to be your mother."

"Of course he meant it. Haven't I said so myself often enough? I'm no judge of people. I've never been around anyone like him. I shall have to be very careful, I think."

"He will always dine with us, won't he? I don't see why not. He is, after all, a gentleman. It will be such fun having someone to talk to in the evening."

"Well, thank you very much," Justi said and laughed.

It was agreed that the afternoons would be reserved for study since Justi's mornings seemed to be the most crowded with farm business. This also gave Gerard the luxury of sleeping as late as he wished.

They tackled German ambitiously and, at the end of only one week, both could be said to be satisfied with their progress. In the matter of mathematics they were not so fortunate. Since Justi was interested not in theory, but in accounting and bookkeeping, she could be said to be ahead of Gerard. At least she understood that one had to have more income than expenses.

Because of the fencing lessons, Justi took the precaution of bandaging her chest under her shirt. She could always give the excuse of cracked ribs, which had happened often enough. She was an apt pupil but not as aggressive as most of the young blades Gerard had instructed.

"It's just that you look so serious when you're coming at me with that foil," she complained to him, "as though you don't really like me and you mean to do me in."

"Never let your opponent get the advantage of you in that way. You must learn to look fierce, too, not like a startled rabbit."

"I can't see what possible use this will be to me. It's not as though people fight a lot of duels around here. Even so, I'm not likely to let myself get involved in one."

"Who can say, when the blood is hot? Now, again with the riposte." After half an hour Justi was exhausted. By then it was time to clean up for dinner.

"I don't understand. You have muscle to spare in your legs, from riding, I suppose," Gerard pointed out. "But you haven't the strength in your shoulders and arms."

"At least I am quick."

"Yes, at retreating, Rabbit." Gerard grabbed her by the back of the neck and shook her.

His physical familiarities startled her, at first, but she soon schooled herself not to show surprise at his touch. She supposed young men did touch each other and that it meant nothing but that they were friends.

But, when her mother came into the library one day and surprised Gerard with his hand on Justi's shoulder as she read out her German, she saw a slight look of shock on Miriam's face. She cornered her mother later. "His touching me while he read over my shoulder, you didn't like it. Why?"

"I'm not sure. It just made me uneasy." She looked into Justi's intent eyes. "How does he make you feel? You're not in danger of betraying yourself?"

"Certainly not. It was strange at first. I've gotten used to it now."

"He probably means nothing by it. It must be because I know you're a girl and he doesn't that it makes me uncomfortable."

By the beginning of August they had already gotten two cuttings of hay off most of their fields. The lambs had brought a decent price in Stowmarket, and Justi had sold a team of workhorses to Colonel Allen. All income from the farm she conscientiously turned over to Mr. Baird or had the drafts made out to the estate.

Her progress with German was such that she felt confident in writing Meecham for an assignment. She began to take a certain amount of delight in fencing. It was a good deal like chess at lightning speed. Everything depended on knowing what your opponent would do if you set a certain trap for him. Gerard was becoming very predictable.

The only time he was bothersome was after Miriam had retired. If Badger left too much wine in easy reach, Gerard was apt to get drunk and insist on Justi playing cards with him. Badger didn't like these goings-on. He was careful to always escort Justi to her room when she retired to work and wait until he heard the key grind in her lock. What did Badger imagine Gerard would do, get her drunk and fleece her? All the same she was touched by the old fellow's concern for her.

*   *   *

One sweltering day in August, the kind of weather they rarely had, Justi was almost falling asleep over her lessons.

"Let's quit for today. I can't concentrate in this heat."

"You've convinced me, Rabbit. Are you going to take a nap?"

She had worked late the night before, copying out a final draft, and the close heat had begun to feel like a comfortable blanket.

"It's too hot upstairs. I think I'll take a walk." She went upstairs for her sketchbook with the intention of going to the woods and finding a shady tree.

"Where are you going? I'll go with you," he offered as he waited for her in the downstairs hall.

"The woods, I think. It's cooler there." Justi rather resented having Gerard intrude upon her walk so she decided to make him pay for it with an hour's tramp through the rougher parts of the woods. There was one place she would never take him, the oak grove. It would seem like a sacrilege. By the time they came within sight of the house again they were both hot and tired. "I thought you said it was cool in the woods," Gerard puffed.

"Usually, if there's a breeze. We may as well go back to the house."

"Wait, the pond's right down there. Come on." Gerard grabbed her sleeve. "We'll go for a swim."

"Are you mad? The thing stinks in this weather."

Undeterred by the murkiness of the water, Gerard began stripping off his clothes. "Come on."

"I don't swim," Justi said, flushing with embarrassment. She should have left him and gone inside, but she did not think that was what a man would do. Not able to decide what to do, she sat down on the grass and opened her sketchbook. She leafed past images of old barns, broken walls and animals grazing to a blank page and began to draw. What if I treat him like a vase of flowers? she thought,

starting a studio sketch of him from the back as he bent over
to shed his breeches.

Thinking about how his muscles lay, the length of his
torso, she realized that, well muscled as she was, anyone
seeing her nude from the back would certainly realize she
was a girl. She now realized that a greater proportion of a
man's height was made up of torso, whereas she had longer
thighs.

She had completed the drawing from memory by the time
Gerard dragged himself from the water and threw himself
down on the grass to dry off. She turned the page and began another drawing, thinking of him as a reclining statue
and trying to suppress the pulsing deep in her stomach. Even
though she did not find Gerard appealing, she began to
consider the course to which she had committed in a new
light.

Not only could she never marry, but she could never even
make love to a man, except anonymously. And such a thing,
though a common enough way for a man to get satisfaction, seemed repugnant to her. It never would do to trust any
man with the secret of her identity, especially not someone
like Gerard, to whose mind the thought of blackmail would
leap as naturally as a frog into a pond.

Besides, a pregnancy would spell disaster. The vision of
herself growing old alone at Homeplace without even the
comfort of a child brought such a hopeless despair as she
had never known. The past and all she had accomplished
seemed futile, the future a blank wall beyond which she
could not penetrate. And the thought of this present moment in which she could not reach out to a man, even if she
wanted to, must have brought such a confused sadness to
her face that Gerard could not resist teasing her. He reached
over, hooked his fingers in her hair and dragged her toward
the pond.

"No!" She wrenched herself free. "You reek and you've
got slime in your hair."

She gathered up her tablet and stalked resolutely to the house away from his laughter. He wouldn't dare follow her away from the screen of trees until he had dressed.

Safely locked in her room, she considered her position. Her embarrassment had very nearly given her away, she thought. Whether it had or not, she was getting more and more uncomfortable around Gerard. It did her peace of mind no good to realize that this was because of her reaction to him, not because of any change in his behavior.

One way or another, she would have to get rid of Gerard. She didn't want to upset her mother so instead she began a letter to Mr. Baird. It wasn't an easy letter to write, and after reading it, she wasn't sure she conveyed her desperation to him. She could only speak of Gerard's excessive drinking making her mother uncomfortable.

"Where were you?" Justi inquired of Gerard, who was emerging from the basement door one afternoon. Justi had taken to spending even more time with the farm work just to keep out of Gerard's influence. Unfortunately, this gave Gerard more time to get into trouble. It was only three o'clock and it was obvious that he had already been drinking.

"Looking for a cool place. I found some more burgundy. I thought Badger said it was gone?"

"It's all one to me. You know I don't drink the stuff."

"Maybe you should try it. Come on, fencing lesson today in the coolest place in the house."

He dragged her by the coat sleeve down the stairs and, to avoid a scene, she went with him past the stillroom and box room, past the now depleted wine cellar, to the old armory. It was a totally windowless vault with a rotting plank floor. It had served in earlier times as a sort of dungeon for the enemies of the House of Mallory. So the rusting bits of armor, pieces of broken weaponry and unidentifiable wreckage of centuries was set against a background of damp mossy wall with, here and there, depressing manacles still in place.

Even with the door open, the damp air was rank with the odor of rats. It was, however, cool. "You can't be serious. We'll probably get sick down here."

"En garde!" Gerard threw her a rapier and they commenced the lesson in the area he had lately cleared.

Of all the things she routinely did, fencing with a man who was half-drunk was neither the safest nor, by any means, the most dangerous. Shoeing a young horse for the first time was more dangerous, she thought, parrying a thrust, because of the unpredictability of a frightened animal. Her only fear was that Gerard would accidentally break the weapon and run her through.

It did add an element of excitement to the session, and with his reactions slowed by drink, she managed to press an attack that left him gasping for breath. "Enough, enough, you are much improved, Rabbit."

"Perhaps, it's just that you...are not yourself today." He followed her out slowly. "Leave the door open," she said. "If you want to use that room, at least let it air out."

The last cut of hay had been made and the culled lambs sold at market. Only the oats remained to be harvested before the work of the farms shifted from summer toward the more leisurely pace of preparing for winter. Spare hours then would be spent laying in a store of firewood for winter, not only for Homeplace, but for the tenant cottages, as well. Repairs not done in the spring would be put forward now in case of heavy rains in the fall.

It had been a month since she had written Baird, and she had received no reply to her letter except a short note in his own hand commanding Justi "not to make a nuisance of himself." There were four months left on Gerard's contract. She supposed she could see her way to the end of it, but it would be just like Baird to renew it without giving her a choice in the matter. Either he didn't believe her or he did not think Gerard's drinking was dangerous.

Each day Gerard began drinking earlier. If there was nothing to be had at Homeplace, he laid in a stock from the Ram's Head. Justi was angry that this lot of burgundy and brandy had been ordered by Gerard in her name and warned the proprietor not to give Gerard credit again.

When he appeared for dinner one evening, half done up already, Justi decided to get rid of him herself. Precisely how, she was not sure. She followed her mother into the hall when she retired from the dinner table and asked her to go to her room early so she could have it out with Gerard.

"No, I won't leave you alone with him. I can't believe I ever thought he was pleasant."

"Don't worry. Haven't I managed so far? Besides, there's Badger to help me throw him out. And I can call on Ned and his boys if I get desperate. I'd just rather not make a stir, if I can help it. The only good thing is he hasn't annoyed you with his attentions."

"I think he goes into Brinley for that sort of thing."

"Mother! Who told you that?"

"Cook. I am not the innocent you suppose me to be," said Miriam, seeming all the time more like Justi's sister than her mother.

"They should not be babbling to you about such things. I just hope they don't give him any credit in Brinley."

"How could your cousin send such a person here? I don't want you to be alone with him."

"Gerard cannot possibly have any designs on me. He doesn't suspect me in the least."

"Are you quite sure?"

"What makes you ask?"

"The way he stares at you sometimes."

"Surely it's your imagination. Now go to your room. Perhaps he'll be gone in the morning."

Justi entered the dining room as Gerard drained the port decanter. "I want you to leave," she said abruptly, resting her hands on the back of one of the chairs.

"What you want, Rabbit, does not weigh with me. Remember that I'm in charge here. You'll do as I say."

"I'm willing to pay out the rest of your contract."

Gerard snorted. "Miserable wages, anyway." He got up from the table, his fair hair falling over his bleary eyes.

"I'll even give you an extra fifty pounds."

"Is that your final offer?" he scoffed, slowly walking around the table.

"You had better take it. It's all you'll get from me."

"But I haven't completed your lessons." Gerard lunged, but Justi sidestepped, pushing a chair in front of him and tripping him. Gerard stood up slowly, now between Justi and the door.

"Besides, I've written to Mr. Baird about you and he'll write to my cousin. I shouldn't be surprised if he wasn't on his way here right now." Even to Justi this sounded like schoolboyish tattling.

Gerard detected the bluff and laughed scornfully. "I haven't taught you to box yet."

"I've learned everything from you I want to know," she said, retreating to the far side of the table. It wasn't going well, she thought. She had allowed him to maneuver her into a position with no retreat. One of the first lessons he taught her was to know what was behind her. Even as she pictured the room at her back, she came up against the sideboard. The bump distracted her slightly and gave him a chance to lunge across the table at her. A glancing clip to her chin dazed her and, as she sank, he caught her up over his shoulder.

"I think you should strip to advantage," she heard him say distantly.

It was only the worst bad luck that did not take Badger into the dining room to clear away. Hanging upside down and dazed, Justi vaguely thought he was carrying her upstairs until he threw her up against a cold, dank wall. The bump on the head further disoriented her and she did not realize until too late that Gerard had carried her to the armory. She saw him light the branch of candles they had left there from a single taper he must have brought with him. She stood and pushed herself away from the damp stones, but hung there helplessly. What had given him the malicious inspiration to chain her to the wall? The manacles worked by slipping a pin through holes in the hinged halves, secure enough if one did not have a free hand to withdraw the pin.

She swayed against the rusty chains, frantically trying to pull her hands through the openings. "What are you going to do?" she asked desperately.

"Give you a lesson."

He put the fingers of one hand behind her neck and hooked his thumb under her jaw, forcing her head back painfully. "I could snap your neck if I wanted to. Just remember that." His face was so close the fumes from the drink covered the musty rat smells of the room. She lunged against the chains, futilely. He unbuttoned her shirt to reveal the bandages underneath, then stripped those off as well.

"Just as I thought," he said contemptuously of her young breasts. "There's not much of you, but you are a woman. How did you expect to get away with this?"

"I was doing fine until you came along." In spite of her fears at what he meant to do next, she was curious enough to ask, "How did you find me out?"

"I searched your room."

"I can't have left anything about. I own nothing that belongs to a woman."

"No, but you don't own something that all men have about them—shaving gear. Even if you didn't have to shave yet, you would be trying it out, if you had really been a lad."

"Damn!" she said as he stroked her face and grinned.

"I wonder what the rest of you looks like."

"I can pay you enough to get whatever you want in that line in Brinley," she offered, generously sacrificing some other woman rather than herself.

"I'll have you and your fifty pounds," he said, suffocating her with a drunken kiss.

"If you get me pregnant, this farce will be over."

"That's not likely to happen after the first time."

"It doesn't matter. You do this and I'll tell my cousin myself."

"You never will, not the way you love this crumbling old house."

"I'll do it to get my revenge on you." Finally she had struck a chord, something he could understand.

He looked at her, considering, then down at himself. "Too late," he said, leaning against her.

If she couldn't keep her secret, at least she would make him pay for it. She caught him a groin kick that left him moaning on the floor.

She pulled desperately at the chains then, hoping the old sand mortar between the stones could be loosened or that the chains would be rusty enough to break. The thought of being chained there helpless when Gerard recovered was too much for her. She pulled down with all her weight, sacrificing the skin on her left hand. The manacle was made for a larger wrist and, by squeezing her hand together and pulling down, she eventually tore it through.

Unpinning her right hand was difficult, but Gerard was on his knees now. She forced her left hand to work, got the pin out and detoured around Gerard to strike over the branch of candles. A fire was too much to hope for. She scrambled for the door, wrenched it open and ran up the stairs, holding her coat together.

She did not go immediately to her bedroom, however, but shut herself up in the small gun room. She chose the smallest pistol she could find and loaded it. She did not want to kill Gerard, but she would never again take any chances with him.

* * *

"I want to talk to you," Gerard said accusingly when he caught up with Justi at the stable the next morning.

"You're up early for once," Justi remarked, as she felt for the small pistol lying comfortingly in her coat pocket.

"It's almost noon. You've been avoiding me all morning."

"I've been doing my usual work. You wouldn't know anything about that."

"Then you don't mean to tell your cousin?" he asked.

"I suppose that's up to you," she said in confusion.

"Where can we go to talk?"

"I am riding into Brinley. If you want to talk to me get Jim to saddle that mare for you."

Gerard did not like to ride, especially not with Justi, for he had to look up at her on her great black beast, which had tried to bite him when he got too near it once. Justi rode across country part of the way since the crops were all in. There was no opportunity to talk until they turned onto the last mile of road before the village.

"What will you pay to keep your secret?" he asked abruptly.

"I have been thinking it were best ended anyway," she said perversely. "If you saw through me surely this cousin will."

"No, I was not at all sure. You are very good, really. You act the part to perfection."

"Thank you," Justi said hollowly.

"I wouldn't bleed you dry," Gerard offered generously. "It would just be something to tide me over from time to time. With references from your cousin I could get another position as a tutor."

"You wouldn't stay here then?" she turned to ask hopefully.

"No offense, but it's a trifle flat."

"I have never found it so."

"How much?" he asked as they dismounted in Brinley.

"Let me think," Justi said as she went into the receiving office for the mail. She knew she was making a mistake to pay Gerard. But she did not at that moment see an alternative. She returned opening a package.

"I thought you got your mail in Glenncross."

"I do, except the stuff from Meecham and Bates. They have been sending me some translation work I'd as soon my mother did not see."

Gerard reached for the book out of curiosity. He leafed through it with raised eyebrows, then glanced at Justi speculatively as she mounted Bluedevil.

"How long does it take you to translate one of these books?"

"I can generally get through two a year," she lied. Actually, in the last year she had finished four.

"And what do they pay you?"

She handed him the check.

"Sixty pounds—not a fortune," Gerard said thoughtfully. "Sign this over to me and I will consider it a down payment."

"We'd best forget the whole thing," she said, taking the check back as they left the town. "You could never live on a hundred and twenty a year."

"No, but it's something. If I tell your cousin about you, I get nothing."

"You'd get worse than nothing if I told him what you tried to do."

"I was drunk."

"That's another thing. You'd have to quit drinking and let me alone. You have to agree to that or there's no deal."

"Who the hell are you saving yourself for, anyway? It's not like you'll ever marry if you continue with this charade."

"You don't have to remind me of that. I know it better than you."

They rode in silence for a time with Gerard considering. "Seems an absolute waste," he said finally, by way of a backhanded compliment.

"You can buy what you want in the way of companionship and they would be willing—not so likely to kill you as I would," Justi said harshly.

"You wouldn't dare. You're still a woman under all your bluff."

"And being a woman I wouldn't be so particular how I got rid of you—poison leaps conveniently to mind. The way you drink, no one would even inquire into your untimely death."

Gerard watched her determined back as she rode off and scowled. He didn't believe her, of course. In some strange way he even admired her. Such a spirited girl would make him an admirable consort after she was discovered, which was sure to happen sooner or later. Until then she was good for a hundred and twenty a year. After that, well, he could already think of one or two schemes where an attractive young woman who was constrained to obey him might be a useful tool. His future had never looked so bright.

As they dismounted in the yard he said, "I agree then. Is it a deal?"

"Yes," she agreed, but turned her back on his outstretched hand. He laughed at her.

For two days Gerard behaved tolerably well, even convincing Justi to let him teach her the rudiments of defending herself without a weapon. Not in the armory, though. She could never go down there again with a quiet mind. She insisted they practice in the stable with Jim looking on. She grasped the theory, but still did not think her small fists would be much good against two or three of the village boys.

Gerard's efforts toward seducing her she treated as tiresome jokes. At sixteen her desires were only vague achings, not the full-blown hunger of a woman. She knew from the books she translated all the mechanisms involved and she found them more often amusing than exciting. She had none of the passions to make such acts meaningful, nor were such passions likely to be aroused by Gerard. She did not know many men, not young ones, at any rate, and she made the mistake of assuming Gerard was representative of the entire class.

Justi shrugged off his arm thrown casually across her shoulders on the way back from the stable. "All right, I'll be good, but things will be different once you come of age."

"What are you talking about?" Justi snapped.

"We'll have more money then. If the war's over we'll be able to travel."

"We? You said you were going away."

"For now. When you have control of your fortune I'll come back."

"Get this through your head. There is no we! There is no fortune! Homeplace could never support that kind of extravagance. All you get is what I pay you and you better be glad for that."

"Your grandfather must have left you something."

"I have no idea. Now leave me alone." Justi stomped up the stairs and locked herself in her room. What had she done? Gerard would never leave them in peace. And the only defense she had was a threat to reveal her identity herself. How could she have let herself get trapped this way? She went over it all in her mind, but she couldn't think what she could have done differently. And she certainly could not think of a way out of the mess short of murdering Gerard.

She managed to compose herself by dinnertime. Gerard was his charming old self again and took himself off to Brinley after dinner, rather than annoy Justi and Miriam.

"What happened with Gerard?" her mother asked. "He seemed almost pleasant tonight."

"Came to his senses, I suppose," Justi said distractedly into her teacup.

"Because you talked to him?"

"I...encouraged him to look into the future."

"What do you mean?"

"Without a reference from my guardian, Gerard will not be able to get another such position as this."

"I hadn't thought of that."

"Neither had he. I think we can in good conscience send him on to someone else. In another household there will most likely be a father to keep him in check. And he did make an effort to teach me German...and a few other things."

"But he's not staying?" Miriam asked brightly.

"No, he will leave in November and behave himself until then."

"Everything's all right then," Miriam said joyously, pouring some more tea.

Justi looked at her mother and forced a smile. "Yes, everything is fine." She could never tell her about the deal with Gerard. She was in this thing alone now.

Chapter Three

It was as well for Gerard that he was behaving himself, at least in the daytime, because Richard Mallory arrived in midafternoon. Gerard presented to Richard the appearance of a tired and serious young man in charge of a sulking boy.

Richard had come east from Amberly in easy stages driving his curricle hitched to his famous grays. He was accompanied only by his valet, Firth, and his groom, Haimes, who was astride one of Richard's hunters and leading another.

Gerard greeted Richard and escorted him into the sitting room as though he owned the place, leaving Justi to make arrangements for Richard's servants, his magnificent horses and his baggage. Justi went from the stable yard in the back door to warn the cook. Mrs. Morrisee, not in a good humor at the best of times, greeted her news with a crash of pots and pans. Justi encountered Badger in the hall and asked him to see if the maid could dust and air out the old master bedroom upstairs.

"I already set her to it, my lord."

"My lord? Oh, practising for company. Thanks, Badger. What would I do without you?"

Justi could not tell how much Gerard had said to Richard, but when she entered the sitting room, she had the feeling the cards had already been stacked against her. Oddly enough, now that Gerard was a party to her secret, he lost his ability to put her out of countenance and make her blush. She merely stared at him with cold patience when he said anything she disliked. And in her cousin's presence Gerard said a great deal she didn't like.

Justi studied Richard Mallory, looking for something to disapprove of, but he only looked bored, or perhaps tired. He listened to Gerard's ramblings about her "studying when he had a mind to" or about "boys being boys." She was looking quite resentfully at Gerard when he smiled at her in a conspiratorial way that conveyed he was trying to help her.

The thought of Gerard making himself useful was such a novelty that she was hard-pressed to wipe the surprise from her face and replace it with what she considered a suitably resentful look. If her cousin thought she was a troublesome boy, he wasn't likely to expect her to be anything else.

Miriam's entrance broke the tension as she made Richard welcome.

"If only we had known you were coming, we could have had a better dinner planned for you."

"Didn't Baird let you know? I'm sure my secretary wrote to him weeks ago."

"I'm afraid Mr. Baird needs more lead time than that to move communications through his office," Justi informed Richard truthfully.

Richard looked at her like she had spoken out of turn. Justi was unaccustomed to being treated like a child and felt a surge of anger, but by the time dinner was announced she was thoroughly enjoying the spectacle of Gerard acting a fool. Richard gave nothing away, so Gerard was just as unsure as she was about what Richard was thinking. Neither of them could tell if Richard had received the letter complaining of his drinking.

Gerard behaved throughout dinner with deference and propriety. He refused wine at first, but when he saw Richard nod at it in approval he took a sip and looked surprised. Even Justi, who didn't care for wine, tried it and found it to be agreeable. Old Badger must have sized up

Gerard early on, and hidden the good stock. A secret wink from the aged retainer, as he helped the maid serve, confirmed Justi's suspicion. She turned her face away to hide a smirk.

Most of the dishes served clearly did not come up to Richard's high standards, but even Mrs. Morrisee could not ruin the tender leg of lamb with which they were supplied in such abundance.

After Miriam retired to the sitting room Gerard loosened up over the port and apologized for not making more progress with the boy, especially in the area of mathematics. He did think Richard would be pleased with the skill Justin had developed in fencing, however.

Justi made monosyllabic replies when queried so as not to run afoul of Richard again and, as soon as was decent, begged leave to join her mother in the sitting room. Miriam thought they should have some music and, although Justi hated the thought of being put through her paces like a young colt in front of a buyer, she arranged a program of piano music to please her mother.

After the gentlemen joined them, she played for nearly an hour, first her most practiced pieces and finally venturing to try a rather faster work she had only been learning a few weeks. Justi got some pleasure from any mechanical skill she could master so long as she was sure it was not a feminine thing.

Technically she played quite well, but she never lost herself in the spirit of a work the way Miriam would. She never let herself feel anything very much. It was too dangerous. Justi surprised a scowl on Richard's dark countenance and wondered if she had made an error. But she recollected he probably heard concerts in London that made her simple efforts seem like an impertinence.

Richard was frowning, however, because the boy played so surprisingly well. If he found the performance colorless, a mere exercise at showing off, that was the only fault he detected. It seemed the lad had been left too long in his mother's charge, the way she doted on him. It would take some doing but he would loose the boy from his mother's apron strings. A Mallory, and an earl at that, would have to behave like a man, not a fop, or he would never bring him to the notice of London society.

Since Justi did not introduce any topic for discussion and Miriam's inquiries concerned the rest of the family, Richard's impression of Justi as a pampered brat was reinforced. He had no doubt that the boy would try his patience as much as Harry ever had.

It was a strange feeling for Justi to have someone think she was bad when she had tried to be so responsible all her life. If Richard was this gullible she should have no trouble deceiving him after Gerard was gone, but what then? Justi felt a pang of guilt at conspiring against her cousin in this way. But what she was doing tonight was trivial compared to what she had already done. She had best quash any remorse and concentrate on saving Homeplace.

Justi was tired and she thought it fit her role well to retire early in a sulk. As soon as the tea tray was disposed of, Justi bid them all good-night and went to her room to work.

She neglected to lock her door since she expected no more trouble from Gerard with Cousin Richard in the house. She was surprised, then, when Gerard pushed her door open without ceremony and shut it behind him. He noticed the key on the mantel, took it down and locked the door. Justi felt in her coat pocket for the pistol and withdrew it under cover of the desk.

"So far, so good, Rabbit. If you behave as well for the rest of your cousin's visit we may just pull this off." He moved toward her.

"Keep your distance," she warned.

"I think I've convinced him to keep me on for another half year."

"You promised to leave!" she almost shouted.

"With everything going so well. You like me. You know you do."

Her desk by the window, with its bookshelves on the wall behind, normally such a comfortable nook, now seemed like a trap. She moved out from behind the desk and drew the weapon on him. He laughed. "Just what do you intend to do with that thing?"

"Shoot you, if you come any closer. You will leave Homeplace one way or another." When he lunged she pulled the trigger, but the hammer clicked uselessly.

She tried then to hit him with it but he caught her wrists and, keeping safely clear of her kicks, threw her down backward on the bed.

At that moment Badger went to remove the tea tray and asked Richard point-blank where Gerard was.

"Gone to bed, I suppose," Richard said in annoyance.

Something about the old retainer's hurried exit aroused Richard's curiosity to follow him. By the time Richard gained the top of the stairs, Badger had already found Gerard's room empty and was calling at Justi's door, through which came sounds of struggle.

"Break it down, sir," Badger pleaded.

To be ordered about by a servant rather set Richard's back up, but he did as he was bid. The door sprang open under his weight to reveal Gerard pinning both of Justi's arms to the bed, half kneeling on the struggling legs and trying to silence a stream of invective by kissing Justi hard on the mouth.

Richard pulled Gerard off and delivered a single blow that knocked him cold. "Get him out of here," he said in disgust to Badger. "As for you—" he directed a menacing look at Justi, who was wiping the blood from a split lip "—give me that pistol, and get to bed. I'll deal with you later."

After they left she staggered to the washstand to clean her face. She did not want to get caught undressing and she was sure Richard was coming back, so she sat behind her desk gazing out into the blackness.

It may have been an hour before Richard opened the door unannounced. His black look deepened when he found he had been disobeyed. "Dumont claims you seduced him."

"What? Are you mad? Surely you don't believe him!" Justi thought for a frantic moment Gerard had revealed the whole plot. "I hate Gerard. He disgusts me." Justi read complete disbelief in Richard's cold blue eyes and recalled how convincing Gerard could be.

Richard, who was not in the habit of having striplings doubt his sanity, was even further inflamed.

"He's leaving, of course, but he wants the sketches you made of him. He doesn't want to leave those in your hands."

Justi looked at him blankly at first, but then recalled Gerard's swim and blushed as she moved numbly to the bookshelf to hand over her sketchpad.

Richard leafed impatiently past her barns and bridges, haymaking and other innocent pastimes to stop at the two nude male figure studies. He tore them out and said ominously, "I'll deal with you in the morning."

Justi dressed for riding as usual in the morning, but found that her door had been repaired to the point that it could be locked from the outside, so she had nothing to do but pace and look out the east window to the horse pastures or the north window into the stable yard.

Justi had never been locked in her room, even as a child. She could never, in fact, remember doing anything bad enough to require punishment. So, by ten o'clock, when her carriage team was being hitched, presumably to take Gerard to Stowmarket, she had worked herself into a lather over the injustice of her treatment.

The key sounded in the lock, and Richard entered looking stern and tired. "I'm sending Dumont away, of course. I've had to pay off the rest of his contract since what happened does not appear to have been entirely his fault."

"Nothing happened!" Justi spit out. "If it had, you would know..." Richard would know she was a girl, for Gerard would have told him. It occurred to her that confession would still be the wisest course in view of what Richard actually thought of her.

"Would know what?" Richard prompted coldly. Justi's inner turmoil resulted in a tight-lipped silence that told him nothing. "I have also had to pay him extra wages to buy his silence in this matter."

"You let him blackmail you? That bastard!"

Activity could be heard in the stable yard, and Richard checked Justi's start for the door by grabbing her arm. He was ill-prepared for a determined right elbow smashing into his ribs with the added strength of Justi's left arm pushing against her fist. The blow knocked the wind out of him and sent him reeling.

Justi was down the hall and taking the back stairs two at a time before Richard recovered enough to pursue.

"Gerard! Wait till I get hold of you, you little bastard!" she yelled at the departing carriage, then sprinted after it, determined to drag Gerard out of it and make him tell Richard the truth. She had caught the back of the carriage and got one leg up on the footman's perch. Jim checked the team when he heard Richard yelling from behind.

It's difficult enough to hang on to a moving carriage, but when someone grabs your coat it's impossible. Justi came down stiff-legged, stoving her right knee so badly she could do nothing but writhe on the ground for a few minutes, stifling a groan.

"How dare you make a fool of yourself over him! Get up!" Richard wrenched her to her feet by the coat collar and twisted the offending elbow behind her back to protect his ribs. He waved Jim on, then force-marched her to the back door of the house, mistaking her numb limp for resistance.

The stairs were a painful climb since she actually had to bend the knee and get it to work. She went down twice, gasping, only to be dragged mercilessly onward and finally thrown onto her bed. The sound of the key in the lock left her stifling a curse into her pillows.

She could hear her mother in the hall. "What is all the commotion about?"

"Nothing. Go down to breakfast, Lady Mallory."

"But I want to see Justi."

"Your son will not be joining us for breakfast, or any other meal, until he has mended his manners." This was said loudly enough to have been intended for Justi's benefit.

It was quiet then for a while. Just when she thought the edge was wearing off the pain in her knee, attempting to turn over woke it up again. Sitting up took several attempts. She eased off her left boot, but only removed the right one by hooking it on the bedrail, holding on to her knee and pushing back with her left leg. That done, she lay back, trying to calculate how she had gotten into this mess. There was something so high-handed about Richard that she thought her anger had been more at his stupidity than at Gerard's underhanded trick. If Richard was arrogant and stupid he would be all that much easier to fool, but not if he called the doctor to her.

When she woke up her whole leg was thumping, and her knee was rapidly swelling. She eased a pillow under it to keep it slightly bent. She heard the door opening then and, reaching for a book on her nightstand, pretended to read.

It was Firth, Richard's valet, who saw only a sulky boy, lounging on his bed. He left a lunch tray and locked the door behind him. Justi had played this game many times before. No matter what, there could be no doctor. Now, even her mother could rarely tell if she was in pain.

She didn't touch the tray. Too much effort to reach it. And it was gone when she woke up again. Richard was standing by the bed looking down at her. She twitched when she saw him and bit her lip to stifle the pain.

"Just how long do you intend to make a nuisance of yourself? If you apologize and give me your word you'll behave, I'll let you out."

Since being locked in her room was the best thing that could happen to her at the moment, she spit out, "I don't make promises I can't keep."

Richard's blue eyes hardened. "You are distressing your mother."

"Something tells me you are the one who is distressing my mother." She pulled herself up on one elbow.

"If you were innocent in this matter, you would have told her what Dumont was like."

"I didn't want to hand her that worry on top of everything else."

"What do you mean, everything else?"

Damn, she would have to be careful. "His drinking. I'm pretty sure he doesn't remember what he does when he's drunk, but that doesn't make him less dangerous."

"Then you should have told someone," Richard reasoned.

"But I did. I wrote to Baird, our lawyer. Isn't that why you came?"

"No. He conveyed nothing of this to me."

"Then he didn't believe me, either. Why do you believe Gerard, and not me?"

"Because you're hiding something. And until you're willing to tell me what it is, I don't feel that I can trust you." With that pronouncement, Richard turned to go. "Oh, by the way, your pistol misfired because it was inexpertly cleaned and carelessly loaded. You really have got a lot to learn."

A dinner tray appeared in due course, from which she ate sparingly. She managed to change into her nightclothes, but her whole leg was in spasm most of the night. She thought sleep would be impossible. She had to keep a folded handkerchief in her mouth to keep her teeth from chattering together.

A voice and a cool hand on her forehead woke her. "You're right, Firth, he is feverish. Ask Lady Mallory—

No, find out from the butler who the local doctor is and send for him. Tell him I've got a cracked rib." Without even blinking, Firth left to carry out these instructions.

"Have you?" asked Justi curiously, for she was feeling better now, the knee just a dull ache that only throbbed when she moved it.

"Have I what?"

"Got a cracked rib?

"I'm not sure. Where did you learn a move like that?"

"Gerard. The local lads used to beat me up on occasion and he agreed I would never stand a chance against them in a fair fight."

An involuntary chuckle escaped Richard. Justi made the mistake of trying to move, and wrenched an "Ouch!" from herself.

"Why didn't you tell me you were hurt?"

"I'm all right. I just stove my knee." She propped herself up and was beginning to think it didn't hurt all that much, until Richard laid his hand on it. "Ow!"

"Liar."

"What's the point of the doctor, anyway? He'll just say stay off it for a few days, which is what I'm doing."

Dr. Trent's verdict was as Justi predicted, but also no riding for a week. Justi bore the sentence with fortitude and used the time to advance her work, scribbling out a rough translation in pencil to be copied out later in ink.

The fall had happened on Tuesday, and by Saturday Justi was hopping around her room without much difficulty. She was still locked in, which puzzled her, since she couldn't have run off anyway. The only possible purpose could be to keep her away from her mother and the servants. If it was to punish her it was a wasted effort. Since she could not ride or walk anyway she would as soon be closeted in her room doing something useful. She did hope Richard would not guess this so she kept most of her work in her desk drawer and a book of history handy to fling open when she heard anyone approaching.

After her breakfast tray was taken away by Firth, she saw her carriage team being harnessed and led around front. She didn't dare hope that Richard was leaving but merely assumed him to be going some distance. This could not have been the case, however, since he came to her room a few minutes later dressed for riding.

"If you want to say goodbye to your mother you can wave to her from the window. I'm sending her to Amberly."

"You're sending her away? But why? None of this was her fault."

"She mentioned how much the smoke bothers her now that fires are a daily necessity. I merely thought it would benefit her health to spend the winter in a house where the chimneys do not smoke as wretchedly as these do."

"The winter? And did you bother to tell her why you were sending her there?"

"Yes, of course, but I don't think she believed me. She seems to think I'm trying to drive a wedge between you two, to lessen her hold on you."

"Well, aren't you?"

"Yes, but I didn't think it was that obvious."

Justi groaned in exasperation. "Have you no conscience?"

"Not anymore. It comes from having to deal with relatives like you."

"What makes you think whipping me into shape will be easier with Mother gone from here?"

"Let's hope it doesn't take a lot of whipping."

Justi looked at him worriedly, for he did sound as though he meant it. Justi saw her mother and Nurse in the yard then. Miriam was looking anxiously at Justi's window. Justi struggled with the stiff sash and finally Richard came and opened it for her.

"Sorry I was not up early to breakfast with you. Have a safe trip," Justi called as bravely as she could.

"I don't want to leave you, Justi," Miriam protested with tears in her eyes.

"Leave the boy alone," Nurse said, letting Jim help her into the carriage.

Justi smiled valiantly. "Nonsense, Mother. You have not been away from this old house since I was a child. You deserve a holiday. Besides, Richard and I will be so busy with the estate we would very likely bore you."

"Justi, are you sure?" Miriam asked, getting into the carriage only to hang out the window.

"Yes, and I will write you every week, I promise."

"Goodbye, then." Miriam waved until the carriage was almost to the road. Justi finally turned from the window. It was the first time she would be without Miriam and, rather than a sense of loss, she felt only relief that her mother would be someplace safe.

"That was well done of you," Richard said, coming to close the window.

"Considering so little has been well done of me, you mean?" she countered.

"As to that," he said, turning to face her, "if you give me your assurance of good conduct in future, I will not hold the past against you."

"A clean slate? It's not that easy," she said bitterly.

"It is as far as I am concerned." He went to the door and turned, expectantly.

She almost told him the truth then. She would have if not for her mother. Richard would never believe that Miriam was as much a victim of this scheme as Justi, that they were both trapped by half-mad old Nurse, who did not even remember what she had done. Their deception was actionable by law and she did not know Richard well enough to have any confidence in his mercy over this.

"I want you to go to church with me tomorrow," he said finally. "Do you think you can manage it?"

"Yes, with a walking stick. Trying to make a good impression?" she chided.

"Someone should. Do you go regularly?"

"Yes, with Mother and Nurse."

"Not with Dumont?"

"No."

"That's no surprise."

She flinched a little at the remark.

Richard left, but did not bother to lock the door.

He could be very forgiving, Justi thought, but it was these little cuts that hurt more than they should have. Had her grandfather sniped at her she would have shrugged it off. Why did Richard's opinion matter so much to her? She scarcely knew him. And what had he meant by sending her mother away for the winter? She had expected him to stay no more than a week or two. Justi now saw that the little act Gerard had put on, and the much bigger lie he told to cover himself, was working against her. Richard was convinced she was a boy but not a responsible one. To correct that impression could take some time.

As she did not leave her room that day she did not see Richard again until the next morning, when he solicitously helped her navigate the stairs and the climb into his curricle.

"You sent Mother by hired post chaise then?"

"Yes, from Stowmarket on. It's been my experience that women like to accomplish journeys as quickly as possible so as not to have to stay at inns more than necessary. She has that old nurse of yours with her, if that's any comfort, and I have written my stepmother, Julia, to expect her. Why do you keep that old woman about? She is past doing any useful work."

"Nurse? She is very much a fixture here. Where else would she go?"

"Not only that, your butler is half-deaf, the stable boy is slow-witted and the cook is the most abominable person I have ever had to deal with."

"I'm sure she found you charming, too."

Richard looked at her sharply. "I can't believe you actually pay these people. They either talk back or stare at you as though they are demented."

"Where else would they go? It would cost me a great deal more to keep Nurse somewhere else than here. Badger was able to put up with Grandfather. That alone should earn him a sainthood, but if I offered to pension him off he would be terribly hurt. He is the sort to die in harness."

"And what about Jim?"

"He gives me a fair day's work and he's gentle with the horses."

"But he can't think of anything for himself."

"No, except to help me home when I'd been beaten too badly to walk. He as good as saved my life, Richard." Justi looked at Richard but found no ready sympathy or understanding in those dark blue eyes. "I know you can do what you please here," she said helplessly, "but when it comes to speaking of turning off Jim or Badger, I wish you would consider their loyalty and what is due them. No one would like you for it. How long do you mean to stay, anyway?" she asked tiredly.

Richard Mallory was not in the habit of being lectured by anyone, least of all a troublesome boy. He took his time over answering. Until Dumont's extraordinary revelation Richard had not planned on more than a few months at Homeplace. Now it looked as though it could be a life's work to look after this flamboyant Mallory who could give him more trouble than Harry had ever done if he did not make a push to scotch such strong-willed behavior from the start.

Not being a parent, Richard's approach to the rearing of children was the same as he would use on training young horses. He knew he had to win every battle or lose control altogether. He optimistically calculated that it would take no more than a few months to break Justi to bit, although he did not say so. Then Christmas would be upon them. What he would do with himself after that he did not know.

Justi fell quiet for the rest of the drive, except to comment, as they neared the church, "The vicar may ask you to stay to lunch."

"Indeed! Why?"

"He usually invites me to lunch on Sunday. I spend part of the afternoon with him and walk home myself, later. I'm sure he'll want to talk to you to find out your views. He's quite a scholar and surprisingly open-minded."

"Even about Dumont?"

"He never met Gerard," Justi said defensively.

"How did you manage that?"

"It wasn't easy," she let slip.

Richard looked pointedly at her.

"I only meant that Gerard was an embarrassment," she corrected.

"Best see that you do not follow in his footsteps."

Justi could not help but dart him a belligerent glance for that.

They sat in one of the front pews and, owing to Justi's limp, they were the last to leave the old stone church. The vicar greeted Richard warmly. "And what have you been up to, Justin. No doubt you came off that black colt of yours."

"Actually I . . . fell off the carriage."

"You must learn to be more careful, lad."

After enjoying the modest but delicious lunch prepared by the vicar's housekeeper, Justi was treated to the vision of Richard floundering among the classical allusions that populated the vicar's discourses. Richard frankly had to ask for clarification more than once before he could reply.

On the whole, Mayfair seemed to approve of Richard since he thought just as he ought to on current politics. Richard, with his London perspective, had current news of Napoléon's machinations on the Continent. When Mayfair learned the *Times* now had a correspondent reporting on the fighting in the peninsula he vowed to subscribe.

Richard must have caught Justi smirking into her teacup and inquired as to the lad's progress.

"Justin doesn't actually study with me anymore. On philosophy and religion I'm afraid we disagree on too many points for him to learn anymore from me."

Richard cocked an eyebrow at his cousin.

"In Latin and Greek the boy has gone about as far as he can. Justin, you say Latin helps you with other languages."

"Yes, Mother taught me French, of course, but from taking Latin I can pretty well make out Italian and Spanish when I need to."

"Did he tell you how he got started working for Meecham and Bates? No? Well, he brought me this French essay in support of a philosophical argument we were having. Eventually he ended up translating the whole of it so that I could see his point. He lost the argument, but I made him copy the work out nicely and send it to a printer in London. Before we knew it Justin was receiving plays and poetry to translate. What are you working on now?"

"A series of German lectures. I'm not sure I follow them even once they are in English."

Enlightenment dawned on Richard. "So that's why you wanted to know German. You know you don't have to keep working at that. I mean you shouldn't be expected to be earning a living."

"But I like doing it. Besides, it passes the time. Winters can get very long here. That puts me in mind of something I've been wanting to ask you. Can you find out from Baird how badly off we are? He won't tell me a thing. I can pay off the local tradesmen and day laborers, and even manage the repairs, but I really need to know how deep in debt we are."

"Does Baird know you've been using your own money like this?"

"Well, I don't know."

"But you must stop it. There's no point in your worrying about such things."

Justi looked downcast. "You mean I'm going to lose Homeplace."

"No, of course not. I only mean that the debts are not your responsibility."

"Well, I would have done the same in any case. People must be paid."

"Are you sure you're not a changeling?" Richard inquired.

Justi choked on her tea.

"Mallorys do not generally feel that way about debts, even their own," Richard explained.

Justi recovered herself. "It's not just that. People here also need to have confidence in something, to see new building going on, not everything falling to ruin. It does make a difference to them."

Richard looked at the boy incredulously, then turned to thank the vicar for his hospitality. When Justi was sent to tell Haimes to hitch the team, the vicar said to Richard, "He's always been like that. So serious and responsible. He knew what was going on at Homeplace long before he should have. His grandfather must have done that to him. He never really had a childhood. So if he seems different from the lads you're used to, please remember, it's not his fault."

Richard was thoughtful on the return journey. Even allowing for Justin to be a pet of the vicar's, he realized he had misjudged the boy. Whatever else Justi was, he was not a spoiled, indolent brat.

"He likes you, Richard. We can look forward to Mrs. Harrison's excellent lunches every week, if you like. You won't mind going, will you? He has so few people he can talk to."

"No, I shall enjoy it, but I do see that I shall have to study up a bit. I felt like I was back in school."

"Yes, it was heavy weather for you until you got away from literature and philosophy. My lack of interest in war and politics, so long as they don't affect Homeplace, is a severe disappointment to him. In fact, I can see that you will quite cut me out as his favorite.''

Sunday dinner was the first meal Justi had taken downstairs since Gerard left, and she was impressed with the spit-and-polish appearance of Badger and the maids, and the deference with which they treated Richard. Apparently seeding London troops into a relaxed country establishment had a beneficial effect.

Her first mouthful of soup brought an exclamation of delight. "Mrs. Morrisee never made this. You fired the cook!''

Richard had steeled himself for a condemnation of his high-handedness. "The new cook has just arrived from Stowmarket. And, on the subject of Mrs. Morrisee...''

"No, I mean how did you manage it? Grandfather had been trying to get rid of her for a decade. I can't count the times he told her to pack up. She just ignored him, except for cooking tripe, which he hated.''

Richard smiled smugly. "I did have to resort to at least the threat of physical violence and it necessitated my invasion of the kitchen area.''

"This calls for a toast. To the victor! Whatever happens after this, Richard, I shall never doubt your courage.''

Richard took the jest good-naturedly, as it was meant, and thought how well the boy looked with a playful smile on his lips rather than a sulky pout.

They had just moved on to a well-turned-out brace of pheasants when Justi slipped in, "Of course, there may be repercussions...''

"What?'' Richard looked horrified. "You don't mean she will come back?''

"No, I rather think Mrs. Morrisee has been permanently routed from Homeplace. But, you see, she's the blacksmith's sister and he already drinks.'' Justi chewed a succulent mouthful. "I just can't decide if having her move in on him will ruin him completely or drive him stone-cold sober. It should be interesting to await developments.''

As it turned out, Mrs. Morrisee did not stay with her brother for more than a few weeks but was taken on as cook at the Ram's Head, the only inn Glenncross boasted. In the meantime, however, Masters sobered up and went back to work and Richard Mallory began to be regarded in the light of a local hero. His embarrassment at the congratulations that came even from the vicar he hid under the guise of modesty.

Richard had just admonished Justi for wandering away from the breakfast table with a cup of tea and for not eating enough to keep a mouse alive.

''Here comes Ned. He's rather late today, no doubt in deference to your gentlemanly hours.''

''Who's Ned?'' Richard scarcely looked up from the farm account books he'd been perusing during his meal.

''Ned Thompson. He's sort of the farm manager. He's come for his orders for the week. Would you like to do the honors?'' Justi teased.

''Why, I wouldn't know what to say to the fellow.''

''Don't worry. He'll tell you. You'll see.''

''Morning, sir, m'lord, fine day.

Justi performed the introductions and Richard waited.

''I was just wondering, sir, if the men should keep on with the wood gathering.''

''Yes, I think so, unless there's anything more pressing.''

''There's two or three sections of field wall that's come down, but you may want to leave that till the hunting's over, else we could be doing it twice.''

''Yes, I think that should definitely wait, then,'' Richard agreed.

''Shearers will be here again this week, of course. So we'll probably need all the lads to herd and handle. Do you want fleeces taken to Stowmarket or Newmarket?''

''I shall have to give that some thought.''

"We took spring fleeces to Newmarket and got a bit better price."

"Let's try that again, then," Richard decided.

"If there's nothing else then, sir..."

"There is one thing, Ned. Now that I'm here, I'll be taking care of paying out the wages—not Justi."

"Right, sir."

"Oh, and one other thing. The chimneys. They want cleaning while we still have some warm days."

"Afraid we have to get the sweeps from Stowmarket for that job. No one hereabouts will go up on roof, except Justi."

"I see. That's all, then, I think."

"What are you chuckling about?" Richard inquired of Justi as they walked out to the stable.

"Ned's face, when he thought you were going to make him go up on the roof."

"What does the squire do when his chimneys need cleaning?"

"I don't know. I never thought to ask him."

Owing to Bluedevil not being ridden for a week, and the fact that Justi seldom rode him slower than a canter, she was having some trouble managing his high spirits at Richard's sedate pace. A series of bucks that got Bluedevil only a laughing reprimand from his owner brought down a severe rebuke on Justi's head for keeping such an ill-trained hunter.

They had just passed the pond and were riding toward the sheep farm in the center of the property when Richard inquired, "Where did you come by that black monster, anyway? You don't breed hunters here."

"Bluedevil? At the sales in Newmarket. He was a bargain."

"But that's near... This is never that black colt that killed old Makepiece!"

"Well, yes, actually, but I've cured him of his tricks."

"Get down!" The vehemence of the utterance made her jump, even though Justi was accustomed to being shouted at.

Her puzzled "What?" was cut short when Richard shouldered his horse up to her mount and grabbed her off by the coat collar.

"You will not ride that horse again! Do you understand?" Justi looked at him resentfully from her seat on the ground. By the time she got back on her feet and gingerly dusted herself off, Richard had dismounted and was holding his chestnut for her to mount. If she had known how few men had ever been permitted to ride Major, she might not have felt so ill-used. Richard mounted Bluedevil himself and curbed the horse's antics with a firm hand and a swat from his whip.

She never carried a whip herself, and Justi eyed it suspiciously as they completed their tour of the farm.

"You have only the horses and sheep—no cattle," Richard commented critically.

"Just the milk cows Mrs. Thompson cares for. She also feeds some chickens and pigs for us, and the boys help me with the butchering."

Richard cocked an eyebrow at her. "What do you do when you want beef?"

"Usually buy it from the squire. If you mean to visit often we can buy some young stock from Squire Coates. Mother and I never kept a ponderous table for the two of us. Even with Gerard here, he drank more than he ate. It's easy enough to use up a lamb or pig, if we smoke part of it, between us and the servants. But if we slaughtered a beef we would have had to try to sell part of it and that's not easy, times being what they are. Also I know nothing of cattle." Justi looked at Richard expectantly after this long speech. She had begun to realize that she had only to agree with him or display an open mind for him to rethink his views.

"I suppose a herd of beef cattle would be regarded by Baird as an extravagance right now," Richard said, staring at Bluedevil's arched crest.

Justi's eyes traveled to the shining black horse, the one extravagant thing she had bought in her young life, not so much because she had fallen in love with him, but because he made the village boys afraid to cross her path. Bluedevil made her look taller, stronger and more dangerous than she was. But he was only part of her costume, the trappings of a life of deceit. "What are you going to do with Bluedevil?" she asked as they rode into the stable yard. "You don't want him."

"It would be too dangerous to sell him to someone else. I'll keep him for my own use until you come of age. He may have settled down by then."

"I can't see that a few years will make that much difference unless you mean to have him cut."

Richard smiled sadistically. "You can't possibly know the terms of your grandfather's will."

"Not the latest one, why?"

"Because you do not come of age, my lad, until you are five and twenty."

"Oh, my God," Justi whispered. "I'll never make it."

Justi darling,
I think about you all the time and hope Richard is not too hard on you. I don't see why you should be punished because of Gerard.

They are quite spoiling me here and your cousin is right. None of the chimneys at Amberly smoke.

Julia is such a comfortable, understanding sort of person and her daughter Alicia is the sweetest child imaginable. Her son, Harry, is a dear boy and so considerate.

Cousin Clara is a little vivacious but she causes us no end of amusement. I find myself laughing at her witticisms even when I know I shouldn't.

I did not realize how much I missed female companionship. You know what I mean—someone to discuss fashions and hairstyles with, and the latest gossip.

I am so looking forward to seeing you at Christmas. We are all to gather here at Amberly.

Love,
Mother

Mother,
Richard has sold the last pair of two-year-old work colts to the squire for two hundred pounds. Can you imagine? I'm sure I wouldn't even have gotten the hundred and fifty that they are worth. His technique bears studying.

He is not really hard on me, just a little unpredictable. He seems satisfied with my education, especially after getting to know Vicar Mayfair. I think he is beginning to suspect that Gerard took him in and that I am not a total reprobate.

We get along comfortably enough most of the time. He has quite a sense of humor, which he attempts to hide. And when he smiles he looks so different from when he puts on his stern face.

Also, I think he is realizing that I am competent to run Homeplace. He seems surprised that I am so docile and eager to learn. If he only knew how often I have trouble holding my tongue. I can't imagine that he will feel like riding herd on me for eight more years so it's only a matter of time before he leaves me to manage on my own. He is much easier to handle than Gerard. Also, he never drinks too much.

I am happy you are having such an enjoyable visit with the Mallory women.

Justi

Harry,

I have a job for you, that is, if it seems safe enough to leave Julia in charge of Clara. I want you to come to Homeplace and help me with your cousin's education. Don't groan! I don't mean Latin or Greek. He has had quite enough of that.

He seems to have never had any male friends his own age. He rides decently enough and can manage a team safely, but has no interest in fighting or cocking, and, I believe, is actually afraid of guns.

As a temptation I offer his pheasants and rabbits that have not been hunted much in seven or eight years. They are practically begging to be potted. There will be several hunts hereabouts this fall and the country is rough enough to challenge your horsemanship.

Come post chaise to Newmarket, which is the closest big town between here and Amberly. Let me know what day you will arrive.

As ever,
Richard

P.S. You may ride my spare hunter.

A rainy day in late September found Justin and Richard both looking disgustedly out at the weather.

"Well, since it's not likely to stop today, why don't you give me a tour of the house so we can make a list of repairs?"

"All right," Justi groaned. "May as well start in the attic. See if we have sprung any leaks."

The stairs to the attic were grimy and echoed hollowly under their boots. "Mind your head!" Justi warned as they ascended the last flight of steps to the short attic space. "Except for the dormer, there's only space to walk upright down the center."

"What is the dormer for?"

"Light, I suppose, and access to the roof."

"The wood looks sound enough." Richard seemed surprised.

"It's a slate roof and it's been kept up, unlike the rest of the place. There aren't any leaks, but I see daylight over by the northwest chimney."

"What is it?"

"Couple of missing slates. It probably won't even leak as long as the wind is from the east."

They did not spend much time on the third floor. "A dozen servants' bedrooms, all unheated," Justi reported. "Do you want to see them, or should we ask Badger what needs done?"

"Firth and Haimes have already given me a graphic account of the state of the servants' quarters."

"They must be very devoted to you, to put up with such privation."

"Let's see the second floor."

"Seven bedrooms and two dressing rooms," Justi continued her catalogue. "The two rooms in the northwest corner are unusable in winter since their flues are completely blocked with brick."

"How do you know? Did you have them cleaned?"

She almost told him she had dropped a candle in from the top and seen the bricks, but thought better of it.

"The top of that chimney collapsed two years ago and the bricks didn't all go into the yard."

"We'll see," was his only reply. He made more notes, as though he were planning on using the rooms. Once all the sticky doors and loose floorboards had been noted, they descended to the main floor.

"You've seen everything on this floor, including the kitchen regions. There's only the storerooms in the basement."

"May as well have a look." Richard turned over a new page in his notebook.

Justi lit a branch of candles for their descent. "This is the stillroom, cheeses, hams and so forth. The box room is over there. Here's the wine cellar." She pushed this door open also and exclaimed, "Good God, did you bring all this?"

"No, wasn't it here before?"

"Not when Gerard was here. Badger must have cached it away somewhere."

"What a comfort to you to have such an honest butler."

"What a compliment to you that he trusts you not to drink it all."

"What's down here?" Richard's voice echoed in the passage.

"A sort of junk room—the old armory."

As Richard pulled open the heavy door, ominous scurryings and squeakings gave notice of the disturbance of the inhabitants.

"Rats," whispered Justi. "We can keep them out of the stillroom, but they've tunnelled into the armory from the rosebush in back of the house."

Richard took the candles and walked past the cleared area to examine a cobwebbed crossbow and some broken pikes leaning against the wall.

"I don't even know what most of this stuff is," Justi said.

"Harry would have fun poking about down here. It looks like a dungeon."

"It was once, actually." She followed him past the cleared area reluctantly.

Richard turned from an examination of the chains and manacles on the wall to catch Justi involuntarily massaging the fresh scar on the side of her hand as she looked uneasily about.

"So, that's how this happened!" Her breath jerked in as Richard yanked her hand up to look at it again.

Justi's lips were dry. "He got drunk a few nights before you came, and knocked me out. I woke up down here." She shivered.

"What did he do to you?"

"Nothing!" She said it a bit too hastily, her eyes wide with the memory of her close call. "He must have fallen asleep, then forgotten me." The lie sounded lame even to her.

Richard's jaw tightened. As they got to the door, he made as if to push her in and close it.

"No, please. Don't do this," she begged in a whisper, pulling ineffectually at the door against his much greater strength.

"I want the truth," Richard demanded.

"Nothing happened. I swear it."

"Tell me and it will be over with."

"To tell you would be to betray someone else, and you would hate me."

"I will find out eventually," he warned.

"I know that," she said desperately. "I am not so naive as I used to be."

"Then what is the point of delaying? I will have the truth out of you in another day or ten days or—"

"But if I tell you now I won't have those days and I do want them," she choked out.

"What are you imagining, that I will murder you?"

"I would not blame you if you did," Justi said forlornly.

Richard could see whatever trust the boy had in him rapidly dissolving, so he pulled Justi through the door. "Come, it must be near lunchtime."

Justi ate little, she was feeling so wretchedly sick. She had not thought about the armory in all this while, she had been so occupied. She was shocked to realize how much the experience had affected her.

"Justi," Richard said halfway through the meal. "We all have something we can't face."

She swallowed. "Even you?"

"Yes."

"What is it?"

"It should amuse you trying to find out." The apprehension in Justi's face was replaced by puzzlement, which was all Richard wanted.

Dear Julia,

Things are shaping up well here, but I hope you will be able to let me have Harry until December anyway. For several reasons I think it would be advisable to postpone Alicia's coming-out until she is eighteen. See how she feels about it.

I have a plan for next season: to spend the spring and summer here at Homeplace. You will find it quite different from Amberly, but I'm sure you will be amused. We intend to spare no effort in refurbishing the rooms here for you. I think you will find them pleasant enough, during the warm weather, anyway.

This new charge of mine is a puzzle to me, one day reckless beyond belief, the next childishly fearful. He doesn't want for sense and, considering his upbringing, could be a good deal worse. He does things almost designed to provoke me, and yet looks so innocent, I must in fairness attribute his follies to ignorance, not malice. Heaven help him if I ever find he is trying to put one over on me. I shall be eager to see what you think of him after Harry and I have had him in hand for a few months.

I hope this finds you all in good health and spirits.

As ever,
Richard

Most of the repairs Richard set forward were not all that expensive, just unnecessary as far as Justi could see. It looked to her almost as though he was intending to hold parties in the house.

He was especially incensed that the residents of Homeplace had either to make use of a chamber pot or the "little house" at some distance from the building. Evidently both Amberly and the Mallory town house were provided with the latest conveniences in this line. But Justi refused to apologize for something she was powerless to mend.

"I have studied our site," she said, pulling a roll of plans out of the ancient desk in the library. "I considered the idea of a stacked loo like one sees built up the outside walls of castles, but the only way to keep the stuff from leaching into the basements, which are already damp, is to build it on the downhill side, and that would let it flow into the stream."

"That's too makeshift, anyway," Richard said, looking at her crude topographic map and finally carrying it outside to pace off measurements himself.

Justi trailed after him, giving a running step every once in a while to keep up with his long stride. "Really there is no good solution that does not require a great deal of digging," she said, "and the purchase of a quantity of clay tile and gravel for a leach bed. There is no way to justify the expense with only Mother and a half-dozen servants."

"I don't think it will cost so very much. Some of your men need employment this time of year anyway," said Richard, rolling up the paper with finality.

"I don't think Baird would like it," she said as a finishing touch, and saw Richard's jaw jut out. The words were like a magic wand. She had only to speak them to push Richard into any little scheme she had been wanting to undertake, but had put off for fear of censure.

"I am not concerned about what Mr. Baird likes or dislikes. I'm in charge here, and you had better get used to the idea." He thrust the drawing at her, almost knocking her down with it, and strode toward the house. She stood looking at his back long enough to wipe the smile off her face, then followed him innocently in the back door.

Chapter Four

"How old is that harness?" Richard asked disdainfully when he finally ran Justi to earth in the stable workshop. She was astraddle a bench with the carriage harness spread out around her, sewing the torn stitching on one breast piece with an awl.

"Older than me, most likely," she said, looking at last year's patch with satisfaction.

"Or me," Richard jibed, looking around the walls at the odd bits of harnesss and other leather pieces hanging about in case they might be needed for patching. "I'm riding into Brinley. Do you want to go with me?"

"Yes, but I had better finish this instead, now that I have made a start."

Justi could tell that Richard was irritated she did not drop everything to go with him, but she could not dance attendance on him all day long. She had things she had to do, and he had no patience at all about letting her finish a task. Everything had to be done when he wanted it.

"This is not fit work for you."

"Jim has enough to do with keeping the stalls clean and taking care of the horses. Besides, he has no turn for this."

"We should get someone who has a turn for it."

Justi's face went quite bleak, and she regretted irritating Richard. You never knew what his mind would light on when he was in a bad mood.

"What is it? You look ill," he said.

"It's only that when you talk like that, about getting rid of Jim, or even Badger—do you really mean to do it?"

"I suppose I could, couldn't I?" Richard teased, a little intoxicated with the power he wielded.

"Please don't!"

"You have never said please before."

"Nothing else you have wished to change mattered."

"Very well," Richard said, no proof against that pleading look. "What I was actually thinking of was hiring more help."

"Oh, you gave me a turn there," Justi said in relief and went back to her sewing, then looked searchingly at Richard. "If anything were to happen to me, would you keep them on anyway?"

"What are you talking about? You're just a child. What could possibly happen to you?"

"I don't feel like a child. Sometimes I feel quite old. But anything could happen. My father died when he was not that many years older."

"Don't even think of that," Richard commanded. "Do you imagine I am heartless? Of course I would not turn anyone off."

Justi smiled at him without thinking and let her dimples show, then looked shyly away.

"You are a strange boy," Richard said, smiling back at her.

"Wh—why?" Justi asked, casting a cursory look over herself. She was always trying to correct any discrepancy between her behavior and that of a man.

"All the work you do. I don't know many lads who would bother, let alone do it voluntarily."

"How many do you know with a house falling down around their ears?"

"None. But that is not your concern."

"It may be some day," she said ominously. "There, finished."

"Oh, good. You can ride to Brinley with me, after all."

If Richard was puzzled by Justi, she was even more confused by him. He seemed to want her to engage in all sorts of manly activities, but he guarded her safety with a violence that usually got her more bruises than if he had not intervened. She had gotten used to his hot but short-lived fits of anger, but could not steel herself not to jump when he shouted at her.

She instinctively knew he would not approve of the Earl of Mallory patching his own roof, so she neglected to mention that for the past two years it was she who replaced the broken slates and ran the sacks of bricks up and down the chimneys to knock down the soot.

The roof of the old house was not particularly steep nor even slippery on the warm, dry days she chose to work on it. It puzzled her that no one else was willing to do the minor patching required to keep it in good order.

Even on her first day up she had begun to enjoy the perspective her perch afforded. She could see the young colts at play in the pasture behind the stud farm and the flocks spread out over the west pastures, grazing in the warm sun.

She asked Jim, who fetched for her on the ground, if he wouldn't like to come up. He blanched. "I can't even stomach breakfast when I know you're going up there."

"But it's not like you could possibly fall."

"If I passed out nothing would be more likely."

The more Justi learned about slate napping, the more she was convinced a heavier person would do more damage than good on the brittle surface, so she gave up trying to get anyone else to do it. In fact, she began to take a good deal of pride in her new skill.

She was itching to clean the chimneys and fix the missing slates but knew she had to put it off until a day when Richard left her alone. The morning he was getting ready to pick up his half brother in Newmarket, he inquired, "Want anything from town?"

He had not asked her to go since three would crowd him in the curricle. Also, he probably wanted to talk to Harry alone. She could guess the subject of the conference. She toyed for a second with the idea of inviting herself along to see what shifts Richard would make to leave her home, but it was a warm day and the roof beckoned.

Her hesitation prompted Richard to say, "I'm afraid there won't be room in the curricle for you since Harry will have his valet along."

"I'm sure I shall find something to occupy myself."

Richard turned suspiciously. "You're not going out, are you?"

"Why, no. I have already had my ride and it's getting hot. I don't imagine I shall leave the house," she said quite truthfully.

"See that you don't."

She raised her brows at the command, but merely said, "I don't need anything. Shall I check with Badger?"

"I already have his list."

"You say that as though you don't normally handle the household shopping."

"No, I do not!" Richard left then, but wasn't even well down the drive before Justi had Jim busy heating pitch in the stable yard.

"So you think Justin only needs to learn a bit of shooting and hunting to give him more confidence?" Harry inquired of his half brother as Richard drove his prancing grays along the hedge-lined road.

"Another two stone of weight wouldn't hurt, either, but I think that's past hoping for. Let's just start with what we can mend."

As they turned in at the untidy drive Richard's attention was arrested so abruptly by the sight of Justi in shirtsleeves walking along the top of the roof that he jabbed his grays in the mouth, drawing an exclamation from Harry.

"Richard, what are you about?"

"Justi!" Richard bellowed. "Get down from there."

Justi looked up, waved, then sat down by one of the huge chimneys and started nailing a slate in place, effectively covering Richard's subsequent shouting.

"So this is the timid lad you wanted help with?" Harry chuckled. "If I'm expected to go up there after him, you can turn around and take me back to Newmarket."

In a rage, Richard lashed the horses up the drive and pulled them up short in the stable yard. Throwing the reins to Harry, he bolted toward the house, yelling, at the same time Justi chose to get rid of some cracked slates by letting them slide off the roof with a clatter and crash into the courtyard below.

"Mind where you go, sir," Jim said, solicitously. "One of them slates could give you a nasty gash."

Climbing three flights of stairs at a run did nothing to improve Richard's humor. Banging his head in the low attic was the final straw. When he finally flung open the dormer window, he hardly had breath to yell. "Didn't you hear me? Get in here!"

"What? It's too windy. I can't hear you," Justi lied. "I'm almost finished."

Richard watched in impotent fury as Justi scored a piece of slate with a straight edge and neatly chipped the excess off with her hammer. She then tacked it in place by the chimney and applied some pitch. He toyed for a moment with the thought of going out after the boy but feared that in his present mood he might knock Justi off the roof—the very sort of accident he was attempting to prevent.

Justi carefully loaded her tools into a canvas bag and lowered the pitch pot over the edge to Jim. She had sent the ladder down already. She untied the end of her rope from the chimney, coiled it up and threw it to Richard.

"Here, catch." Richard almost fell out the window grabbing for it, only adding to his temper. As she stood up and walked to the dormer, Richard's face turned pale.

When she slid down beside the dormer and was reaching around for the window frame he grabbed her arm and dragged her in. Tipping her over his knees, he delivered three sharp smacks to her bottom.

"Richard, what are you doing?"

"Get to your room. That's only a sample."

Thinking she had gotten off easier than she expected, she scampered downstairs to wash the black smudges off her face and change her dirty linen.

Richard did not, however, come to beat her, but to let her out for dinner. He had interviewed her hapless accomplice, Jim, who testified that Justi did this sort of thing two or three times a year.

"Why didn't you tell me you were going out on the roof?"

"I didn't think I needed to. Besides—" she grinned "—I planned on being done before you got back."

"You knew I wouldn't approve?" he thundered.

"Considering the number of activities you disapprove of, it was a good bet. Did you, by the way, succeed in hiring sweeps in Newmarket?"

"No, I did not."

"No matter. The upper flues are cleaned now. All we have to do is run the long brushes up and down the individual flues, and we can do that before each room is cleaned."

"You planned to defy me."

"I did not. You never told me not to go on the roof."

"I'm telling you now. If I ever catch you up there again, you'll get the beating you deserve."

"Does this mean you're going to be cross all through dinner? You'll have Harry thinking we are at daggers all the time."

"Aren't we?" he demanded.

"No. Occasionally you can be quite reasonable."

"Me?" Richard sputtered. "You're the one who starts these things."

"I'm sorry I don't live up to your expectations, but that's a little difficult to do when I don't even know what they are."

"Very well. When you are not in my company, or Harry's, I want to know ahead of time exactly what you plan to do."

"Fair enough."

Though somewhat mollified, Richard had decided it was his duty to be stern throughout dinner, so it was left to Justi to draw Harry out about Amberly and his trip to Newmarket. Harry was a good storyteller and made her laugh all through the meal. The high spirits of his two companions, with the help of good food and wine, managed to charm Richard out of the sullens. Also, Harry started telling tales on him and he had to defend himself.

"Remember when Father's bull was after me and you stopped it with a pitchfork?" Harry reminisced.

"You faced down a bull with a pitchfork?" Justi stared at Richard.

"Oh, no. He impaled it," Harry crowed. "We thought it was killed."

"What is worse, so did my father," Richard put in. "I was nearly eighteen, but he beat me half to death anyway."

"After you saved your brother's life!" Justi was incensed.

"Well, the bull was worth a hundred and twenty pounds," stated Richard flatly. Harry howled.

"I take it the animal recovered?" Justi asked.

"Yes, and so, eventually, did I."

"That must have happened when I was ten." Harry passed the port to Richard. "That's not the worst scrape I got Richard into. When I was six I climbed up this tree after Clara's cat and got stuck. Father made Richard get a ladder and come up after me."

"Why?" asked Justi.

"Because he wouldn't let go of the cat. Besides, I was supposed to be looking after him," Richard supplied.

"It does sound like he needed a keeper."

"Anyway, Richard got partway up and froze," Harry continued. "I thought I'd be up there forever."

"It was the ladder," Richard explained. "I didn't realize it bounced worse when you were in the middle of it. I really expected it to break."

"What happened?"

"Harry started to cry."

"I did not. But anyway, Richard finally climbed the rest of the way up and got my foot unstuck."

"You were afraid." Justi turned to Richard. "But you went up anyway. How did you manage it?"

"It was the thought of my father waiting for me at the bottom that encouraged me to complete my mission."

"Once he got down, he lost his dinner in the yard," Harry reported with delight.

"So that's it," mused Justi.

"Confess, you would never have figured it out on your own," Richard said.

"Not till the next time the roof needed repairs, anyway."

"What are you two talking about?" Harry asked.

"Irrational fears," said Justi.

"I would hardly call the fear of falling and breaking your neck irrational," stated Richard.

"Off a horse, no. Off that roof, yes."

"Depends on your point of view," countered Richard.

"I'm sorry about today. I didn't mean to worry you," Justi apologized.

"Sometimes I wonder."

"Well, you have to remember, nobody ever worried about me before, except Mother. And she had no idea what all I did."

"A fortunate circumstance for the good lady's sanity," Richard said dryly.

"I think it's rather nice to have someone worry about you," said Harry, "especially if you get hurt."

"You don't mean you would tell your mother if you got racked up?" inquired Justi.

"Of course, you get no end of sympathy."

Justi shook her head and looked at Richard.

"Don't look at me. I didn't have that luxury. My mother died with I was seven," Richard said, "but I came to love Julia as well."

"Mother needed all the help she could get," Harry said gratefully. "I don't know how often Richard took her part against his own father. That's what got him thrown out."

Justi flinched and looked an inquiry at her guardian, but he merely shrugged and went back to his meal.

Justi learned more about Richard and the rest of the Mallorys in one evening spent in Harry's company than in the whole month before. Richard seemed to come alive with Harry, to lose his reserve.

Over tea Justi found out about Clara. "She was married at sixteen to Albert Redmond. I tried to talk Father out of it—" Richard shook his head "—but he thought it was an excellent match."

"Clara killed him," Harry reported matter-of-factly.

Justi choked on her tea and looked to Richard for confirmation, but he was smiling. "Not literally."

"No, she pestered him to death."

"Were you fond of Clara's husband?" Justi asked.

"No," Harry considered, "but he didn't deserve Clara."

Harry was determined to take his task seriously, and directly after breakfast the next day he dragged Justi off to the gun room. It would have been a chancy day for riding anyway, reflected Justi. It was threatening rain, and there was a cold wind whipping down the valley.

After disparaging both the condition and antiquity of the various weapons, Harry selected two fowling pieces that still looked serviceable and instructed Justi in the disassembly and cleaning of them.

She was surprised at the simplicity of the mechanisms, and after taking apart and cleaning all the other guns and pistols that were not past mending, she felt that the insides of a gun, at least, no longer held any mystery for her.

When Richard went to roust them out for lunch, the room reeked of gun oil, and the hands and faces of the two youngsters, bent over the guts of an ancient pistol, were smutty enough for Richard to demand that they go upstairs for a wash.

"I'm going into Stowmarket this afternoon," Richard announced during the meal. "Anyone want anything? And, no, I haven't told Badger. I plan to sneak off without his shopping list."

"Could you pick up some fresh powder?" Harry requested. "What's in there looks damp. I don't know how old it might be."

"I wonder if that's why..." Justi started, then looked embarrassed.

"Your pistol didn't fire? Possibly," supplied Richard.

"You shot at something? What?" Harry wanted to know.

"Just...a rat."

Richard laughed. "Justi hates rats."

"Here's your powder." Richard handed over a package to Harry later that afternoon. "And some number seven shot. I didn't think there was any."

"Right. We'll use up the heavier stuff at target practice."

"Harry, do be careful."

"Come now, Richard, it's not like I haven't been doing this since I was twelve."

"Yes, I know. Just remember, if you manage to shoot each other, I'm the one who has to answer to your respective mothers."

They spent an hour firing at broken and chipped crockery, liberated from the kitchen with the connivance of the cook, who had her eye on a new set of dishes for the servants' hall.

"How did he do?" Richard stopped Harry on their way in to clean the guns.

"Well, I wouldn't say it's hopeless. If he would keep his eyes open, it would help."

"Oh, Lord."

"He did shatter a saucer toward the end."

"But was it an accident?"

"Oh, I never thought of that."

"Perhaps I'd better come with you tomorrow."

"No, no, you'll just make him nervous."

After filling their shot pouches the next morning, Justi asked, "What should we do with this old powder? Just throw it away? There must be pounds of it."

"Best not dump it." Harry considered. "I know. Do you have any stumps you want blown out?"

"There is this old bush outside the kitchen I'd like dug out. The rats have holes under it. I think it's their outside entrance to the basement."

"Perfect!" Harry exclaimed. "If there's a tunnel down into it, we won't even have to dig." After constructing a long fuse from linen, candle wax and fresh powder, Harry really warmed to his task.

"What should I do?" asked Justi.

"Make sure everyone keeps a safe distance."

Harry thrust the fuse down what looked like the main tunnel under the old rose canes and spilled down as much of the old powder as would fit. He used the remainder to pour down the other entrance holes.

"Ready?"

"I suppose. Harry, what's a safe distance?"

"Oh, twenty-five feet."

"But the house is closer than that."

"Yes, but the windows are high on this side. I don't think any pieces of wood will fly up there."

Harry lit the fuse and ran along the wall of the house with Justi, but not too far to prevent a good view. Nothing happened for half a minute.

"What a letdown. I guess we'll just have to set fire to it." Harry started toward the fuse when a tremendous explosion rent the air, knocking both of them flat.

The noise of the blast and the rattling of all the windows in the house brought the kitchen staff out the back door and Richard bolting around the house from the library. He was in time to see the last of the rat parts raining down on Justi, who was sitting up, disgustedly brushing fur and pieces of tail off her coat sleeves.

"Where's Harry? Never mind."

Between coughs, Harry was rolling on the smoking ground in hysterics. "Did you ever see anything like it?"

Richard teetered for a second on the brink of delivering a thundering scold, but it would clearly have had no effect on his giggling sibling, and Justi already looked half scared to death. Besides, his relief at finding them both in one piece was so great that he, too, found release in laughter, and walked with Harry down to examine the crater in the yard.

What is this fascination with destruction? Justi wondered. She was still a little stunned when they came back chuckling.

"Justi, I know you hate rats," Richard said, laughing, "but really!"

This was too much for her, and she laughed a little weakly. She secretly suspected that if she had done this, instead of Harry, Richard wouldn't have found it nearly so amusing.

Tenants, neighbors and villagers came all day to observe the destruction, and Jim proudly shoveled up the rat corpses. By his count they had bagged fifty-six of various sizes, though how he could determine this was a puzzle to Justi.

"By counting the tails," he said seriously.

The mass burial of the remains was conducted by Jim and the lads from the stud farm with what Justi thought was undue fascination. "Interesting method of exterminating vermin," Squire Coates commented later that afternoon.

"Squire, let me introduce my half brother, Harry, the perpetrator of the destruction," Richard offered.

"Hello, sir." Harry shook his hand. "Actually killing the rats was an accident. We just wanted to blow up their tunnels."

"Take my advice, lad. Get yourself a fast terrier or even a ferret. Much safer."

"Actually," a more composed Justi put in, "we were looking for a safe way of disposing of some old gunpowder."

"Safe! By God, you're lucky you were not killed. I would have thought you had better sense, Justi."

"Me?" Her eyes widened. "I don't know anything about powder."

"All the more reason you shouldn't fool with it."

The squire took his leave, and Justi walked him to his horse. "Harry's your guest, now," he said in a fatherly way. "You must keep him out of trouble so your cousin can get on with his work."

"Yes, sir," she said with a rueful smile. "I'll do my best."

"Of course. I know I can count on you."

"What did he say?" Richard asked, still chuckling as she walked back to them.

"I don't know which of you is the worst. He's counting on me to keep Harry out of trouble."

This set Harry and Richard off again. And, for days, the mere mention of the word "rat" sent them into fits of laughter. Justi supervised the filling of the hole with rock and dirt, in preparation for its transformation into a flower bed for her mother.

The next day it rained steadily all morning. Justi, in the throes of translating another French novel, easily managed to keep busy. But Harry, with only cards as a recourse—he didn't feel like reading and there wasn't even a billiards table—got on Richard's nerves long before the grass was dry enough to go hunting.

Justi, who roamed Homeplace nearly every day, either on horseback or on foot, certainly knew where there were birds to be had. She did not, however, volunteer this information to Harry. She knew better than to tell him that she would rather watch the pheasants than kill them. He would never understand.

She had no qualms about the slaughter of sheep, pigs and chickens when their time came. They would not, after all, have existed, if not intentionally bred and raised for food. But there was something about the wildlife that seemed sacred to her. There was a balance there in the woods she was reluctant to disturb.

In matters of the farm, control was necessary and good, in so far as it was possible. You were still always at the mercy of weather and disease. But in what she considered the wild part of Homeplace, amid the great oaks and berry thickets, she preferred not to disturb anything. Even the gathering of wood for winter fires consisted of picking up dead limbs and culling dying trees.

Harry and she had penetrated into the densest part and he went, unerringly, to the best cover for the birds.

"You take the first shot."

To please him she went against her instincts and fired when prompted. To her amazement, a bird fell.

"You got it!" Harry pounded her on the back.

She had been thinking since his arrival how different Harry was from Gerard. It wasn't just that he was five years younger. Everything was open about Harry. When he touched her on the arm to get her attention or slapped her shoulder after a good shot, she felt safe to take it at face value. He meant nothing more by it.

She thought this must be what it felt like to have a brother and, in spite of the dead bird he was gleefully carrying to her, she was glad Richard had sent for him. He was a very comfortable person. You could trust him and tell him anything, except that one thing. She hated to deceive him, but she had tricked people she cared about all her life. She thought perhaps it had hardened her somehow.

"Well, I'm afraid it's full of shot. Next time, try for the wing. Here."

"At least it died quickly," she said, gently laying it to rest in the game bag.

They hunted until they had scarcely enough light to find their way home, but the unfamiliar sounds of gunfire must have sent everything to cover. On the walk back she had time to think about Richard, not so open as Harry, except in Harry's company. He was very much in control of himself and those for whom he felt responsible. No wonder, since the burdens of a family and estate had been thrust upon him when he was only twenty. Any flouting of his authority brought on a violent outburst. She tried to fix him in her mind as some kind of father figure but that wasn't how she felt about him.

At first he was her enemy; now, a friend. But the give-and-take conflict with him continued. What's more, she liked the conflict. As much as she had initially wanted him to go away, she now realized she would miss him desperately if he went. His jokes, more subtle than Harry's, even his fits of anger, which she had begun to be able to manage, were endearing. When he touched her it meant more; when he cuffed her it hurt more. He had begun to awaken a hunger in her, and a temptation to tell him the truth about herself.

But she was also a person dedicated to control. She would not throw away her whole life and Homeplace for a man, even an endearing one. Also, the thought of his contempt for her deceit was too much to contemplate. She couldn't stand the thought of him hating her. So an older brother he would have to be to her, and nothing more. Women made such sacrifices all the time for the church. She was at least that strong.

The specter of accidental discovery was a risk she had lived with all her life. Perhaps it was a greater risk now, staying alone here with Richard and Harry, but what choice had she? That Gerard had rumbled her disguise and that Richard and Harry had not rather surprised her. But then, Gerard had the sort of mind that would look at a situation obliquely. Richard was suspicious of her in the beginning, but then Gerard had thrown him onto the wrong track by suggesting that she was an effeminate male.

Now Richard made allowances for little things like her dislike of shooting. She understood why Gerard had concocted the tale, not just to blackmail Richard, but to cover for her. Gerard was dangerous and was probably still hatching schemes to plague her with. Life never used to be so complicated. And her attraction to Richard was like to land her in the soup if she was not careful.

"Any luck?" Richard asked, when the weary pair returned.

"Justi shot a bird."

"Let's see it." Richard feigned disbelief.

Justi reluctantly revealed the mangled remains of the woodcock. Richard unkindly burst into laughter.

"The whole breast is gone. If you know what's good for you, you won't take that to the cook."

"I told you we should have gotten a spade and buried it behind the garden wall," said Justi.

Chapter Five

Since the next day dawned dry and clear, Richard thought they should show Harry some of the country. Harry was surprised when Justi mounted Major and Richard got on an unknown black brute. He didn't mind riding Richard's second-string hunter, but began to think Justi must be something on horseback to be allowed to handle Richard's favorite horse.

They worked their way upstream past the sheep farm and pastures, jumping gates, hedges and ditches, then took Justi's favorite track through the woods. Even the air was delicious today. Mature ferns brushed nearly to the horses' knees as they made their way through the cathedral formed by the magnificent oaks. The jingle of their bridles echoed off the canopy of leaves.

They were going the back way to the squire's to try his jumps out on the way over. The squire had invited them to his hunt in November so it would be good to check the lay of his walls and fences.

They were cantering downhill with the squire's house in distant view when Harry placed his mount wrong for a stone wall. Beau took off too early and caught the stones with his back hooves, pulling part of the dry-laid wall over with him. He stumbled on landing, went down on one shoulder and spilled Harry off.

Major, close on his heels, managed to avoid stepping on Harry or Beau, but came down on a round rock, upsetting himself and Justi. He couldn't help rolling on Justi as he got to his feet, looking apologetic and standing in place.

Richard took Bluedevil over the wall farther along so as not to add to the tangle. He was at Justi's side in a minute. She lay conscious, eyes open, but unable to breathe.

This wasn't the first time she had had all the air squeezed out of her and she knew she shouldn't panic—that eventually her lungs would remember what they were for and start working again. Harry was staggering to his feet, and Richard's face, bending over her, looked so worried she wished she had the breath to tell him she was all right.

The first lungful she got was blood, not air, and caused explosive coughing and wheezing. Richard's natural impulse to keep her still made it almost impossible for her to get any air. She struggled, in a panic, got her right arm free, made a tight fist as Gerard had taught her and swung at him.

The desperate blow sat Richard back on his heels long enough for her to roll over and cough the worst of the gore clear of her lungs. She was still coughing, spitting and almost retching when he bent over to hold her by the shoulders.

"So, you're not killed."

"You nearly drowned me," Justi gasped.

"I thought you had a ruptured lung."

"Don't be stupid. I bit my tongue."

"You really scared me," Harry chimed in.

Looking at the ravages to her neck cloth and coat, she chuckled. "What a mess." She was still wiping blood away from her mouth with her handkerchief. "Did I black your eye, Richard?"

"No matter. Can you ride?"

She struggled up beside Major and automatically ran her hands over his front legs. "Wait. We can't leave the wall like this. The squire's sheep may get out.'' She picked up a rock, but Richard took it from her.

"Go sit down over there, both of you. I'll take care of this.'' He removed his coat and, in a short space of time, made a respectable job of relaying the wall. This gave Harry time to wet his handkerchief in a nearby spring, and half laughing, he and Justi cleaned each other's faces of the worst ravages of the fall.

"All done,'' Richard reported. She noticed his shirt was wet with sweat between his shoulder blades.

"What do you think?'' He was obviously expecting a compliment.

"I know day laborers who couldn't have done as well,'' Justi said with a devilish half smile.

"That's the last time I do manual labor for you.''

"Maybe we shouldn't stop at the squire's,'' Justi suggested as they mounted.

"What's the matter? Are you hurt?'' asked Harry.

"No, but I'm a wreck and so are you. If he sees us now, he won't want us hunting on his ground.''

"I'm inclined to agree with Justi. Let's take that track back to the road.''

Justi caught Richard watching her on the way home with his brows knit.

"What's the matter? I know I'm a mess.''

"I was just wondering if we should have the doctor out.''

"What for?'' She tried to sound calm. "Haven't you ever had the wind knocked out of you? If you're expecting me to keel over, it's not going to happen.''

"For God's sake, let him alone, Richard. He's all right.''

"The voice of reason speaks,'' Justi joked.

"No, the voice of the idiot who knocked over the wall speaks.''

Harry swung at Richard. "Watch it, Harry. Justi only got away with it because I thought he was dying. I won't go so easy on you.''

They stopped at the stud farm on the way home to see how the training of the yearling colts was progressing. All were halter broken and being worked in long reins.

"You bit these horses at six months?" asked Harry.

"Actually, we use a leather thong instead of a bit the first year and we only work them a few minutes a day. They are more mature physically than mentally right now, but it's amazing how quickly they get used to being harnessed."

"So, by the time they are sold, they are pretty well broken?" Richard asked.

"Yes, but not so set in their ways that they can't be trained by their new owner. The three pair sold this year won't be worked hard until they are going into their third year."

"Do you always work the same two together?" Harry was sitting on the fence watching a groom take a team down the paddock and turn them.

"Not initially. We work them in as many different combinations as we can. They should be used to being harnessed up with anyone. But they do develop preferences, and it's amazing how often the two that have paired off themselves end up being sold together just because they work better that way. The other thing is we may not have an even number every year. Last year we got six out of six mares. This spring, only five."

"This isn't like any workhorse I've ever seen," Harry said.

"No, they are much smaller. Grandfather had them brought over from Ireland, a stud and six mares. They only eat a third of what a shire would eat. Also, we haven't got bad rocks or hills around here so they are strong enough to plow our fields."

"So, you just sell your two-year-old crop and work on the batch for next year. Seems so simple." Harry mounted his horse and they rode through the pastures toward the house.

"Unfortunately, we can't go on this way forever. The breeding stock is all between twelve and sixteen years old.

Darvin is already starting to throw more mares than colts, and for some reason they don't bring as high a price. We either invest in new breeding stock or look for another income in three or four years."

"How much for a new stud?" Richard asked.

"More than your father's bull."

Harry came in to lunch the next day great with news. "Jim tells me there's to be a match near Newmarket Saturday between Butcher and Hanley. Can we go, Richard? Most of the lads are taking a half day to go see it."

"Which recommends it highly to me. What time?"

"Four o'clock."

"I suppose we could book rooms in Newmarket and stay over."

"What? Miss church on Sunday just to watch a mill?" Justi put on a saintly air.

"Not just a mill—a real match."

Harry could hardly eat for excitement. During the rest of the meal Justi endured an unappetizing discussion of famous fights, none of which Harry had witnessed, but of which he had evidently memorized a blow-by-blow account from Richard and other sources. "Won't this be something?"

"Yes, with lots of blood, and maybe some teeth flying. A high treat by all accounts. But is this really a necessary part of my education?" asked Justi.

"You don't mean you would miss it? Richard, tell him he must go."

"No, he needn't, if he doesn't care for it." Richard's jaw looked set, and he treated Justi with cool civility the rest of the day as though she had not measured up in some crucial way.

At breakfast Saturday, Justi asked Richard if she might go with them after all.

"You changed your mind. I knew you would." Harry was really happy she wasn't to miss such a treat.

"I began to think it might not be so bad, compared to shooting holes in birds or blowing up rats. Besides, Saturday is race day at Newmarket. We should get to see a couple of races before we have to find this farm where the fight's to be. The day won't be a total waste."

Harry laughed, and Richard looked secretly pleased. He was to drive his grays. They were taking Haimes to watch the horses. Harry and Justi were to ride so as not to crowd Richard, but they preferred this, anyway.

They had lunch at an inn near the racecourse, where Richard was accosted by an acquaintance who had been imbibing freely of the local ale.

"Going to the match, I suppose, or have you had one of your own?" He indicated Richard's eye. "Who did this to you? Young Harry, I'll wager. Slipped one in over your guard, eh?"

Harry chuckled. "Actually, cousin Justin gave him that eye."

"You're joking! He's hardly more than a boy. Nice work, lad." He slapped Justi on the back, nearly pushing her face into her food.

"Well, really!" Justi exclaimed when he had gone. "What sort of person would commend me for doing something I actually feel rather guilty about?"

"A sport such as Bentley would, or any one of Richard's crowd."

"And you set yourself up as such a paragon of moral behavior."

"I never did!" denied Richard, laughing.

"You certainly gave the vicar the impression that you were a model of propriety. You even acted stuffy when you first came. I must say you had me fooled."

They arrived at the course in time to lay bets for the second race. By dint of knowing the local horses, Justi managed to turn her modest limit of ten pounds into nearly forty by the fourth race. Harry, who had begun to bet with her, did nearly as well.

Richard was adamant in picking for conformation and lost modestly and without rancor on each race. "Who could have thought that old screw would beat so many young colts?" he asked.

"Sarabande nearly always wins on this course, especially if the front runners fall like they did today and clear the field a bit. I don't recall Sarabande ever falling, and not for want of taking chances. He just knows the course. As long as his jockey doesn't interfere, he can usually pull it off."

For Harry the day was one of unalloyed joy. He had cheered two winning horses home and was now on his way to a fighting match for which he was already rehearsing the story.

"Who are you backing, Justi?"

"Neither. I know nothing about it and should do as badly as Richard at horses."

"My money's on Butcher."

"Nonsense! Hanley will take him in five rounds or less." Richard's claim started an argument that did not cease until they had followed the flow of traffic to the farm where the event was to occur. Although scarcely the first to arrive, they had no trouble finding a good vantage point for observing the makeshift arena being set up in the hollow of a valley.

Richard and Harry went off to find stakeholders and, since these two had clearly taken leave of their senses, Justi asked Haimes if he would hold her winnings. The press of the crowd that was building would cover the work of more than one skilled pickpocket.

"Very wise, my lord. I shall be staying here with the horses, so your blunt will be quite safe with me. Mind you keep track of how to split back here in case we have to leave in a hurry."

"You mean after its over?"

"No, I mean if the local law shows up to stop it."

"Good Lord! Do you mean to tell me this isn't legal?"

"Well, let's say it's frowned upon."

"But not by you, I take it? No, how could you, since Richard brought us. Well, thanks for the warning, at any rate."

Justi went to observe the roping off of the temporary ring and the throwing down of bundles of straw for the first ranks of spectators to sit on. Those farther back would have to stand. She was privileged to witness the arrival of the combatants. She would not have guessed from their size that they were fighters, since neither was much bigger than Richard. But the scars on their faces and the scattered applause pointed them out for her.

She was offered several times two-to-one odds against Hanley, and hoped Richard wouldn't be out of temper if he lost. Harry and Richard's heated argument was repeated throughout the crowd, many of whom she reckoned to be from London or thereabouts. Some of the language that was flung about was an education in itself. She was raptly following one such discussion when a hand grabbed her shoulder, and she started guiltily. It was Richard, of course, but he seemed more amused than annoyed at her mixing with the rough crowd.

"Seen Harry lately?" he shouted above the din.

"Over there, I think." Justi pointed to the other side of the arena.

"Let's go back to the curricle. We can see better."

The first few rounds passed with a lot of sparring and, as far as Justi could see, no damage to either party. They seemed to be sizing each other up. To her surprise, she began to anticipate the movements of the combatants as though they were fencing. She had almost begun to think it wasn't such a bad sport till Hanley started bleeding from a cut over his eye.

Any injury she could empathize with made her stomach lurch. From her encounters with the village boys she knew how miserable it was not to be able to see to defend yourself. The end of the round saved Hanley.

The fifth began with both opponents sweating and breathing heavily. Hanley switched tactics and began to drive away at his opponent's stomach. Butcher lost his wind and was on his knees. He got up once more, but another series of rapid punches flattened him.

It was over. Half the crowd cheered, half moaned. All went to collect or pay off bets. She pondered whether Hanley had just been toying with his opponent and only got serious when the outcome of the match was in question.

Richard came back smiling with satisfaction as he counted his money. "Where's Harry?"

"Last time I saw him, down— Oh, no!"

A fight had broken out around one of the stakeholders, and Justi had picked out Harry in time to see him go down under a cruel blow to the head.

She jumped out of the curricle, but Richard stopped her. "Stay here. I'll get him."

She and Haimes watched helplessly as Richard fought his way through the crowd. Harry had not come up again and might be getting trampled. Then they saw Richard stagger under a blow and take out his assailant with one punch, but two more jumped him. This was too much for Justi.

She flung herself up on Major.

"Where do you think you're going?" Haimes demanded.

"After them. We have to do something."

"You're not taking yourself nor a horse down into that melee. They may have knives."

"All the more reason to go. Haimes, what would the magistrates say if they were going to arrest everyone?"

"I don't know, m'lord."

"Well, think of something and shout it as loud as you can. I'll part the crowd with Major and Beau. You bring the curricle through."

"They will never move aside for us."

"Of course they will. People are mostly afraid of horses. Now, come on." With that she spurred Major into the crowd, dragging Beau behind her. Haimes drove the team in her wake with their heads tossing and their mighty hooves thudding the ground. The parting of the mass of struggling bodies was as much the result of Haimes booming out "Stop! In the name of the law!" as a fear of being trampled.

She laid about her with Harry's whip when necessary. She almost caught Richard with it when he came up for air. He was standing astride Harry's unconscious form, protecting him from the crowd. She dispatched Richard's current assailant with a sharp kick to the side of the head so Richard was able to hand Harry up into the curricle. Richard mounted Beau and led the way out of the struggle, but the crowd was beginning to scatter. Richard called a halt when they reached the road to determine how badly Harry was hurt.

"We have to go back," Harry insisted after Richard had tipped some brandy down his throat. "Fellow didn't pay me my winnings."

They got him to the inn by dint of Haimes holding him down and driving one-handed. Richard was laughing most of the way, and Justi seriously began to fear for his reason.

"What is so funny?" she demanded after Haimes had gone off in search of a doctor. "He could be scarred for life."

"I'm not hurt." Harry struggled up from his bed. "Fellow welshed on the bet."

"Wait a minute. I thought your money was on Butcher," Justi said. "Surely, you lost."

"Mostly, but when they started offering three to one against Hanley, I took a bit back on him."

"Lost your nerve, I see," Richard observed while ruthlessly stripping off Harry's coat.

"You should have seen what I did to the bugger who hit me."

"If you think you can handle this lunatic," Justi said, "I'm going for bandages and cold water."

"I'll manage. Bring a bottle of brandy with you."

By the time the doctor arrived, Justi had Harry resting with a cold compress over his forehead and was unsuccessfully trying to look at a gash on Richard's jaw. Haimes offered to help hold him down but was deterred when his employer demanded to know what gave him the idea to drag his horses down into such a fray.

Haimes almost snapped to attention and began a longwinded explanation that would result in him taking the blame when Justi cut him short. "I made him do it. He had no choice but to follow me, since you told him to look after me."

"So the cavalry charge was your idea?" Talking around a split lip, Richard sounded more menacing than usual.

"Yes, and even if I never got to ride again, I'd do the same thing all over."

"I was merely going to commend you on your ingenuity. You two probably saved us from a much worse thrashing."

"Are you sure that wouldn't have merely added to the day's enjoyment?" Justi asked, starting to dab at the bloody bruise on his cheek.

Richard spit out an oath in gutter German that surprised Justi into staring at him in openmouthed admiration. She turned aside to laugh at his embarrassment.

"I suppose I don't have to ask where you learned the meaning of such language," Richard said accusingly to cover his lapse.

"No, from Gerard," Justi supplied, "but where could you have picked it up without spending a considerable time on the Continent?"

Haimes seemed to be trying to back out of the room.

"What did he say?" Harry demanded, sitting up in spite of the doctor's protests.

Justi had opened her mouth to answer Harry when Richard begged, "Spare us your translation. I learned it from a soldier."

"A Prussian?" she asked.

"No, an Austrian."

"When were you ever around an Austrian soldier?" Harry demanded.

Haimes did slip out the door then, making Justi suspicious.

"Richard—you were never in the Austrian army!" she demanded.

Richard was looking mulish.

"A mercenary!" exclaimed Harry. "But this is wonderful."

"I had to have something to do when Father cast me off," Richard said lamely.

"Were you in the fighting in Italy?" Harry asked eagerly.

"Yes, and I don't want to talk about it."

"What was your rank?" Justi demanded.

"Enough, I said!" Richard may have thought he put an end to the discussion, but once his secret was out Justi knew that Harry would worry him like a puppy at a rag until they had the whole story from him.

Neither Richard nor Harry began to stir much before noon the next day, so Justi had a chance to walk about town and hear the gossip about the previous night's adventures. To figure so centrally in these she found a point of embarrassment. She did discover, to her relief, that no one had been killed, nor, it seemed, seriously wounded.

"In short," she reported to a bleary-eyed Richard, "a good time was had by one and all, but where people got the idea the match was raided is beyond me." Her innocent look as she poured more tea set Richard chuckling, which he thought better of, since it aggravated all the bruises on his face. For once, he did not make a hearty breakfast. Harry ate nothing at all, but Richard refused his request for a brandy for breakfast. "I'll not have you throwing up on the way home in the curricle."

"I can ride," Harry insisted, but he made no protest when Richard consigned him to the curricle and mounted Beau himself. Harry couldn't have been feeling very well, since no sooner had they gotten into the house than he discovered he was still very tired from the night's raking, and lay down for a nap that lasted till dinner. Richard forced himself to stay up and write letters with a fist that could barely grasp a quill, while Justi worked on her translations in the library.

"You're not telling his mother, are you?" she asked.

"No, not the whole story. I think he will enjoy telling her that himself. Are you going to tell your mother what happened?" he asked as casually as he could manage.

"Of course not. I can think of nothing that would worry her more. I shall tell her, as always, that my education is progressing to your satisfaction."

He threw a book at her, then winced.

It was several days before either of the combatants felt like doing more than loafing about, so Justi rode and saw to things on her own, remembering to warn Richard where she was headed. Her conscientiousness in this made him a bit uncomfortable, since he was taking himself to task for leading Justi into danger. He also suspected that Justi was laughing at him a little for being so pompous, then falling so short as a model.

Harry was as pleased with his wounds as could be, asking hopefully if the cut on his cheek would leave a scar. Justi merely shook her head.

Every time Harry told the story of the night's adventure he grew bolder. He did not stint in praising the rescuers, however, and offered them full credit in his account.

"Don't," said Justi. "If some of that mob found out who had done all that kicking, I'd never be able to go to Newmarket safely again."

In this, Richard concurred. Harry promised Justi anonymity but thought it very poor-spirited to hide such deeds. Perhaps it even ruined the story.

Justi was surprisingly sensible, Richard thought, far more so than Harry, who was five years older. Harry was the only youngster Richard had much experience with, but he had always considered his brother to be rather typical of the reckless lads he had known in his youth. It seemed such a long time ago, even though only seven years separated him from Harry.

Justi was different. There was no lack of courage in the boy, but it tended to be of the cold, calculated variety, not the reckless bravado that got Harry into trouble so often.

Growing up with only an old man and a female for company may have influenced Justi, let alone having responsibility thrust on him at such a young age. But Richard was more inclined to consider it part of Justi's character to be more sober than Harry.

He was amazed at Justi's ingenuity in getting around him. The lad was more inventive than Harry had ever been. He was only glad that Justi's tricks were merely playful, not costly or dangerous. Still, he considered the young earl to be his greatest challenge.

They were getting on well together, Richard thought. Justi might turn out all right, after all.

Chapter Six

It was one of those rainy days that threatened to ruin the ground for hunting for a week or more. "It will be just too bad if the squire has to postpone his hunt." After hearing this for the twentieth time, Richard drove Harry from the room, and Justi paused in her work to thank him. She had brought her latest job, *La Petit Innocent,* down to the library to work on it. She had not gotten more than a dozen pages into it, however, before she had discovered it was not a lukewarm novel, as she had supposed, but a rather mature piece of pornography.

Having been raised in the country where one saw stallions and rams at work, it took a good deal to impress her. She was puzzling over a complex ménage à trois scene and how best to express it without making it funny when Richard bent over her shoulder and happened on the succulent passage.

"I thought you were doing lectures, or something."

"Not for a while, now. This novel is not what I expected. Some of these things sound stupid in English."

"Some of these things sound impossible in any language." He was leafing through her completed pages. "Does this publisher know how old you are?"

"I don't know. Does it matter?"

"You said you started doing this when you were fourteen. Has he been sending you salacious literature all this time?" Richard was unconsciously raising his voice.

"Oh, no, this is the worst I've had to deal with so far. I hope it isn't a trend." She felt Richard to be on the point of composing a lecture on the dangers of reading such filth, and she was composing herself to hear him out with patience, when Harry burst into the room.

"Guess what I've found. All these old weapons in the basement. The place looks like a dungeon. Why didn't you tell me about it, Justi? I could spend hours down there."

"Then do so and relieve us of your company," commanded Richard.

"I found these foils down there, too. You don't care if I poke about, then?"

"Is that where you practiced?" Richard turned to ask Justi, who was looking uncomfortable.

"Only when it was too hot outside."

"Come to think of it, we haven't tested your skill in fencing yet," Richard remembered. "Dumont said you looked promising."

"Come on, Justi," Harry suggested. "A match between you and me. What do you say?"

"Why not?" she agreed, to divert Richard from the translation. "But can't we practice in the hall? The air is bad down there and there's no light."

"Nonsense. If there's enough space, that's all you need. But I claim the right to test your skill." Richard lit extra candles and carried them down. She followed in the wake of the excited Harry.

The armory was as Justi remembered it, damp, reeking of rat droppings and filthy with cobwebs. She and Richard took off their coats, and Harry volunteered to hold them since there was no clean place to lay them. Richard fenced politely at first, almost as though he was putting her through a series of exercises. Her arm tired long before he was through with her and he dashed the foil from her hand. She breathed a sigh of relief, thinking it was over.

"Again, *en garde!*"

"Richard, for God's sake," said Harry, laughing, "give him a chance to rest first."

Her right arm was aching so badly she tossed the weapon into her left hand. She had done so often enough when practicing with Gerard, since her arm usually gave out before they were finished. She wasn't quite as fast with the left, but neither was she with her right when her arm was this tired.

Richard paused in his advance. "You switched hands."

"It's allowed."

"You fight with either?"

"I learned with both. What difference does it make?"

"None at all."

Richard, true to his words, seemed to experience no difficulty. Again and again he drove her back, making her fall over lumber and crash into old pieces of armor. She had no time to think about what was behind her nor light to see it by. She was too busy keeping his blade away from her. His rushes reminded her of Hanley's attack on Butcher. He was just toying with her, each time pausing to let her get to her feet before he began pushing her again.

"You retreat too much."

"That's the best way to study someone," she panted. It wasn't a good bluff and it didn't work.

His next rush knocked her backward over a pile of rubble, but she got her blade up to guard her throat.

"Get up, Rabbit."

"What did you say?" She gasped at the cruelty of the jest.

"Wasn't that Dumont's pet name for you?"

"Why did he tell you that?" she asked, struggling up. "What did he tell you?"

"Everything."

"It's a lie."

"How do you know, if you don't know what he told me?"

She wasn't even thinking clearly now. Why was he doing this to her?

She switched the blade to her right hand, but Richard backed her into the wall and disarmed her with a practiced flip of his weapon. She knew he could have done it at any point in the practice.

"Tell me the truth." He held the capped tip to her breastbone. She touched it as she breathed in and out.

"I can't."

"You will."

"For God's sake, Richard. Can't you see he's had enough?" Harry pushed the blade away impatiently, handed them each their coat and carried the candles upstairs. Justi followed hard on his heels, afraid of being left behind with Richard.

She went to her room to wash up and calm down. When she returned to the library, trying to fix the shambles of her neck cloth, Richard moved to the table where she had been working and deliberately began to gather up her translation.

"What are you doing?"

"You are not continuing with this," he stated flatly.

"But if I don't finish it I won't get paid." She came toward the table, moving slowly. It didn't do to make him angry when he was in one of his moods. He might chuck the whole thing in the fire.

"Richard, please," she pleaded. "I'll write him that I won't take any more like this."

"You are finished with this now. Write out the man's address for me."

She wrote out Meecham and Bates's London address, thinking frantically what to do to save the situation—how to joke him out of it.

"Come on, Richard. Don't be such a prude. This is nothing to the sort of language I heard at the match."

"Yes, I'm surprised you didn't take notes. I was wondering how long it would be before you threw that up to me." It was as though he had pounced on her.

"I should say you've been looking forward to me throwing it up to you," Justi countered heatedly. "You must have your defense pretty well prepared by now."

Since this was exactly the case, and Richard hated being outguessed, it set the seal on his anger. "Get to your room!" he thundered.

She knew not to push him any further. The damage was done. No point in getting him really angry. How had she let him provoke her? It was only that he was looking for some fault in her to make him feel better about his own shortcomings. If she could see that so clearly, how could he fool himself about it?

Some while later a soft rapping came on her door. She knew it wasn't Richard. He usually entered without knocking. "Come in, Harry."

"How did you know it was me?"

"No one else would dare come here without his orders when I'm under house arrest."

"You mean he's kept you here before?"

"Lord, yes, under lock and key."

"Justi, I'm sorry I caused all this trouble. I didn't mean to."

"No, it's my fault. I usually manage him better than this."

"You? Manage Richard?" He looked at her appraisingly. "If you do, you're the first to boast of it. It's always Richard who manages us and gets us out of scrapes."

"I'll wager you never got into anything as bad as me."

"Actually, in the spring he had to buy me out of a breach of promise suit." He smiled engagingly.

"And was there cause for such an action?"

"What do you mean?"

"Did you make love to the girl?"

"No, of course not. I only wrote her some letters."

Justi rolled her eyes heavenward. "Did you tell Richard this?"

"A fellow doesn't like to admit a thing like that."

"But don't you see? If he had known this, he would only have had to buy the letters back. He might not have had to pay so much."

Harry was looking miserable.

"Never mind," she said, thinking that if she or her mother had told Richard the truth that first day, he wouldn't have had to buy off Gerard.

"Who was this Gerard, anyway?"

"Richard didn't tell you?"

"No."

"Just a tutor Richard hired for me. He told Richard I had seduced him."

By his indrawn breath she gathered she had shocked Harry. "It was a lie. Gerard said it to get more money out of him, but Richard won't believe me. And, if he's as good as his word, I could be stuck in this room a very long time without anything to do."

"This is all my fault."

"No. Never think that. This has been at the back of his mind ever since he sent Gerard packing. He said sooner or later he would get the truth out of me. It was just a matter of time before it came to this."

"Well." Harry brightened. "If he won't believe the truth, why don't you tell him something he will believe?"

"Lie to him? I couldn't." It suddenly occurred to her that she lied to Richard every time she came down the stairs in her coat and riding breeches.

"What have you got to lose?"

"The ability to sit down for a week, if he catches on. And Richard is no fool."

"It was just a thought. If you made up a story, and wrote it all out, and memorized it, don't you think you could pull it off?"

"I suppose it's worth a try. You would have to promise never to give me away."

"You have my oath on it." Harry was very solemn, as though swearing allegiance to a wronged monarch in exile. Justi successfully resisted the temptation to laugh.

"You had better go now. This will be hard enough to do on my own."

Since Harry could see he would not be of much use in composing this sort of a story, he crept out of her room with the stealth of a conspirator. Justi hoped Richard didn't catch him lurking along the passage or he would be sure to know something was up.

She paced the small room thinking over all the things that had happened with Gerard. As soon as the luncheon tray came and was taken away again by Firth, she wrote it all out. It was something of a disadvantage not knowing what Gerard had told Richard, so she decided not to paint him as black as she might, conceding that she might have unknowingly seduced him. She was just wondering if there was any truth in this when she heard a footfall on the stairs. She raked the papers into her desk drawer, but it was only Harry. He had sneaked up before to ask how it was going. This time he couldn't be waved away.

"Really, Justi. What a piece of work you're making of it. If you don't hurry and talk to Richard, you'll miss the pork pie tonight."

"What— Harry, you don't imagine he keeps me on bread and water?"

"He feeds you?"

"Of course. He's not a beast." Even she was surprised to hear herself defending her persecutor.

"Try the story out on me." He flopped down on the bed. "I'll tell you if he'll swallow it."

She looked over the confession and shook her head. "No, it's going to be hard enough saying this to Richard. It's too embarrassing."

"But it's not real."

"No, but while I'm telling it, I have to pretend that it is—like an actor. If he even suspects it's a lie, he'll half kill me."

"Well, are you ready?"

"I think so. Where is he?"

"He's been in the library going over the accounts all day. Even Firth felt the edge of his tongue just now."

"Good. Get someone to give him this note—not you, mind. I haven't spoken to you since this morning."

"Right." Harry seemed mollified to perform even this small part in the conspiracy.

"Read it first. Do you think it sounds contrite enough?"

"Lord, it sounds like you've been crying into your pillow all day. If your story is this convincing it should be something like!"

Badger duly delivered the note to Richard without comment. He wasn't sure what Justi and Harry were plotting, but that it involved Justi's release was a sure bet.

Richard read the short missive with a self-satisfied look. "I'll go up to him now. Oh, Badger, this may take some time. Tell the cook she may have to put dinner back half an hour."

"Yes, sir."

"So you've decided to come clean?" Richard said on entering the room.

Justi was standing at the east window looking out at the finally clearing weather. Richard seated himself at the desk, and Justi checked nervously to make sure all her scribblings had been put away. She turned from the window, wondering if Richard's choice of seat was unconscious or if he always deliberately sought to put himself in control of a situation.

"When I said nothing happened with Gerard, that wasn't quite true."

"Yes, I know."

"What did he tell you?" she asked.

"I simply knew you were hiding something."

This was going to be tougher than she thought. It took her back to that first night, when he had come for the drawings. He had not believed her, and he had not forgotten. In spite of all they had shared, and as much as she had come to care for Richard, there was still this wall between them. He could tell she was lying about something, and she could never tell him the truth about herself.

"When Gerard first came here..." She swallowed. "I didn't know what to expect. I mean I'd never been around anyone like him before. I didn't think anything of it when he touched me. Or, at least—" she flushed "—I tried to get used to it."

"But you felt it was wrong?"

"Yes," she whispered.

"And you told no one?"

"No, not then."

"You did not, in fact, ask for help until he had already violated you?"

Her eyes flew to his face and she turned away from the condemnation she read there. He was not following her script.

"After that, I was more careful not to be alone with him. Badger had some idea what was going on. He helped all he could."

"Were you aware that Dumont had never approached a man before?"

She looked sharply in his direction.

"He usually takes his pleasure with women," Richard said.

"Why me, then? Did he say?"

"He said, because you are small, and sensitive, and weak."

She closed her trembling lips and set her jaw. "I have had to fight all my life because of these things. I suppose it will always be harder for me."

Richard rose. "Tell me one thing." He advanced toward her. "Did you enjoy it?"

"No. It made me throw up." She turned to face him but could not look him in the eye. Her reaction to Gerard, at least, was genuine.

She caught the movement of his hand out of the corner of her eye and, remembering Gerard, cringed against the window, flinging her arm up to block a blow that never came.

"How could you think that I would punish you for merely doing as I asked?"

She looked up at him, and his eyes showed the hurt.

"Do you think I am unmindful of what you suffered at his hands? Recollect I sent him to you."

She had forgotten that. "It wasn't your fault. How could you know?"

"It was my business to know." He took a deep breath. "We need not speak of this again. Change for dinner now."

At dinner Richard was so much in command of himself, or appeared to be, that Justi managed to still the trembling she felt inside and lose the color from her face. He joked and laughed with Harry, who seemed to think Justi had turned the trick. Justi responded mechanically and hardly tasted what was put before her.

She had not planned to hurt him. A few months ago she wouldn't have thought it possible. Richard had obviously forgiven her, but she doubted that she could forgive herself for tricking him in this way. Perhaps the guilt she was feeling would dull with time, but any joy she might get in the future from Homeplace would be linked in her mind with Richard's pain.

Justi valiantly tried to be cheerful. But it was days before Richard's brave face didn't give her heart a sickening thud. She had betrayed him, and continued to do so every day she stayed at Homeplace. She thought that if she had been alone in this thing she would simply have left. But her mother was deeply involved, could be said to have plotted the whole thing and drawn her child into it. Richard would never believe she was the one who decided to continue the pretense after her grandfather's death.

What Richard did with the translation she never asked him, knowing it would be useless to try to change his mind. Once Richard made a decision he stuck by it, right or wrong.

The day before the hunt Harry thought everything was back to normal between Richard and Justi. They joked and laughed as much as before. The only difference was that Justi wasn't forever with his head in a book or scribbling away at something.

Richard knew there was a difference. Justi was torturing himself with something, for all the boy's pretence of gaiety. He almost wished he had not wrung the truth out of Justi. He wouldn't have if he'd known it would make the lad feel so guilty. But he was young. Justi would get over it and lead a normal life. On that Richard was determined. He felt as much affection for Justi as for his own half brother.

Harry asked who would be at Squire Coates's, and as Justi named her few neighbors she had a sudden fear about the impression Richard might make with his barbed comments. About Harry she had no qualms. Richard had been polite enough to the vicar, but how would he treat the rest of them?

"Richard, you know these are simple country people."

"What are you talking about?" The smile faded from his face.

"Only that they would not understand some of your little quips, or they might take them in bad part."

"Quips?" he asked suspiciously.

"Grandfather was so rude to everyone, we really had no friends except Squire Coates and Colonel Allen. I don't know why they did not take offense, but they have been very kind to me and I wish you would not cut at them, even in fun, or—"

"Just what are you trying to say?" he seethed.

"Simply that I have not many friends. I would appreciate it if you did not offend those two in particular."

"God's death!" Richard brought his whip down on the leather chair so hard Justi was surprised the seat did not split.

"It's only that you can have a damned nasty tongue sometimes, and they would not even know you are sniping at them." She stood up, prepared to bolt if necessary.

"Do you imagine I have no manners at all?"

"I don't know you well enough to know what to expect of you around other people, but even when you are coldly polite you have a way of showing your contempt—"

"I have heard enough. I will not be lectured by some whey-faced boy on how to behave in polite society. What did you imagine I would say to them?"

"I don't know. That's why I brought it up."

Harry looked from one to the other in awe and said goodbye to any thoughts of hunting the next day.

"If I were to enumerate all the points of your behavior that don't suit me we would be here all day." Richard advanced on her but this time she stood her ground.

"Yes, but I try to change," she said defensively.

"No, you do not!" Richard shouted. "You wait until my back is turned and do as you damn well please."

Justi looked at him in surprise, for this was quite true. She simply did not think he realized it.

"I have had to hold this place together without worrying Mother about the straits to which we are put. Far from making that task easier, you have made it a damn sight harder. If I do work that does not jump with your notions of gentlemanly pursuits it is because it is the only way to get it done."

Richard was looking at her in something like shock, and a slight tremor shook him. Harry held his breath.

"I'm sorry," Justi said. "I should not have shouted at you, but it's the truth. I should have known it would be a mistake to say anything to you. You will do as you please. I simply did not want people to think you would be like

Grandfather." Justi walked from the room, defeated, she supposed.

She left behind her not a victorious Richard, but a thoughtful one.

"Bit hard on him, aren't you?" Harry risked asking.

"I won't stand for being insulted," Richard said coldly as he poured himself a brandy.

"I only meant the way you shout at Justi he has no idea what good company you are most of the time."

"When someone is not irritating me. I think he does it on purpose," Richard complained.

"Who would bait you on purpose? I would as soon poke a stick at a bull. You seem to jump on everything he says. Don't say it. I'm taking myself off before you read me a lecture, too."

Richard sank into a chair with a tired sigh. Oddly enough he thought of Evelyn and his stillborn son. He wondered if it was not better for them as things fell out. Had he shouted like this at Evelyn he would have shattered her nerves. If his son had lived he might have brutalized him or, at the very least, beaten the spirit out of him. He was more fit to command a troop of soldiers than raise a sensitive boy.

He drained his glass. A night in a woman's bed would have taken the edge off his nerves, but only for a day or two. In spite of Richard's position, his admirable management of his properties and relations, he was, at bottom, extremely discontented with his life. And he saw no future for himself but to become just such a lonely recluse as Justi's grandfather had been.

Richard realized that the boy had finally dropped his guard and shown a glimpse of the real Justi. Not a weak, helpless creature, but a young man of considerable strength of character. He could only imagine the lengths to which the boy had been put to contain such an outburst until now.

All things considered Richard was glad it had happened, though he could hardly admit that to Justi. For he then might be led to admit that he could be stiff-rumped with strangers. He determined he would a make a supreme effort to charm Squire Coates and Colonel Allen for Justi's sake, though why it would occur to the boy to care about the impression he would make was a puzzle.

He was about to swallow his pride and go talk to the lad. He usually just let things cool off, and Justi always looked so uncertain the next time they met, as though surprised he was not still angry. He was interrupted by a soft rap at the door.

"Come in," he commanded.

Justi opened the door hesitantly, with that so childishly serious expression.

"There is no need to knock in your own house," Richard said, and noticed Justi cringed a little.

"I wish to apologize for what I said. It was inexcusable."

"Yes, it was," Richard agreed. "Nevertheless I accept your apology."

"Then we can consider it unsaid?" Justi asked hopefully.

"Such things can never be unsaid."

"I see," Justi said in some pain and turned to go.

"I want to know why you expected the very worst of me," Richard challenged.

Justi turned with her hand on the doorknob, opened her mouth to speak but took a moment over her reply so as not to stir Richard's coals again. "I never know what to expect of you. I'm not used to so much uncertainty. It makes me nervous, and you are always surprising me."

"Did it not occur to you that I might surprise you agreeably sometimes?"

"No," Justi said, startled. "That is, with my upbringing, I am, in general, expecting the worst. Surprises are very seldom agreeable."

"Then we must contrive to adjust your expectations."

"Pardon me?"

"Prove to you that the world is not quite so grim as you imagine it."

"I doubt that is possible," she said in amazement.

"Nevertheless it is my goal."

"Once again you surprise me. Why should you bother?"

"Because, in general, I am not displeased with you, but rather surprised that you have managed so well given the considerable trials that have come your way."

Justi was looking confused and a little suspicious.

"Still waiting for the barb?" Richard asked with a tired smile.

"No, of course not, I just don't know what you want of me—to be less responsible?"

"No, perhaps less controlled, not so tightly reined in, if you know what I mean."

Justi looked at him a little dubiously, nodded and left. If he meant she should be more open with him that was dangerous. She was beginning to realize that there were more than physical differences between men and women. They thought differently, had different fears and joys. They shared so little it amazed her that men and women ever got together.

Haimes came up to the house early the next morning as they were getting ready to leave for the squire's.

"Beau has loosened a shoe, Harry," Richard informed his brother. "I'm afraid you won't be riding with us today."

Harry groaned but took his disappointment like a man. Justi knew better than to offer Major for Harry's use. Richard might have done so. But she did suggest, "Let me shoe him. That is, if you trust me to work on him, Richard. I've done ours lots of times. I'm no hand at making shoes, but as long as he hasn't lost it I can put it back on. We won't even be late."

Harry looked doubtful, but Richard gave his consent, so they repaired to the stable where Justi donned a heavy leather apron before quickly cleaning the frog and prying off the shoe. Jim handed her the nippers, and she trimmed half an inch off evenly around the hoof and rasped the surface flat. She tacked the shoe in place and clinched the nails.

"I'll have to do the other front foot or he'll feel uneven, but we can let the back ones go until later." She worked quickly, her small, strong hands using the tools with confidence.

Harry was impressed. "You could do this for a living."

"Let's hope it doesn't come to that," Richard said, chuckling.

When they arrived in the squire's courtyard the dogs had not been loosed yet, so one could still hear conversation as hot punch was passed around. Horseshoes rang on cobbles as the anxious steeds moved about, snorting. It was just cold enough for the horses to be gently steaming already.

Colonel Allen's two daughters, Meg and Sally, rode with them today. Justi scarcely knew them since the Allens were comparative newcomers to the district and she watched with fascination as Harry flirted with the two girls. This was a side of him she had never seen before. What a cake he was making of himself. Surely women could see through such banter, but perhaps they chose not to.

Richard, too, rode over to the girls to be introduced. Apparently Harry wasn't the only flatterer in the family. It occurred to Justi that, except for the few sentences Richard had exchanged with her mother, she had never seen him talking to a woman before. It bothered her so much more to hear Richard utter such inanities than Harry.

Colonel Allen sidled up to comment, "I suppose you will be running in the front of the pack with Richard and Harry?"

"Actually, I thought I would stay behind and pick up the pieces. If I am any judge, they will both make fools of themselves today," Justi said, glancing at the Allen girls.

The colonel laughed and rode off.

Richard must have observed her scowling at him, so he pranced over on Bluedevil. "Why are you over here all by yourself?" He actually seemed to prefer the big black, and she had to admit, Richard looked good on him.

"You'll find out when they loose the hounds. By the way, there's something I forgot to tell you."

"Yes?"

"It's about Bluedevil. I don't know how important this is."

"What?" He was getting suspicious.

"I wish I had remembered to warn you about this earlier."

"Out with it," Richard commanded.

"He doesn't like dogs," Justi said simply.

"You mean he's afraid of them."

"No, he hates them. He's subtle about it. But he never misses a chance to step on one. I had a devil of a time keeping him from overrunning them last year."

Richard was looking incredulous. A rising din signaled the release of the hunting pack. Bluedevil's ears pricked forward.

"So, if you want me to ride Bluedevil today, I'd understand. I mean, I'm used to his tricks."

"Certainly not!" Richard had misread her offer as the sort of trick Harry would play to get his own way, and as a sort of challenge.

Harry chose to stay at the back of the field with the Allen girls. It would serve him right if he had to baby them the whole way, and missed all the fun. Justi stuck close to Richard all the morning, and Richard rode up near the squire and Colonel Allen.

After a long chase the fox eventually worked his way home, so they were not far from the squire's when Richard fell. A young hound had gotten distracted by some animal other than their quarry and was trying to dig it out of the other side of the wall they were jumping. Allen and the squire avoided him, but Bluedevil must have been trying to kick him, because the buck with which he completed his jump dumped Richard hard on the ground.

Justi pulled up and was the first to reach him. He was obviously in pain, his eyes closed and brows drawn together.

"Richard, can you move your legs?"

"I'm all right! Go catch the horse!"

"I can't leave you."

"I'll stay with him," volunteered Colonel Allen.

"Justi, go!"

She mounted doubtfully and went to rescue the hapless hound, running in circles, trying to avoid the black hooves bent on squashing him. She was lucky enough to grab one of Bluedevil's loose reins on the fly, so she soon had him under control. When she returned to the wall Richard was standing, none too steadily, she thought, but he mounted stiffly and wordlessly.

"I'd say it's over," remarked Colonel Allen. "Let's head back for dinner."

"Richard, if you would rather just go home..."

"That would be rude."

"I mean, if you're hurt..."

"I am perfectly all right."

Richard drank more at the dinner than he usually had in an entire evening at home. It must have been enough to stave off the pain for a while, Justi thought. She began almost to hope that her worry had been misplaced, for they were nearly the last to leave, and Richard seemed to be at his most amiable. Was he going through all this just to please her? She would never have asked it of him if he was in pain.

When they dismounted in the stable yard at Homeplace, Richard staggered against Bluedevil.

"Lord, Richard, this is the earliest in the day I've ever seem you half sprung."

"Don't be stupid, Harry. He's not drunk. He can hardly walk. Get under his other arm."

"I don't need your help." Richard tried to shake them off.

"Can't you ever bring yourself to lean on anyone?"

"I'm just a little drunk, that's all."

"If that's what you want the servants to think, fine. Now lean on us," Justi commanded.

He allowed them to support him into the house and up the stairs where they delivered him into the hands of his valet, Firth. This worthy was ejected from Richard's bedroom a few moments later by a stream of German that impressed Justi and caused Harry to raise an eyebrow at her.

"He won't have a doctor," Firth said in some desperation, "nor even let me take his boots off."

"I didn't hear that," Justi said. "I'm going for Trent."

"He won't see him."

"Trying to wrestle his own boots off may make him more tractable."

"What the devil!" Richard growled when Trent invaded his room an hour later. "Who sent for you?"

"Actually, young Justi came for me."

"Wait till I get my hands on him."

Dr. Trent laughed. "You should have heard what the old earl threatened Justi with."

"Don't compare me to that old crank."

"Then stop acting like him. If nothing else, I should think you would set a better example for the boys."

Richard scowled at him.

"Is this the way you want them to act next time one of them gets laid up? No, you wouldn't tolerate it, would you? Now, call your man, for I assure you he can make a much better job of getting these boots off than I."

"Firth!" Richard shouted, and the valet standing in the hall jumped. Justi thought he had the look of a man on his way to the scaffold as he slipped into the bedroom.

Harry shrugged and went off to change. Justi sat on the top step with her head in her hands blaming herself, firstly for the accident itself, secondly for Richard enduring several more hours of pain before coming home.

''How is he?'' she asked, when Trent finally emerged.

''Nothing broken, just thrown his back out. Don't worry. A week in bed and he'll be as good as new.''

''How do you suggest we keep him there? Tie him to it?''

''I should think the pain would take care of that.''

''You don't know Richard.''

''What's all this?'' Richard barked the next morning as Justi came in carrying the chessboard and pieces and some packets of playing cards.

''I thought that since you're stuck here anyway, this might be a good time for you to teach me chess.''

''Don't you play already?''

''After a fashion. But I suspect Grandfather made up his own rules.''

Richard was a good enough player not to tax Justi's skill at throwing a game. She could only be glad of this, for she suspected he would tumble to her tricks and would only value a fair win.

''That's an illegal move,'' he pointed out.

''See what I mean?'' Her second choice lost her the game.

''What do you think of my style?'' he asked when he knew he had the second game in his pocket.

''It's the same as your fencing—unpredictable. I have absolutely no idea what you are thinking.''

''Good. Checkmate.''

''Agh.''

Richard didn't tire as quickly as her grandfather, but Justi was an expert at deciding when a patient needed rest, so she resolutely packed the pieces away for later.

''Where are you going?''

''To lick my wounds and try to figure out how I lost that last match. Harry wants a game of piquet after dinner. We have a bet on.''

''What's the bet?''

''I'm not allowed to tell you.''

* * *

Later that day she made the mistake of riding into Brinley for some nails when she could not come by them in Glenncross. There was a letter there from Gerard demanding more money. She had no idea what Richard had given him, but evidently he had run through that and hers, as well. She was right in thinking he would never be satisfied.

She would have told Richard then, thinking it might be a safe opportunity for her to confess with temporary impunity. But when she saw him biting back pain she could not do it. Instead she wrote Gerard a scathing letter, daring him to expose her. She told him Richard had confiscated her work and forbidden her to do it again. There would be no more money. The letter burned in her pocket for two days until she had a chance to post it.

Monday Richard turned his head resentfully away from the last golden days of autumn slipping by outside the window. "You and Harry needn't be cooped up here just because I'm stuck in bed."

"We did take Major and Beau for a ride this morning and we'll probably go for a tramp before dinner. We took Bluedevil down to the stud farm and turned him in with the yearling colts for exercise." Justi gazed out of the window for a minute. "Richard, if you want to get rid of Bluedevil, I won't mind so much, really."

"Get rid of him? What are you talking about? He's an excellent mount."

"But he nearly got you killed."

"So, that's what you've been moping about."

"Richard, I'd rather shoot him than have anything happen to you."

Richard was surprised and touched. Had he heard such an impassioned speech from Harry, he might have doubted the sincerity of it. Justi clearly meant it. And Richard had no idea what he had done to endear himself to the boy.

Running roughshod over youngsters usually did not produce this result.

"Don't go putting a gun to his head on my account. Even Major might have dumped me if a dog had popped up under his nose. Besides, you would probably miss anyway."

By such devices as tournaments and bets Justi, with the eager cooperation of Harry, managed to keep Richard's interest up and keep him in bed for nearly the required time. But by Saturday he announced he was going to have a real bath, and not a regiment could have held him down. Fortunately, it came on to rain again, so his activities were limited to loafing about the sitting room and library.

Richard and Justi spent a good deal of time discussing farming, and although Harry listened politely, he never expressed much more than a mild interest in any aspects unrelated to sport.

"You call Homeplace a farm," he observed one day. "Yet it has more acreage than Amberly, which is considered an estate."

"Does it? I always just assumed Amberly was larger, to provide a larger income, I mean."

"Oh, no," said Richard, "the house is larger, of course, and certainly in better repair."

"That goes without saying."

"Our income is mostly from interest on capital invested in the funds and rents on London properties."

"You mean you don't sell anything?" Justi was confused.

"Not actually. We do try, of course, to grow enough hay and oats for the horses. The home farm supplies us with meat and vegetables."

"What about servants' wages?"

"From the income."

"And you have no tenants working on shares?"

"No, not for years."

Richard's simple confidences left Justi uneasy. She had thought Richard looked on Homeplace as a liability. That she was robbing him of a much-needed source of income had not, until then, occurred to her. That's when she definitely decided she would have to leave and see that Richard got his inheritance. The important thing was not owning Homeplace, but keeping it safe, and Richard would surely do that.

If Mother felt disposed to live with the Mallorys, Justi could set out on her own, travel perhaps. For some reason the prospect of this freedom was rather depressing, since she would have to go alone. She was surprised that this would bother her, having been essentially alone all her life. Richard had changed that.

By mid-December preparations were in train for them to remove to Amberly for the Christmas holidays. Justi and Richard were riding from the sheep farm discussing the merits of the new ram. It occurred to Richard that he had probably learned as much from Justi as the boy had learned from him, and it was useful knowledge, too. At Amberly, they only played at farming. This was the real thing. Rather than dreading his guardianship of the boy, he was looking forward to the coming years with an interest he had not felt in anything for a long time.

"I'm going to ask you a question and I want a straight answer."

Justi looked at him in innocent surprise, then started casting about in her mind for what wrong she might have committed recently.

"How long have you been running this place?"

"But I'm not," she gasped.

"Oh, you don't appear to, I'll grant you that. In fact, you make it look like it runs itself. How long have you actually been in charge?"

"Well..." She swallowed and gave it some serious thought. "I suppose it happened gradually. Grandfather used to interrogate me before I relayed his orders, to see if I could guess what they would be. I'm not sure when I started giving them and he just agreed.''

"So my presence here is superfluous."

"That's not true!" Justi said passionately. "It was you who got rid of Mrs. Morrisee and . . . Gerard. I never properly thanked you for that."

"Are you forgetting that I'm the one who inflicted him on you in the first place?''

"I'm sorry. I forgot I wasn't supposed to mention him."

If the very mention of Gerard's name could cast a pall of gloom between the two friends, it was nothing to the consternation a letter bearing his name caused.

Harry slipped into Justi's room as she was trying to decide what to pack. "Richard's looking black as thunder. He's got a letter from that tutor of yours. I'm not supposed to tell you."

Justi looked pale. "I'm glad you did, Harry."

"What's it about?" Harry asked

"He must want more money." Justi sat on the bed dejectedly.

"Well, Richard says he's going to stall him till after Christmas, so there's no need to worry."

"Harry, that will be in a month. Never mind. I know what I must do."

She went to see Richard with every intention of confessing, but when she entered the room he put away his anger and spoke only of the coming holidays with a joy that was somehow much more touching for being forced. In the end she decided to consult with her mother first, or at least warn her. But she must put an end to the masquerade. She would not have Richard bled for her sake.

Chapter Seven

They left Richard's curricle and grays at Homeplace, since they were coming back in a few weeks, and traveled to Amberly by post chaise with job horses. Haimes and another groom were bringing the hunters behind them at an easier pace.

They arrived in the late afternoon with the red winter sun lighting up Amberly's beige and pink sandstone. It was an inviting place that looked like it had known many happy hours. In contrast, Justi realized Homeplace must look dark and secretive behind its mask of ivy.

When they pulled up around the neat loop of drive embraced by the east and west wings, two footmen sallied forth to move baggage, and a dignified butler welcomed them warmly. After ushering them inside and relieving them of their greatcoats, hats and gloves, this worthy opened the door into a well-lit drawing room, and Miriam leaped up and threw herself on Justi as she followed Richard in.

"Mother, why are you crying? I know for a fact you have been well treated."

"I'm just so happy to see you. I really think you have grown some."

"Must be the new cook," joked Justi.

Richard introduced the rest of the family.

"Cousin Julia." Justi took her hand. "I am grateful to you for being such a friend to Mother."

"Miriam has been a great deal of company for me."

"Hello, Alicia. I've heard much about you. I'm looking forward to getting to know you."

Fair Alicia smiled shyly and murmured her greeting. Alicia looked the least like a Mallory, with her delicate features and gold ringlets.

"This is Clara," Richard said finally.

Justi had barely delivered her rehearsed greeting when Clara embraced her and kissed her full on the mouth. Justi staggered back in some confusion. Perhaps this ardent greeting was not out of the ordinary in their society.

"Clara!" said Julia sharply.

Justi looked to Richard for guidance and almost cringed under the stern gaze bent on her, but Richard said only, "Stop teasing the boy, Clara."

"You'll have to forgive Clara." Julia was composed again. "She is quite a joke smith. She embarrasses us no end."

"Oh, you know she makes us laugh." Miriam did not think the situation beyond saving.

They spoke then of the journey, the weather and the coming festivities at Amberly. Richard followed Clara to her room when they all went up to change for dinner.

"Go easy on the boy, will you, Clara? He's just turned seventeen this summer, and he's not used to women, except his mother. In fact he was never around anyone his age until I took Harry out to his estate. Believe it or not, he's not nearly as shy as he was before."

"I don't find him shy at all. Did you notice? He didn't blush when I kissed him. I think this should be a very entertaining holiday." She sat at her dressing table.

"Clara. He's just a boy. It would serve you right if he fell in love with you and made a nuisance of himself."

"Well, you said his education needed rounding out." She pouted at her reflection in the mirror. "Who better to teach him about women than me?"

"Who better to ruin him, you mean?"

"I won't eat him, Richard. I just want a little fun. Besides, he'll grow up much faster once he's through his calf love."

"You just want an adoring swain to fetch and carry for you."

"Oh, come on, Richard. I've been cooped up here since spring. I need a diversion."

"Just don't go too far," Richard begged.

"I shall be gentle."

After Richard changed he visited Justi, who had dispensed with the footman assigned to serve her, changed into her evening clothes and was struggling in the mirror with her neck cloth.

"What a disaster. Let's start over." Richard tore the mangled cloth from her grasp. "Do a simple tie if you can't manage anything else creditably."

"Richard, you're strangling me," she complained, with her face pointed toward the ceiling.

"I really came in to explain about Clara."

"Explain?" Justi noticed that Richard had not taken time to shave again and thought how attractively sinister half a day's growth of dark beard made him look.

"She's a bit of a tease. It's what she got used to in London, always being courted and having a train of admirers."

"You mean she's spoiled, like me," Justi concluded.

"I haven't thought of you as a spoiled brat for some time now."

"Well, she better not expect to bring me to heel, because I have no liking for laying about the drawing room watching women embroider."

Richard chuckled.

"What's so funny?"

"The thought of Clara doing embroidery. You do not find her beautiful?"

"I suppose she is, but Alicia is prettier."

"Don't tell Clara that," Richard said with a smirk. "There will be no living with her."

Clara was at her most stunning at dinner and managed to sit next to Justi. Miriam was looking a little frightened, and Richard felt he really could not blame any mother for not wanting her son to fall into Clara's clutches.

But Justi was not impressed with Clara's flirting and maintained an attitude of cool politeness toward her. At one point Richard saw Justi actually wink at Miriam, some private joke between them. It must have conveyed to Miriam that the boy could handle the situation, since she immediately calmed down and was able to enjoy her meal in spite of Clara's antics. Everyone was relieved when Julia rose to lead the ladies to the drawing room.

"Really, Richard!" Harry complained over the port. "Can't you do something about her?"

"I'll talk to her again. Sorry, Justi."

"It's all right. I think it's a game she's played many times before."

"With every man she meets. She told me she's got Sandford dangling after her now," reported Harry.

"No, not Sandy," said Richard. "He's no match for Clara."

"Do you think Justi is?"

"He hasn't managed ill, so far," Richard said, casting her an approving glance.

"But she won't be satisfied until she's got him, then she will toy with him for a while and cast him aside."

"Ha, you make me sound as helpless as a wounded mouse," Justi joked.

"That's what you'll feel like when she's done with you."

"Thanks for the warning, Harry. But I can always choose not to let anything happen."

"You don't know Clara."

"Gentlemen, shall we join the ladies?" Richard suggested.

When they entered the drawing room, Alicia was at the pianoforte and Clara was preparing to sing. She chose a poignant love ballad and so obviously directed the song at Justi that Harry nudged him. Justi listened raptly. Whatever else was wrong with Clara, one could not fault her voice. It was rich and full.

Next, Clara and Alicia performed a duet that they had obviously practiced. Then Alicia played a hauntingly delicate piece that Justi had tried but could never get quite right. When Miriam requested Justi to play, she chose a masculine work, which required a long reach and no delicacy.

The rest of the evening was spent discussing the holiday plans. Richard always gave a hunt the day after Christmas for the close neighbors, so those preparations had to be thrashed out, as well. Justi was surprised to learn that this was to be a comparatively quiet holiday with only the immediate family staying in the house. She could only be glad for this, especially if Clara was going to be a nuisance.

The next morning Harry and Justi had nearly finished breakfast by the time Richard and Julia sat down. Harry was charged with errands in Horwell for both his mother and sister. This was a good time to show Justi the neighborhood.

Richard acceded to this. Miriam and Alicia only came down in time to see them off. Clara's fashionably late appearance for breakfast was wasted since her quarry had already flown. She pouted and complained of cold tea and eggs until Richard threatened to wake her himself the next day with a pitcher of water. Knowing that if he was pushed too far Richard might make good on his threat, Clara subsided into a resentful silence.

Richard sought Julia out in the morning room later that day.

"How has Clara been behaving up until now?"

"Not badly, really. She thinks she is captivating our neighbour, Mr. Sandford."

"So I heard. Poor Sandy. I like him and wouldn't have him running at Clara's heels for anything."

"But it's no such thing, I assure you. He is kind and polite and I suppose he does pay a great deal of attention to her. Well, who could not, as forward as she acts. The truth is he comes here to see Miriam."

Richard raised his eyebrows.

"I won't say he's in love with her, yet, but I wouldn't be surprised if they made a match of it in the end."

"I wonder how Justi will take that. He will continue to live with us, of course, since I am his guardian."

"You had better let Miriam tell Justi in her own way. Has he missed her very much?"

"Not as much as I feared. In fact, I think I was mistaken in him on a good many counts. He is young but, because of having responsibilities thrust on him so early, he is rather mature in many ways."

"Not unlike you, in fact."

"It's true, we do have a lot in common."

"I'm glad you are all getting on so well. Miriam was a wreck until Justi's first letter arrived. That seemed to calm her down. I don't know if it's because she was widowed so young, but she seems to rely a great deal on Justi. Perhaps it's simply that she's not a very strong person."

"So, he had that put on him, as well?"

"He's turned out all right."

"No thanks to anyone."

When Harry and Justi returned without mishap from the village Justi went to her mother's room.

"I have so been wanting to talk to you alone," Miriam confided.

"And I can guess why. I hear from Harry that you are being courted."

"Oh, Justi, do you dislike it?" She turned from the mirror to face her child.

"How could I, Mother? I have seen you unhappy all my life. If Sandford will but change that, I want you to marry him more than anything."

"He hasn't asked me yet." Miriam almost blushed. "I'm not sure I can say yes to him."

"Why ever not?" Justi pushed herself up from her seat on the windowsill. "Oh, you mean because of me?"

"It would not be a good way to start a marriage. And what's to become of you?"

"I need to talk to you about that, Mother. I like Richard. I care more for him than I do for Homeplace. Would it matter to you if he owned it and not me?"

"You're going to tell him?" Miriam's eyes grew wide.

"Yes. But I don't know if I can face him with that. I don't know what he would do. I am going to have to leave."

"But where would you go?"

"London, I suppose. I think Meecham will still employ me if I go and talk to him. Or perhaps I'll travel. Don't worry. I'll sneak back to see you as often as I can."

"It isn't fair. It's like you're being exiled."

"Mother, when I say I like Richard, I mean I'm afraid I can't be around him any longer without betraying my feelings."

"You're in love with him after he treated you so cruelly?"

"I don't quite understand it myself." She looked out the window. "I've never felt anything like this before."

"But if you love him, why leave?"

"Because if I told him the truth about myself he would hate me for the deception. The lie has gone on too long."

"It's my fault." Miriam began to weep.

"No, never say that." Justi knelt by her and took her hands. "My life has been my choice for years now. Think of all the times you begged me to tell Grandfather. Do you imagine I regret the life I've led? I'm better off than any woman I know."

"But you did it all for one reason, to inherit, and now it's all for nothing."

"No, it's not for nothing. Mother, I can speak four languages. I can go anywhere. I can be anything I choose. That's not nothing."

"It is if you're lost to me." Miriam was inconsolable, so Justi left her to get used to the idea. She didn't know, herself, when she would leave. She might just have to slip away. She hated taking the cowardly way out but she had no doubt Richard could and would stop her, even if it meant locking her in her room until she came of age.

The day of Christmas Eve saw many callers drive up to Amberly. It was an open house with punch and Christmas cake served up all day long. Justi tried to stay out of Clara's way so as not to cause Richard embarrassment. Harry assisted by spiriting Justi off on a riding tour of the estate and surroundings before Clara could invite herself along. They had lunch at the Red Dog in Horwell where Harry seemed to be well-known. They then spent a good part of the afternoon with Richard's houndsmen. By dinnertime Justi was in possession of all the information she needed to set up her own kennel. That she had no intention of doing so she did not bother to tell Harry.

Dinner was festive and there was an intense excitement in the air. Christmas had always been a quiet affair at Homeplace. Here there was an anticipation Justi had never known, even as a child.

Clara was quiet throughout dinner. Justi thought Richard must have warned her off. Actually, Clara was studying her. If Justi had really been a man, she might have been flattered to think that she represented something of a challenge to Clara. As it was, had she known the plots and devices Clara was considering to win her, she would have been frightened.

There was a Christmas Eve service at the church. The choir was inspiring. Justi took note of all the pieces they did, thinking to tell Vicar Mayfair for next year. Then it occurred to Justi that she probably wouldn't be at Homeplace or Amberly next Christmas.

Home at Amberly, they sang carols and listened to stories from Christmases past. Clara was so jolly and well behaved she put Justi off her guard. Richard, who knew her better, was glad of the period of good feeling and peace, while wondering how long it would last.

They opened gifts in the morning at Amberly, after breakfast, so latecomers to the breakfast parlor, like Clara, got short shrift from Harry and Alicia, who were as excited as two children. Many exquisite articles of clothing and books were exchanged. The watercolor Justi had gotten framed for her mother found favor with everyone. It was the rose garden at Homeplace with a girl clad in a cream-colored dress and straw bonnet seated on the bench. Everyone assumed it was Miriam.

Harry was ecstatic over the dueling pistols Justi had found for him in Newmarket. For the women she had purchased shawls of figured silk, peach-colored for her mother, pink for Alicia, cream for Julia and, for Clara, a vibrant red that was very becoming. Richard looked puzzled over her gift to him.

"I couldn't think what you would really like."

Richard lifted up a new halter with a brass plate and read, "Bluedevil." He then fished a document out of the box—a bill of sale for one black five-year-old horse, for services rendered.

"My gift to you, Justi, is also in the stable."

"One of your horses?" Harry guessed.

"Don't get too excited," Justi advised. "What if it's a manure fork?"

They went out, laughing, to the stable. It was a beautiful young gray hunter. "She's lovely. What's her name?"

"Gray Dawn. We bred her here, but she will never be up to my weight, or even Harry's. She's an excellent jumper, though, a natural over fences, and nothing scares her."

"She's perfect. Thank you, Richard."

"Now for my present to you, Justi." Harry preceded them over to the kennels. "One of my pointer bitch's pups. You can have your pick."

Justi was not insensible to the honor bestowed on her. "You choose for me, Harry."

The day after Christmas the hunt at Amberly began with a lavish breakfast, with everyone dressed for riding except Julia and Miriam. Clara was not conspicuous among so many other high spirits. Justi examined Sandford with interest. He was handsome enough in a fair way, with curly brown hair and a good-humored expression. His looks were not particularly to Justi's taste, but she couldn't deny that Sandford and her mother made a handsome couple. She really couldn't picture him angry like Richard, and she hoped that Sandford's disposition was always sunny for her mother's sake.

As she turned to look at Richard's dark face, her heart started thumping. What right had she to compare them or even consider her preferences? She was going to have to get herself under control or she would have to leave right away.

Justi asked for her new mare to be saddled. Richard chose to ride Bluedevil rather than Major because, he said, the beast was inexhaustible. Justi kept close to Richard and Harry, but with a watchful eye on Alicia, who seemed to be a competent, if not daring, horsewoman.

Clara plainly took chances, no more so than Harry, but what was put down to high spirits in a young man was regarded in Clara as unbecoming. This was puzzling to Justi, who felt once again thankful that she could enjoy the hunt without reservations.

By midafternoon, when they were miles from Amberly, Justi saw Clara unhook her leg from the saddle, kick out of the stirrup and throw herself off her horse. Justi rode after the loose mare wondering what Clara was up to.

When Justi returned, Richard was kneeling by Clara, looking concerned. "Can you ride?"

"I think so," Clara said tearfully.

Justi wondered how she could be so unfeeling as to ruin Richard's day like this. "I think I've had enough for today anyway," said Justi. "Why don't you let me see Clara home? I'm sure if we just walk the horses it won't be hard on her ankle," Justi suggested.

This must have been Clara's plan all along. "Yes, Richard, you're the host. You must catch up with the others. Justi can take care of me as soon as I've rested a little."

Richard mounted, looking somewhat doubtful, but he was glad to shirk this one responsibility, anyway. Justi waited until Richard was out of sight and said, "He's gone. You may as well get up now."

"What are you talking about? I've sprained my ankle."

"I saw you fall. Do you pull that stunt often?" Justi asked coldly. "It wasn't very convincing."

Clara rose in wrath, brushing her skirt. "I don't know why I bother with you. You're just a boy."

Justi brought Clara's mare over and prepared to help her mount. "What is wrong with you, anyway?" she asked as Justi gave her a leg up. "Any normal man would want me."

Justi's face, when Clara looked at it, was stricken. Justi suddenly realized she was working the wrong way with Clara. Such a wicked rumor could really hurt Richard. Even Clara's heart of stone was touched by Justi's hurt expression. "I was only joking. What is it? Why don't you like me?"

"I don't know," Justi lied, "I suppose you're just too old for me."

The words had scarcely left her mouth when she realized what an insult she had offered to Clara. Richard, at his most furious, looked tame compared to Clara. She cut at Justi with her whip. Justi flinched away, but caught the lash in her eye. By the time she could see well enough to ride, Clara was gone.

She took roads in the general direction toward Amberly and, by dint of asking a carrier, managed to arrive before the boisterous hunting party. After seeing Clara's mare being rubbed down in the stable, she went to knock on Clara's door.

"Come in—what do you want?" Clara said coldly. Justi entered and closed the door behind her.

"I came to apologize. What I said wasn't what I meant." Justi could hardly keep her left eye open. "It just came out wrong. I meant I'm too young for someone like you to be interested in. You see, I'm not used to being around women so I don't really know what to say."

Clara did not look mollified.

"I've been a great deal of trouble to your brother," said Justi, inspecting her boots. "And today is very important to him. I just want to be able to get through it without a scene. Richard has little enough enjoyment out of life without having this day ruined."

"You don't know what trouble is," asserted Clara. "Not even Harry has cost him more or caused him more grief than me." She looked at her dressing table.

"What?"

"Didn't he tell you about me?"

"No, he just said you were lively. He does care about you. He cares for all his family, even me, a stranger."

Clara rose to face Justi. "Your eye is very red. Can you see at all?"

"I blacked Richard's eye once," Justi said, grinning, as she squinted at Clara.

"Never tell me you got over Richard's guard."

"No, nothing like that." Justi told her the tale of the squire's wall and ended up describing how Richard had re-laid the stones. The picture of Richard doing manual labor gave Clara the giggles.

"But I'll never forget his face when I was coughing blood all over him and he thought I was dying. He looked just the same when he was bending over your sprained ankle. He really does care."

"I know, and I do try to be good."

"Well, let us try not to cause him any more grief. Especially, let's not fight in front of company."

"All right."

"And remember," Justi said over her shoulder as she opened the door, "Richard's no fool, so you better show at least a slight limp."

"My goodness, Justi, what happened to your eye?" Miriam asked before dinner.

"It's all right."

"You always say that." Richard came over to inspect the injury.

"It's my fault," Clara said defiantly. "I caught him with my whip."

"Clara, you make it sound like you did it on purpose." Justi laughed. Clara wondered for a moment why Justi was protecting her. Then it occurred to her that Justi didn't want to upset Richard.

"Well, it doesn't look serious, and I'll wager you've taken harder knocks," Richard confirmed.

"What about the time we thought you killed yourself?" Harry put in.

"As I recall, it was your fault Justi fell," Richard admonished.

"Justi told me about that one," Clara volunteered.

Harry told the story again, and after that the hunt supper was regaled with everyone's favorite fall.

Miriam shuddered. "You're mad, all of you," Miriam said. "Why would you want to recall something that hurt so much?" No one could answer her.

Justi smiled across at Clara. She felt they had reached an understanding on some level. They both agreed that Rich-

ard deserved some peace. What Justi didn't realize was that
Clara saw no conflict between Richard's happiness and her
conquest of Justi. She planned to have Justi sitting in her
pocket before they returned to Homeplace. Marriage was
never in her mind. She did like to drive men to the point
where they asked her, though.

The day after Richard's hunt a cold snap set in, which
lasted for weeks. It made the ground iron hard, and although riding was still possible, chasing and hunting for any
time was too hard on the horses' legs.

Thus confined to the house the better part of the day, it
was as well, Richard thought, that Clara's good humor held.
She and Justi had seemed to be getting along well since the
day of the hunt. He toyed with the idea of a match between
them but, besides the age difference, they were not much
alike. Still, he wouldn't discount the idea totally since it
would solve a world of problems for him.

Justi and Alicia might be a better match, but he didn't like
marriages between children. At least one party should know
how to go on, preferably the husband.

The young set, including Clara, organized billiards tournaments that consumed many hours. Since Justi had never
played, and Harry was determined to teach her, the course
of play was often interrupted by lively arguments and
laughter.

In the evenings they played piquet or whist, and unbe-
knownst to the rest of the party, the four younger members
were rehearsing a one-act play they had drafted together,
which included a sword fight between Justi and Harry. Justi
favored the role of villain for herself because she thought she
died more convincingly than Harry.

When Harry and the rescued heroine, Alicia, had left the
scene, and Clara had mourned the death of her misguided
lover, Count Urgo, the applause from Richard, Julia, Miriam and Sandford was quite genuine.

* * *

Clara still meant to bring her young cousin to heel, of course, but she conceded it might take some time to arouse Justi's interest in women at all. In the meantime she treated him with a familiarity that disgusted Harry but amused Justi. Even in a house the size of Amberly Clara could run Justi to earth in a very few minutes. Clara learned not to treat Justi as cavalierly as her other young men by sending her off to fetch mislaid fans or reticules. Justi would never return from these errands, but would be found later reading a book somewhere.

"I sent you for my vinaigrette an hour ago," Clara accused after tracking Justi to one of the gallery rooms on the second floor.

"Is that Richard?" Justi asked of a youngish portrait.

"Yes, when he was seventeen, just before father sent him away. He accused Richard of the vilest things, and they were not true."

Justi did not ask what things. She knew the pain of being wrongly accused. "He bears a strong resemblance to Harry now. It's those penetrating blue eyes."

"Yes, they seem to drill right through you," Clara said, "especially when he has caught you out in something."

Justi looked at her rather sheepishly.

"I see you know what I mean," Clara said.

"He doesn't look very happy," Justi said to distract her.

"He wasn't very happy in those days. Would you like to see your grandfather? Which one is it now? This one, with his brother—that would be Richard's grandfather."

"He looks so different. I would never have recognized him. I can't think that I ever saw him smile in my whole life."

"This must have been while they were still on speaking terms." Clara recited some of the other names, the ones she knew for a certainty and Justi tried to memorize them.

"This is no Mallory," Justi said of a small watercolor in an oval frame.

"That is Richard's wife, Evelyn."

Justi staggered a little. "I never knew he was married."

"She died in childbirth. It must be five years now. He hasn't looked at another woman since."

"No wonder he's never spoken of her then," Justi mused, studying the delicate, ethereal curls and fragile smile. This was not the sort of woman she would have guessed Richard would have chosen. Surely his barbed tongue would have devastated such an ephemeral creature. Perhaps Richard was the one who had been devastated, or perhaps he had not always been so cutting and impatient. He had a gayer, gentler side to him—that she knew. The rough shell he showed the world might just be his way of not getting bruised again.

Could Richard ever be interested in a boyish hoyden like herself? Impossible—even if he knew, even if by some chance he did not hate her for the imposture, he would never love her—not if this was his taste in women, not if he was still grieving.

"Are you going to stand there all day? Come."

"Where?"

"With me, silly. The first interest you've shown in any woman and it turns out to be a dead one."

The only good thing to come of the extreme cold was that the shallow lake had frozen hard enough, even in Richard's conservative opinion, to permit ice-skating.

"Do you skate, Justi?" Richard inquired.

"No, not since…" Justi hesitated. "Well, Mother doesn't like me to."

"Since when?"

"I went through the ice once when I was skating alone," Justi said reluctantly.

"Who got you out?"

"No one. I mean no one was about."

"But how did you get out?"

"I got myself out." Justi was looking back in time, seeing a scene from long ago.

Until that moment, Richard had not understood the emptiness of Justi's life. He knew there was much Justi had to bear alone. But that a child would have to face death alone, to drag himself back from that numbing cold, knowing there was no possible rescue, was a terrible thought.

"You almost died, didn't you?"

Justi looked at him in surprise. "I had to get out myself. There was no one to come for me," Justi said almost resentfully.

"You will never be alone like that again, I promise you."

All her courage deserted Justi then. Richard cared so much, and her repayment was betrayal.

At Richard's insistence they fitted Justi with skates, and under Harry's buoyant influence she applied herself to relearning old skills. They raced, jumped and played crack the whip. Julia and Miriam chose to watch from the shore, but Richard and Sandy joined in the romp on the frozen lake as though they were boys again.

By the third week in January, Richard was beginning to plan the return trip to Homeplace. The ladies agreed to join the men there for spring and summer provided the bedchambers could be got up comfortably.

Sandford was at dinner the night they were discussing Homeplace. He had been looking at Justi all evening in the oddest way. Justi decided something was in the wind.

Just before the ladies retired from the table, Sandford rose and said he had an announcement. "Lady Miriam has consented to become my wife."

Miriam blushed. Justi went around the table and bent over to kiss her cheek. She shook Sandford's hand and wished him well. Sandford blushed. Richard proposed a toast to the happy couple. Alone, among those present, Clara was the only surprised recipient of the news. She was white with shock or anger. Justi couldn't be sure what she would do and feared a scene. Clara rose mechanically and drank the health of Miriam and Sandy.

Since the ladies left for the drawing room then, Justi hoped Clara would have time to compose herself. Sandford was still having trouble meeting Justi's eyes. This is odd, she thought. He wasn't this shy before. Then it hit her. He knew. Her eyes widened and met his. He looked at her helplessly and questioningly. Mother had said she wouldn't accept him unless he knew the truth. But would he tell Richard?

This was the oddest situation, sitting calmly at the table with a near stranger who held her entire future in his hands. She smiled at the absurdity of it. She knew she should be embarrassed appearing before him in this disguise. But, truthfully, appearing in a dress would have made her more uncomfortable. These were her clothes, the only kind she had ever known.

This did decide one thing for certain. She would have to leave. Sandford might not rat on her intentionally, but sooner or later he would slip. It was so much on his mind. Even Mother blundered sometimes.

Richard caught Justi's half smile and was glad that Justi was truly happy with the match. But with those dimples he despaired of Justi ever looking anything but an impish boy. He tried to picture Justi older, married and with children, but he simply could not.

Neither Richard nor Harry thought it odd that Justi hung back to talk to Sandford when they started for the drawing room.

"You know about me?" Justi asked.

"Yes, I'm sorry, I mean, what can I do?" Sandford offered.

"Marry Mother and make her happy. Leave the rest to me."

"Justi, you have to tell them!"

"Will you, if I don't?" she asked.

"No— I don't know. I hate to think what will happen when this comes out. But sooner or later, it will, you know."

"Yes, I suppose you're right. I don't like to think of it, myself. I can't decide if Richard will hang me or beat me to death."

Sandford looked shocked. "I'm sure he will do nothing of the kind."

"You don't know Richard, if you think that. I was considering just leaving."

"That doesn't solve anything, except to make your mother unhappy."

"Yes, I know."

"Tell Richard. Then come with us. Miriam is bringing your nurse to live with us. Everything will be as it was before."

"Why, thank you," Justi said in some surprise, "but that is a kindness I do not deserve. I know you mean well, but I have to work this out for myself. If it's any comfort, tell Mother I won't just split and run. I will always see that she knows where I am. And I will tell Richard. I just need some time to screw up my courage. You can leave on your honeymoon with a quiet mind."

Justi could only be glad that they were not to make a long stay at Amberly. Now that Sandford knew about her, he tended to flush and glance her way when any untoward language was used among the gentlemen. He rode close on her heels whenever he was one of the party riding out, and was beginning to get on her nerves.

Richard's care of her she tolerated, perhaps even enjoyed; Sandford's was marked enough to cause her the embarrassment of being asked by Harry, "What is wrong with Sandy? Doesn't he think you can ride?"

"I don't know," said Justi. "He has become quite fatherly, and I'm not much used to it."

"He knows you are not to live with them. I don't see why he concerns himself for your safety," Richard said almost jealously.

"I can only think Mother has made him promise to look out for me." Justi laughed helplessly. "Why else would he take such a sudden interest in my well-being?"

"Yes, that must be it," Richard agreed. "Well, it's like to get him killed. He can't keep up with us on that slack hunter of his."

Justi took a fall, on Sandford's land, in fact. Gray Dawn lost her footing on some frost-hardened ground and went down on her haunches. It could almost be said that Justi merely stepped off her until the mare recovered herself. But Sandford was all for returning to the house.

Justi's angry flush amused Richard and Harry, who rode on when she said, "A word with you, sir," to her future stepfather. "I am not a china doll to be hurt so easily. I scarcely even scratched my boots coming off that time, and if I had fallen I would have rolled as I have been taught and come up unharmed." She ignored his offer of a leg up and mounted as lightly as a boy.

"But you are a girl."

"A fact that is likely to be public knowledge sooner than I want if you maintain this nonsensical watch over me."

"You promised you would tell him," Sandford said in exasperation.

"When we return to Homeplace. Content you that Richard will know the truth long before you tire of your honeymoon. Do you imagine I want to expose my mother to his wrath?"

"But yourself."

"I can take care of myself," Justi assured him. Sandford looked at her doubtfully as she cantered off to catch up with Richard and Harry.

"Did you get him off your back?" Harry asked.

"I don't know if I've made the slightest impression on him. He's so besotted with my mother he scarcely knows what he is about. I hope I haven't hurt his feelings."

"Not Sandy, I assure you," Richard said. "He is acting oddly, though."

"I expect you have never seen him in love before."

"If that's the result, I hope I never get a case of it."
Richard laughed.

"Something tells me it wouldn't take you quite the same
way," Justi said.

Surprisingly, the few weeks spent in this state of uncertainty were much more wearing on Sandford's nerves than
on Justi's. In fact, Sandford thought she had none. Justi
acted no differently than when he thought she was a boy. If
he wasn't mistaken, she went out of her way to terrify him.

When Sandford remonstrated with Miriam over this he
calmly said that Justi had always taken care of herself. She
assured Sandford that if Justi had said she would take care
of everything, she would do it, and Miriam certainly voted
to delay Justi's revelation until they were well away from
Richard.

This smacked too much of cowardice for Sandford's liking, but as much as he disparaged the thought of leaving
Justi to her fate, he dreaded more the inevitable scene if he
told Richard he had known of the imposture all this time.
Although he was ten years Richard's senior, and they were
the best of good friends, even he had felt the lash of Richard's tongue once and had not relished it.

By an effort of will he managed to restrain himself from
pestering Justi again. He merely did a lot of sweating in her
presence, lest he should let her identity slip. He marveled at
her composure. Justi even teased him rather unmercifully
about his wedding night.

Sandford and Miriam were married quietly in the church
at Northampton. The bride was radiant, the groom over-
joyed, and both had been gratefully lulled into a sense of
security by Justi's promise. Since the projected honeymoon was to comprise a three-month tour of Sandford's
relations, including those in Scotland, Justi felt she had
plenty of time to make good her vow. Sandford left her with

the private assurance that she could make her home with them if the Mallory household became unbearable for her.

Far from finding it unbearable, Justi enjoyed living under the same roof with Richard as much here as at Homeplace. That this far from idyllic situation would soon have to end Justi accepted. She merely garnered what memories she could against a time of future loneliness. She never tired of watching Richard and she savored every moment spent with him.

Richard came upon Justi one snowy afternoon ostensibly reading a book on the window seat in the library. Actually, she was gazing out at the softly falling flakes so raptly she didn't hear him enter.

Richard wondered if Justi would ever give up perching on windowsills. The need to see out when not actually outside seemed to be a passion with the child.

"In summer two lads are kept busy constantly scything that lawn. I suppose you would turn a flock of sheep loose on it."

Justi's low chuckle warmed Richard's heart. "I was just wondering what it was like in summer."

"You will see it next year."

She looked up at him, so close yet so unreachable. "You mean to bring me back here?"

"Of course. You are a minor. If I didn't trust Clara or Harry to live alone, I'm not apt to leave you to your own devices."

"I seemed somehow to manage before." Justi looked an amused challenge at him.

"I didn't mean that I don't trust you. For whatever reason, you are more sensible even than Harry and you certainly have more discretion than Clara."

Justi was coming to realize that Richard had been in control of his odd family for so long he actually needed to have someone to manage. Whether this was healthy or not, she would have liked nothing better than to be by his side forever, but not in her present guise. She really wondered how much longer she could stand to be near him, knowing that she could never share more than a ride or a joke with him.

She watched him as he moved over to select a book for himself. She was in love with every move he made—the way his dark hair came close to falling across his forehead but never quite did. Except for the fight at Newmarket and the fall he had taken at Squire Coates's, she had never seen him disarranged. There was a lot of suspense in being around Richard.

Richard must have felt Justi's gaze, for he turned and gave her one of his rare smiles. "How about a game of chess?"

"Gladly."

Justi was so distracted she fell into the first two traps he set for her easily enough. She shook herself into a more vigilant mood and pointedly did not hasten to snap up all the pawns he sent out to tempt her. He even went so far as to bait her with a bishop, but she saw through that. He was, in fact, so busy setting traps she managed to get him into check and thought sure she would win one match.

She almost didn't want to. Winning was so important to him and meant nothing at all to her. But it was fun to watch his eyes scanning the board, testing every possibility. He flashed her a brief, triumphant look under his dark brows and made a move that achieved a stalemate. One of his black locks had actually dropped across his brow.

"Another game?" she asked, smiling.

"I don't think we have time before dinner. You are much improved."

"Yes, but my mind tends to wander."

"Really, where to?"

"You would be surprised."

Chapter Eight

The beginning of February saw Richard, Harry and Justi driving back to Homeplace to prepare for the arrival of Julia, Clara and Alicia. They were running ahead of a snowstorm, but Richard thought they could beat it.

"Well, are you happy for your mother?" Richard asked from his corner of the post chaise.

"Yes, of course." Justi was thoughtful. "I think in my own way, I've treated her as badly as Grandfather ever did."

"What are you talking about?" asked Harry.

"Well, except for Mother, I've been more or less alone my whole life. I've never known what a real family was like so I never knew what I was missing. But Mother had a family, once. She might have died of loneliness at Homeplace. I should have spent more time with her."

"But you're her son," said Harry. "She wouldn't have expected you to be always underfoot."

"I agree," said Richard. "What she missed was female companionship. The best move I ever made was sending her to Amberly."

"Yes, I know that now." Justi looked out the window.

The snow overtook them before they reached Saint Neots. Justi, who had been watching behind, decided it was fortunate that they had their night gear with them, for she had not seen the chaise with the valets and the luggage for more than an hour. Now there was a wall of white behind them and little visibility in front. She wondered if Richard would force them onward but he signaled to Haimes and said they would put up at the next inn no matter what it was.

Justi and Harry helped Haimes find accommodation for the hunters and a box for Justi's pup while Richard sought rooms for the night.

They stamped into the taproom, shaking snow off their greatcoats to unwelcome news. "They can give us two rooms, no more," Richard announced. "And we'll have to eat in the taproom. You two won't mind sharing, will you?" He sent Justi a searching look.

"Well, that all depends," Justi considered.

"On what?" Richard demanded.

"On who snores."

"I do not snore," asserted Richard.

"I never said that."

"You implied it."

"We'll leave it up to Harry," Justi offered.

"He snores."

"I'll get you for that." Richard shoved the laughing Harry into the taproom and ordered them each a brandy to hold them until dinner. They enjoyed a simple but satisfying meal of pork pie, roast hen, cheese, fruit and ale.

Justi excused herself early, on the pretext of having too much to drink. She wasn't particularly worried about sharing a bed with Harry. She washed, changed and lay under the covers thinking what strange passes she had come to since knowing Richard. Harry tried to get to bed without waking her, but after he staggered into the washstand, upset the chair and nearly dropped his candle on the bed, she was wide-awake.

"You're not asleep, are you?"

"No, not anymore. Has it stopped snowing yet?"

"Yes. Richard thinks we can make an early start, after all."

*   *   *

They began the night back to back, and every time Harry
rolled over on her, Justi resolutely nudged him over onto his
side of the bed like an overaffectionate hound. When Richard invaded their room next morning to rout them out, Justi
looked to have won the struggle for covers but lost the one
for space. Justi lay curled up on the very edge of the bed,
and Harry sprawled on a diagonal with his head nestled into
the nape of Justi's neck. Richard laughed, for they looked
like two tired puppies lying in an exhausted heap. In re-
pose, Richard thought, the boy's face gave no hint of the
steel within.

"Justi. Harry."

Justi's eyes opened slowly and looked vaguely up at him.
She smiled sleepily, thinking him part of some delicious
dream. Then she gave a start.

"Richard, I can't think where we are."

"Farnwell."

"That's right." Justi blinked and sat up. Harry, when
prodded by Richard, merely moaned and rolled over.

"Don't worry," Justi said. "I'll make sure he's up before I come down."

Justi rang for a can of hot water, then she washed and wet
her newly acquired shaving gear and left it lying out to dry.
Gerard had been some use to her. She did not bother to go
through the motions of shaving, since Harry was still sound
asleep. Then she dressed quickly and tried to tie her crushed
neck cloth presentably. Harry was difficult to rouse but responded to the threat of being doused with cold water. Justi
couldn't help wondering what it would be like to sleep with
Richard. The only impression that leaped to mind was the
image of bedding down with a lion.

Richard and Justi were almost finished eating by the time
Harry joined them at the trestle table, nursing his hangover. He got scant sympathy from Richard, who recommended he have some coffee and ham quickly since they had
already called for the horses to be put to. Harry turned pale

at the mention of food and slept for a while in the chaise. When he did awake in midmorning, he was starving, but Richard refused to stop.

"Jasper might be willing to share his breakfast with you," said Justi, pulling out a packet of bread and ham. "I didn't know that Haimes would have time to feed him before we left." Richard looked on in disgust as Harry consumed, without hesitation, all the pup's meal, and reflected that Justi was a great deal kinder to Harry than he deserved.

Richard and Justi spent the rest of the trip discussing plans for refurbishing the unused bedrooms at Homeplace.

"Julia can have Mother's room. There's the yellow room for Clara, and Alicia could take my room. I'll sleep in one of the northwest rooms."

"Nonsense. Harry can move and give Alicia his room."

"All right, what's wrong with the northwest rooms?" Harry roused himself to ask.

"No heat," Richard explained.

"As if I care for that." Harry was playfully teasing the white pup.

"You may if the weather continues like this," Richard said. "Actually, Justi should have his grandfather's room."

"But I like to look out the back of the house. There's more going on."

They reached Homeplace before noon, and there was a rather nasty shock waiting for Justi. It was a package from Gerard. Evidently Jim had happened through Brinley, and they had sent the package by him. Among so much other mail, Richard merely handed it to her without a thought, assuming it to be a book she had ordered. The letter it contained was even more demanding than the last one. Gerard had gone to Meecham and Bates and gotten *La Petit Innocent* back for her and set himself up as her agent in London. Such nerve!

The most distressing part was that he had heard of her mother's marriage and meant to make trouble if Justi did not agree to do the work. He could not know that Sandford was in on the secret. Still, it would cast a pall over their first weeks of marriage to have the scandal broached now. Perhaps if she could hold Gerard off until they went to Scotland . . .

She screwed up her courage and went in search of Richard with every intention of telling him the truth as she had promised Sandford. She found him in the sitting room among a litter of mail and with an empty brandy glass. He dashed it onto the hearth with one of his famous oaths before he noticed her.

"Sorry," he said angrily. "Don't look so frightened, Rabbit. It's nothing you have done."

"Gerard?" she guessed.

"Yes, he wants more money, of course."

"Then it is something I've done," she said bitterly.

"I shall have to pay him," Richard said, hating the words, "not what he wants, of course, but enough to keep him quiet for a few months.

"Until Mother and Sandford have gone north."

"You are quick. I know Sandy well enough to know it would not matter to him—not very pleasant for your mother, of course. But as you are not to live with them, no scandal will attach to them once some time has passed with you in my household." Richard folded up the letter.

"Use my money to pay him, Richard. I have close to four hundred pounds saved."

"No, you keep that." Richard smiled tightly. "You will need that for Homeplace. I will take care of Dumont."

"There must be something I can do. Leave—if nothing else."

"Run away? That won't solve anything. On the contrary, it will only lend credibility to his tale."

Justi's head came up at that.

"There is one thing you might consider," Richard said.

"What?"

"Marriage."

"Me?"

"I know you are young, but—"

"Richard, I can't!" she said in a panic.

"It was only a thought."

Justi went to her room and began work on the translation. If she could finish it quickly and send it to Gerard perhaps he would let Richard alone.

The chaise with the valets arrived late that day. Within two days of their return, they had extra help from the village turning out the bedchambers and giving Homeplace its first thorough spring cleaning in years.

Justi spent every spare moment on the translation, which was to say she got up in the middle of the night to work on it. It was not a task she could let Richard catch her at. Once she finished it and dispatched it to London she really should be gone from here. Everything she did she did thinking it would be the last time. She went to the pond to skate. The fear of the ice and the cold water was an old fear and one she felt she had to lay to rest before she left. Like so many things she dreaded, it turned out to be a joy once she had mastered it. And she knew that if she was careful she would not go through the ice.

When Richard missed Justi and Harry he went to Badger, who reported he had seen Justi walking toward the pond with his skates. Master Harry, if wanted, could be found at the stud farm hobnobbing with the grooms.

Something about the mention of the pond drove a cold stab through Richard's heart. The lake at Amberly was ornamental and only four feet deep all over. The pond here was for watering stock. Although it had more slope to the banks, he thought that it might, near the center, be deep enough to drown in.

He threw on his coat and walked with some urgency toward the frozen pond, but slowed when Justi slid into view, circled the edge and skated to the other end. Richard paused beside a stand of trees to watch. Like everything the boy learned, Justi practiced skating relentlessly. Richard was reminded of Justi's piano pieces, not just because of the repetition of the circles, figure eights, spins and leaps, but because Justi seemed to be listening to music as he skated.

Justi took chances, each time faster, higher. Richard waited for a fall but it never happened. Justi pushed to the limit of what was possible. He repeated the sequence six times after Richard deemed it perfect. Why did the boy care so much about how he did? There had never been a father to nod his approval of how well Justi rode, or anything else. Richard concluded the lad did it to please himself. It was a cold and lonely thought. Even Richard's father, demanding as he was, had at least been there.

Richard could anticipate the succession of moves now—speed up, a leap, spin in the air, land and skate backward, figure eight. Justi used his arms to balance; like a bird's wings, they seemed almost as much as moving feet to keep the skater suspended over the ice. Thigh muscles stood out tautly at each movement. Richard was nearly lulled into a dreamlike state by the rhythm of Justi's movements. As he stood leaning against a tree trunk, he thought, I really love this boy.

Startled, he gave himself a mental shake. Of course I love him, he thought, as a father loves a son, even an adopted one. But he knew in his heart this was not so. He began to understand a little how Justi could have unconsciously tempted Gerard. The sooner the boy was married, the better. He walked to the house without Justi ever knowing he had been there.

Richard was cold to Justi the next morning for no particular reason that she could think of. Harry merely shrugged it off as a mood. Justi couldn't make out what she had done to displease Richard. When she ventured to ask, he snapped at her so viciously, she drew back in silence.

"It's not you—nothing to do with you, Justi. Leave it alone."

Richard maintained his distance all week and only seemed affable when in the company of Harry or others. They were not without entertainment that winter. The squire had them to dine twice. They descended on the vicar nearly every Sunday and reciprocated in turn. Justi almost begged off a dinner at the Allens'. There was to be dancing afterward and she hated that. Harry taunted her into going, but she did not know how she would be able to manage it after a week of very short nights. The translation was almost finished, and she wanted rid of the thing before Richard accidentally discovered it.

He did catch her at it the night before the Allens' party when she thought he had already gone to bed. He must have seen the light under her door. When she heard it open she flipped open a book of history on top of her pile of work and hoped for the best.

"Don't you ever sleep?" Richard asked in a voice thick with drink.

"What time is it?" she asked, clearing her throat. She had never known him to sit up drinking alone before.

"Past two o'clock," he said, putting his candle carefully down on the desk beside her own.

"When I wake up, there's no point in simply lying there."

"Pliny—pretty dry."

"That's what I need."

Jasper set up a howl in the stable, and Justi got up and went to the window. She turned to the desk and snuffed the candles, the better to see into the stable yard. Also it eliminated the possibility of Richard discovering what she had been doing.

"What is it?" Richard asked.

"I can't see anything. I imagine he is just lonely. If he keeps it up I will go out to him. There may always be a fox about."

"It's special to you, isn't it?" he asked obliquely.

"The dog?"

"No, Homeplace."

"It's just a place. I could like another place as well," she said, but not convincingly.

"I could not."

"Not even Amberly?" She turned to him in the dark.

"Amberly is finished."

"What? Done up?"

"No, I mean I've done all I can there. It's perfect and finished."

"Whereas Homeplace needs so much work it will never be finished," Justi concluded. "I always wondered what the attraction was. Now I understand. You've a lifetime of work ahead of you here—and I trust you with it now, no matter what happens to me."

"What could possibly happen to you?" Richard laughed.

"I could go away."

"No!"

"You asked me once to tell you about Gerard and me— what had happened." The darkness gave her courage to broach the subject she had so long avoided. She could not see those blue eyes, for one thing. "I went wrong a long time before Gerard came on the scene. I can't think what else to do but leave."

"Don't be stupid. You had one brush with disaster. You shall come about."

"No, you don't understand. There's a danger that will always be there."

"Nonsense," he said huskily. "You're tired. Get some sleep." Even his brandy-fogged brain knew it was dangerous for him to be there alone in the dark with Justi. He turned to go.

"Richard, I must tell you! I'm not what you think I am."

"I have a pretty fair notion what you are."

"No, you don't," she said passionately. "I'm an imposter." There! She had told him finally.

"Oh, I see," he said, chuckling with relief. "Born on the wrong side of the blanket? But I think you must be wrong about that. You look too much a Mallory."

She gasped when she caught his meaning.

"It doesn't matter," he said. "I like you well enough anyway."

When he left she rested her forehead against the cold windowpane in despair. Where would she find that much courage again?

For Justi at least, the Allens' dinner was a disaster from beginning to end. Everyone else seemed to have a capital time. There were innumerable courses to get through, each one with its own wine. She was so tired and groggy she could not think clearly enough to defend herself against Sally's jokes or Meg's teasing. She was afraid to say much of anything lest she let her irritation get the better of her.

If only Harry and Richard had not to make such fools of themselves over the girls. That was an embarrassment in itself. The dancing exhausted her but helped clear her head of the spirits. She wanted only to go home and sleep. But there was still the late supper to get through and more wine.

It was a relief when they mounted for the short ride to Homeplace. The icy cold air was like a delicious drink, but it could not clear the buzzing from her head. Gray Dawn did nothing untoward as she trotted after Richard on Blue-devil. Justi merely slid off her. Even landing on the frosty ground did not wake her.

Richard turned to see Harry dismounting and the gray mare standing still. He rode back and got off in some concern. It took them a few moments to rouse Justi even to a vacant stare, and then she nearly drifted off again.

"What made you fall?" demanded Richard. "Did your horse spook?"

"No, I must have fallen asleep," she said, struggling to her feet with his help. Harry was a little tipsy himself and laughed.

"You what?" Richard demanded.

"I fell asleep. Too much wine, I think." She took her horse's reins.

"You hardly had any," said Harry.

"Hardly any to you is more than enough for me."

Richard laughed then. "Shall I carry you back?"

"I think I can stay awake if I walk." Justi staggered into her horse then, so Richard picked her up and tossed her on Bluedevil.

"Slide behind the saddle. You can lock your hands around my waist. It won't matter if you fall asleep then."

She did as he commanded and rested against his broad back. If only they could ride on like this forever.

She finished the work, not with pride this time, but in disgust. She sneaked into Brinley to post it. Her short escape went unnoticed because Julia, Alicia and Clara arrived that afternoon with a mountain of baggage and three maids. This threw the household into a flutter for hours. Justi stood back in amazement as poor Jim carried load after load of trunks and valises into the hall. This had all then to be identified by the maids and Jim had to heft it upstairs.

Clara kissed Justi no less passionately than last time, and it took all Justi's resolve not to wipe her cheek like a mulish little boy. Richard must have detected this urge for he laughed at her unmercifully.

Fortunately the weather broke so they were not obliged to spend all their waking hours cooped up inside together. Although the ground was muddy it was possible to ride in some comfort. The lambing had begun—more lost sleep for Justi—but it was comforting to see the ewes turned out on the new green grass with their awkward babies shambling after them, bleating.

Richard seemed to avoid Justi if he could manage it. He frequently took only Harry with him riding or on business. This threw Justi into the company of Alicia and Clara. Alicia was an easy companion to please. She rode well enough to keep up with Justi and Clara. Together they toured the district, including the jumps they would be expected to take if they hunted here in the fall. Justi found herself holding Clara back from dangerous jumps she would have thought nothing of taking on Bluedevil. Her life was now dangerous enough in other ways.

They met the Allen girls frequently for rides, and the silliness of these two made Justi appreciate even Clara. At least the lures Clara threw out had a certain subtlety to them.

Justi had been getting up in the predawn hours to take her turn watching the pregnant ewes, so she was not her normal, patient self.

After retrieving Meg's whip for the third time in an hour, she threatened to use it on her, but that only made Meg giggle. She yearned for Richard's and Harry's company and the times they had had together. Clara started teasing her then, and in spite of Alicia's protests, they pushed Justi to the point where she left them and rode home in a temper. Richard and Harry had just dismounted in the stable yard, and seeing Justi ride in alone, Richard inquired as to the whereabouts of Alicia and Clara.

Even Harry was shocked when Justi replied, "Halfway to Brinley."

"You idiot!" Richard shouted. "That's three miles. What if one of them fell? You don't just abandon the women you are escorting. I don't care what they said to you. Now, ride out and meet them. There will be no not finding them, do you understand?" Richard shouted after her as she mounted and cantered down the drive. She crossed fields toward where she would connect with the Brinley road. A sheepherder said they couldn't be more than a mile ahead since they had just ridden past. Hunting young ladies on horseback wasn't nearly as much fun as chasing a fox.

She rode four miles at a clipping pace before deciding they must have turned off for Stowmarket. It seemed to her Alicia had said something about some lace she wanted. She should have stayed with them for Alicia's sake, Justi thought guiltily. Who could guess what kind of scrape Clara might get her into? If they really had gone to Stowmarket, she might as well take a shortcut though the woods and save time.

As she rode, her mind was busy with the problem of Richard's churlishness. Although he said it had nothing to do with her, she strongly suspected that either there were serious financial problems with Homeplace or Gerard was putting the squeeze on Richard again. She had tried to broach the subject with him several times, but he cut up at her so stiffly she was at a standstill as to how to give him the money she had earned.

She was roused from her abstraction by catching sight of the girls on the road half a mile away. She changed direction and cut down a wooded bank. Gray Dawn had been ridden hard that morning but was still not tired. She jumped some brush on the trail that Justi didn't see, and Justi caught a limb across her throat. This is going to hurt, she thought, as she let go the reins and went off backward.

She lay still for a moment, assessing the damages, but nothing seemed to be broken, and she had not banged her head hard enough to knock herself out. She saw a horse's hooves sideways, and a soft muzzle blew in her face. She reached up and stroked the concerned face, and the mare whickered softly.

"It's not your fault, Dawn." This was the first horse she had that seemed to care about her. Her old hunter would have gone off home. Even Bluedevil would have been grazing nearby, not staying beside her.

She could tell where all the bruises would be already, and her ears were still ringing. She rose slowly, hanging on to the stirrup until she was sure everything was in working order. It did make you half-sick to take a racking fall like that, but she had survived worse without telling anyone. She found her hat and mounted. There was no sign of the girls. Once she put Gray Dawn on the road for home, all she had to do was stay on. A trot was out of the question, so she walked her mare the whole way back. It was unlikely she could catch the girls now anyway.

Jim was walking the girls' horses about the stable yard, and Richard was watching for her out the library window. She took her time about unsaddling Dawn, brushing her and turning her over to Jim to walk, reluctant to face Richard. She dusted her clothes off on her way to the house. As she stepped inside the back door Richard thrust the door to the library open and commanded, "Get in here!"

He looked as black as thunder, and she expected a severe dressing down for not finding the girls, but that was not the only cause of his anger. He sat behind the desk on which lay an open letter.

"Read this!" he commanded, giving it a contemptuous toss in her direction.

"My Dearest Justi," it began in Gerard's bold hand. Her eyes widened as she scanned its contents. It was more than a thank-you note for the translation. Why in God's name would he suddenly decide to write her a love letter? She could almost hear Richard fuming. He snatched the letter from her before she had fully mastered its contents.

"You have kept up a clandestine correspondence with Dumont, all the time pretending to be a wronged inno-cent."

"But I had no choice," Justi whispered.

"You could have come to me!"

"I did try."

"You broke your word."

"What?"

"You promised you would not consort with him again."

"Did I? I can't half remember what I said."

"Don't split hairs. You led me to believe Dumont disgusted you, that you would have no more to do with him. Didn't you?"

Justi struggled for words.

"Didn't you?" Richard demanded so loud he made her cringe.

"Yes," she said weakly.

"I should wash my hands of you," Richard said in disgust, "or is that what you wanted all along?"

"Richard, no."

"Don't lie!"

"I have tried to tell you the truth, but it's so hard."

"To one so unaccustomed to the truth. Yes, I can appreciate that. Get out of my sight. You make me sick."

Had she been feeling slightly better she might have told him the whole even then. Bad as he thought she was as a boy, confessing that she was not would make his condemnation a hundred times worse. She must certainly leave now or as soon as she was feeling able.

Justi had no sooner struggled up the stairs with a bleak look than Julia interrupted Richard's agitated pacing with a quick knock.

"What is it? Oh, Julia."

"Richard, what on earth has happened?"

"Read that. I'm at my wit's end to know what to do with the boy."

After perusing the document Julia merely said, "All that shouting over one letter?"

"Julia, there must have been others."

"How many?" she asked pointedly.

"I don't know."

"You mean you didn't bother to ask. And how many did Justi write?"

Richard paused in his pacing to stare at her.

"I see," she said. "You didn't bother to ask that, either."

"No, I was so angry I did not want to go into particulars. The boy deceived me."

"Intentionally?"

"Of course," Richard asserted. "He knew this was wrong."

"You're sure about that?" she asked sagely. "I mean, Justi is obviously an intelligent child, but he might still be ignorant of proper behavior. And from what you have said of his background, he might have laughed this off or chucked it in the fire. How did you come to open it by mistake, anyway?'' She pursed her lips, straightened her dress and waited for his answer.

''It was no mistake. I just had this feeling and tore it open on impulse.''

''That will hardly set a good example for the boy, opening other people's mail.''

''My God, you're right.''

''He looks to you for guidance, Richard. I have seen how worshipfully he stares at you. Each misstep he takes is new to him. He doesn't mean to make you angry.''

''And I perhaps should not have taken his head off like that,'' Richard admitted.

''It would not seem to serve much purpose. Do you want me to go see him with you?''

''Yes, he is probably terrified of me now.''

Justi had thrown herself down on her bed as she was, falling into a sound sleep, and she could not think for a moment what letter Richard and Julia were talking about. She grunted a little as she got up from the bed and managed to stand.

''What is the matter, child?'' Julia asked.

''Took a toss off my horse,'' she said, sitting down on the bed.

''Why didn't you say something?'' Richard demanded.

''I'm fine, or I was until you rang a peal over me.''

''I want to know how many letters Dumont sent you.''

''Three, counting that.'' She nodded toward the letter in his hand. ''The others were demands for money.''

''And how many did you write him?''

''Only one . . . letter,'' she said uneasily.

''What did it say?''

''That you had forbidden me to do any more translations.'' She shuddered. ''So I wouldn't be able to send him any money. Then—''

"I'm sorry. I read too much into this."

"But, Richard—"

"I should have the doctor out to you."

"I shall do. It was not Gray Dawn's fault. I wasn't watching where I was going."

"Get some sleep then, child," he commanded benevolently.

"But, Richard—"

"That's an order."

Justi didn't know what was worse, having Richard blazingly angry at her, or having him forgive her so humbly.

Justi slept through the day and into the next morning. She could not by then remember if Richard was still angry with her or not. She was tempted to roll over and bury her head and her worries under her pillow. But if Richard and Julia's visit was not a dream then his solicitude might prompt him to send for Dr. Trent if he found she was still abed. She washed shakily, dampened her shaving gear and got herself dressed after a fashion. The effort of tying her cravat with a stiff neck and shoulders reduced her to a trembling wreck. By the time she entered the breakfast parlor she looked very much worse than if she had stayed in bed. She glanced hopefully at Richard, not caring what anyone else thought of her.

Richard saw once again that uncertain look of a punished whelp, not quite sure what it has done wrong, but so eager not to do it again. The look melted his heart and thawed his face into the semblance of a smile. When Richard discovered Justi meant to breakfast on only tea and bread he very nearly embarked on another scold. A warning look from Julia forestalled him.

Justi was too caught up in her own misery to notice this byplay. She must tell Richard the truth but did not think she could handle another tirade from him in her present shattered condition. Certainly she could not leave. She could barely sit a horse. What was she thinking? She could not take Gray Dawn with her, not knowing where she might have to live. Best leave the mare here for Alicia's use. Having to give up Richard and his only gift to her nearly cracked her tight composure. She shivered a little and sighed heavily in an effort not to cry.

"Finished?" Richard asked.

She came to the realization that they were alone and that she had been mindlessly crumbling the toast on her plate.

"You should have stayed in bed."

"You just stiffen up then," she said huskily. "It's best to keep moving."

"But not on a horse. You stay away from the stable until I say so."

She spent the day sorting out what books she should take with her, but in the end put them all back on the shelves. The most she could easily carry was some spare clothes. Unless she could find a way to pack the oak grove in her valise, there was nothing she cared about, anyway.

Richard stopped her going for a walk later in the day by saying that Baird was coming. This was so unusual an event that Justi thought it worth staying in for.

After he was seated in the library, Mr. Baird accepted a glass of sherry. It didn't take Justi long to figure out she was present at Richard's insistence, not Baird's.

"Well, I have done the best I could. It's difficult with little income other than what the farm brings in. A bad year has quite an impact."

Justi didn't need a lawyer to tell her that.

"But the mortgage on the stud farm has finally been repaid. Here is the document. The income from Lady Mallory's dowry just covered the payment. I have always insisted it be used for that and nothing else."

"So, it's Mother who has been keeping us afloat all these years. When I think of the way Grandfather treated her... Wait till I tell her."

"Lady Mallory's second marriage, of course," continued Baird, "puts a different light on things. I do wish I'd had a chance to consult with her before. The capital shall be returned to her, of course."

"I should think so."

"But, as long as there are no unforeseen expenses, Homeplace is in the clear, and I feel optimistic that it shall remain so. Your cousin has given me a good report of you, Justi. He thinks we needn't fear your running into debt or acting irresponsibly where the estate is concerned."

Justi looked at Richard in some surprise. She supposed he might have a good opinion of her business sense and still think her a profligate. And why not? She was much worse than he imagined.

In spite of Baird's reassurances, Justi knew that Gerard could ruin them. She might not care what was said of her, but Richard did and would continue to pay the blackmail.

Richard, for his part, thought that this favorable report would cheer Justi. He had only to put Dumont off until he could get Justi married, and all would be well.

It concerned Richard that the boy did not bounce back as usual from a fall. Justi had not even begged to go riding yet, though he spent hours in the stable with his mare.

"I should have had the doctor to you," Richard observed, when he came on Justi moping about the library.

"Why? I'm all right," she said defensively.

"You don't act it."

"Just blue deviled."

"Don't worry," Richard said kindly. "No matter what you may do, I won't disown you."

This comforting assurance called up to Justi's mind a new, quite unexpected horror. She had always assumed that when she finally screwed up her courage and told Richard the truth, he would disown her, that she would have to leave. Knowing him as she did, she now considered the possibility that he might make her stay. The thought of being locked up at Homeplace with Richard hating her at close range was so much more disquieting than him hating her from a distance, the bleakness must have shown in her face.

"What is it?" Richard asked in some concern.

"Damn you, Richard. Why do you have to be so noble?" she said with a flash of temper and left the room.

Richard did not know what he could do to relieve Justi's guilt, but things could not go on as they were. That was a certainty.

Chapter Nine

Clara halted Richard going into the library the next day. "I want to talk to you, Richard."

"Yes?" He seated himself at the desk while she paced to the window.

"What's wrong with Justi?"

"He took a fall. I thought you knew that."

"That's not what I mean." She turned to face him. "He's not like other men I've known, not even the young ones. He's different somehow."

"He's little more than a boy. Don't expect him to jump to do your bidding. He's just not that interested . . . yet."

"But when I teased him about not being normal, he got this awful look on his face, like I had wounded him. And I was only joking."

Richard's brows came together, and he didn't answer her immediately, wondering what would be safe to tell her.

"Richard, what is it?"

He sighed. "Do you remember that tutor I sent up here last spring? No, of course not. I never met the fellow myself until I got here in August. He became attracted to Justi and . . . started a relationship with him."

"Richard, no!"

"I believe Justi was powerless to stop him and was afraid to tell Miriam."

"But that's monstrous!"

"Believe me, I quite agree. I do not believe Justi naturally leans in that direction. He said the whole thing made him sick."

"How did you find out?"

"Dumont told me. No one else knows about this. I'm trusting you not to speak of it. If you do, you'll ruin Justi."

"Richard, of course I won't tell anyone. Justi is, after all, one of the family. If you want me to let him alone, I will."

"Perhaps I'd better tell you the whole."

"But what could be worse?"

"Dumont demanded money not to make the whole thing public. Now he's trying to bleed me again. Justi knows this and, I think, is brooding over it. If I could get him creditably married, and soon, it would save me being blackmailed and might make him feel better. I know there is an age difference. He isn't eighteen yet, but if you thought you could like him..."

"I don't know, Richard. I wasn't thinking of marriage again yet."

"There would be advantages, a title for one thing, and an estate not far from Amberly. He wouldn't be able to afford a house in town, but you could stay with us in Berkeley Square when you came to London."

Clara looked troubled.

"It's just a thought. Perhaps it would be best if you just ignored him. There is Alicia, too, but she isn't even out yet. I feel strongly that she should have a choice."

Clara looked at him sharply.

"I said the same thing to Father when he set up that marriage with Redmond, but he wouldn't listen."

"I didn't know that." She rose to go. "I will think about it. At least I'll try not to do anything to hurt him."

Richard woke in the cold of a March predawn to lay listening. He heard a door open and close and got up to see what was going on. He just opened his door in time to see Justi tiptoeing toward the back stairs. Had it been Harry he

might have expected a romantic tryst. But, in connection
with Justi, the notion was no sooner thought of than discarded. He pulled on pants and boots and threw his great-
coat over his nightclothes. He could only think one of the
horses must be down with colic and Jim had come for help.

But all was quiet in the stable when he reached it. Past it,
he could see Justi on the trail going toward the sheep farm
where there was a light in the farmhouse and in the byre.
Lambing! Of course!

By the time Richard reached the sheep byre, the Thompson boys were staggering toward the farmhouse. He let
himself into the din of a hundred-odd sheep and lambs all
bleating at the same time. The air was full of steam and
smelled of hay and damp wool. Justi was watching a stout
ewe in obvious distress and didn't hear Richard at first.

"Richard! I thought I took such pains not to wake you. I
try to spell Jeff and Henry each morning till they eat and
catch some sleep. You can lose a ewe in a few minutes if no
one is around to help."

"What do you mean, help?"

"Deliver the lambs."

"That's what I was afraid of."

"This one, for instance," she said, shedding her coat and
rolling up her sleeves. "She's stopped trying. If I don't get
the lamb out, she will die."

Justi soaped her arms to the elbow and asked Richard to
hold the ewe's head while she explored the uterus. Richard
was gritting his teeth.

"What's the matter?" Justi asked.

"Just get on with it. I'm willing to hold the head but I
hope you don't expect any help on the other end."

"No, you needn't worry about being called on as a mid-
wife. Your hands are too big."

"Thank God."

"I think I have one sorted out." She drew two tiny feet
out and reached in for the head. A lamb plopped out,

steaming in the hay. Justi squeezed the fluid from its nose and mouth, and the ewe started into labor again.

"Don't let her go. I may as well get the twin."

"A lot of them have twins?"

"Of course, that's what we breed for. You don't make anything if they have one each. The second lamb is your profit. Oh, no!"

"What?"

Justi reached farther in, looking concerned.

"What is it? Tell me," Richard demanded desperately.

Justi looked at him in surprise, and suddenly the memory of a delicate face in an oval frame swam before her and she knew he must be thinking of his dead wife and stillborn son.

"Too many legs," she said, and smiled.

"A defect?" Richard looked as though he was going to be sick.

"No, triplets," she said and laughed. The second lamb was as large as the first, but the third was smaller.

"You'll double your profit on this one," he said in a more normal voice after they had dried the lambs with straw.

"Only if we keep it alive. A ewe can only reasonably feed two." Sure enough, the ewe rejected the runt, who cried piteously from hunger and loneliness.

"Hold her, Richard." Justi milked the ewe a little into a bowl, dipped her fingers in and let the lamb lick the milk off.

"Won't it take forever to feed it that way?"

"Yes. Fortunately, they can live on cow's milk."

The next few hours saw the delivery of another set of twins and a single big lamb, all of whom arrived unassisted, to Richard's relief. In between, Richard and Justi took turns feeding the rejected lamb.

"Not another orphan!" Jeff Thompson exclaimed as he and his brother entered the shed. "We have got three in the kitchen already and they are driving Mother distracted with their bleating."

"I'll take this one up to the stable. We can't have your mother collapsing on us."

Justi carried the lamb out into the new dawn. The air smelled of young grass and wet earth warming under the sun's rays. "It only smells like this in the spring," she said to Richard.

Richard, whose mind ran along tracks of work and control, seldom took the time to appreciate anything other than a beautiful horse or a fine wine. He did pause with Justi to drink in the new day.

"What will you do with it?"

"I might be able to get Jim to help feed it. I was going to put it in the stall with Jasper for company. In a day or two the lamb will think he's a dog. And it wouldn't do Jasper any harm to get to like sheep. He'd be sure never to chase them."

Jasper and the lamb touched noses and sniffed each other all over. Jim agreed to take on the new charge, and by the time Richard and Justi went in to breakfast, the pup and lamb had curled up together for a nap.

Apparently Clara gave the idea of marriage to Justi some thought and decided it had merit, for she renewed her efforts to win Justi's devotion. She didn't tease this time, though. She decided to try a different approach. She had thought about Justi's concern for Richard's well-being and wondered if she could inspire the same feelings toward her. It wouldn't do to fake another fall. Justi had seen through that right away. When she thought about her ruined life, she thought she might deserve a little compassion. That she had brought many of her problems on herself through her irresponsibility she conveniently shoved to the back of her mind.

Her tactics absorbed her so much that she was quiet all through dinner. Julia went so far as to ask if she was feeling well. She did confess to having the headache, and Justi looked sympathetic, but no more so than if Julia or Alicia was not feeling quite the thing.

Richard merely recommended that she go to bed early and give them all some peace. This almost drew a retort from her, but she managed to change her black look to one of long-suffering, and excused herself.

Richard no longer treated Justi so coldly, but he spent no more time with Justi than before. It was too hard on him.

When she was not out riding with the girls, Justi resumed her solitary walks with only Jasper for company. Having become accustomed to going about with Richard, or the livelier company of Harry, Justi missed them now, and was in something of a melancholy mood herself when she rounded the pond late one afternoon to hear someone weeping softly on the small rustic bench.

"Clara? What's the matter? I thought it was Alicia crying."

"Nothing. Let me alone."

Ordinarily, knowing Clara's temper, this would have been enough to send Justi packing. But there was such a hopelessness about her that Justi was moved.

"Isn't there anything I can do?"

"No one can help me. I can't talk about it."

Justi's initial guess, that Clara had been jilted by a lover, she discarded because she couldn't think who it could be.

"Things can't be that bad."

"Everyone hates me."

"That's not true. Your family—all of them care about you."

"I'm not stupid. They hate me too, and with good reason." She looked up from her damp handkerchief. "I wish I could make people like me the way they like you."

"I don't think you can make people like you." Justi sat down on the bench. "If you behaved better, why wouldn't they like you?"

"But they expect me to be bad. If I'm not, they think I'm ill."

Justi thoughtfully considered if there wasn't some truth in this statement. "You mean you do all those outrageous things because they expect it of you?" Justi was still confused. "You can't always have been like this."

"Richard said I was spoiled by my father and no one could do anything with me after that. That's why my stepfather made me marry so young."

"Did you love him?"

"Redmond? I barely knew him. And he was twice my age."

Justi looked shocked. "I didn't know. Surely, Richard and Julia don't blame you for his death."

"Yes." She was still sounding watery. "They said I should have managed better. But he drank and . . . and he hit me!"

"Does Richard know this?"

"I told him, but he didn't believe me."

Justi, who had some experience of Richard only believing what he liked, began to think more kindly of Clara. "But none of this is your fault. Can't you put it behind you?"

"But my whole life is ruined, and I don't know what is to become of me."

"Talk to Richard sometime when you haven't put him in a rage. He can be reasonable."

"I know what he'll say. I must live in the country, either here or at Amberly. I shall grow old and never meet anyone or ever marry again!" This brought on a fresh burst of tears that were not entirely faked. Clara was by this time feeling genuinely sorry for herself. Justi, quite naturally, put her arm around Clara's shoulders, and Clara threw herself on Justi to enjoy a good cry. Although it was a dead bore to have someone weeping all over your neck cloth, Justi endured it all with fortitude and decided to try to be kinder to her cousin in the future.

Justi finally persuaded Clara to go to her room and lie down before dinner so that her eyes would not be puffy. Clara thought she had never set such a skillful trap before. She was inside Justi's defenses and spent several hours planning her next assault.

Clara dressed demurely for dinner. Justi seated her and they exchanged confidential smiles. All this did not go unnoticed by Richard.

The next day, Justi returned from her tramp to find Clara waiting on the seat by the pond, not crying but shivering in a light mist.

"Clara, are you mad? You'll surely catch cold."

Justi pulled off Clara's damp shawl and draped her own coat over the girl's shoulders. Justi was inured to the weather, and frequently walked in drizzles she would not have taken her horse out in.

"It doesn't matter."

"Of course it matters." She buttoned the top button of the coat and pulled Clara up to lead her to the house. "Has Richard been at you?" she asked suspiciously.

"Why do you ask?" Clara neither confirmed nor denied.

"Because you look just like I feel after he's been ripping and tearing at me."

"He's usually right," Clara said in mock defeat.

"Not always," Justi said gently, taking Clara's hand.

The rain grew heavier before they reached the house so that they were both soaked by the time they came in. Richard was just ascending the stairs. "Get caught in the rain?" he asked unnecessarily. He ignored Clara's guilty look and Justi's resentful one, smiled and merely said, "Better change for dinner."

Richard thought Clara must be making progress. It would be as well if she could turn the trick. His conscience stabbed at him a little when he thought how easily she could ruin the boy, not financially—he could see to that for the time being—but through disillusionment. Young men were never the same after their calf love. His approval of the marriage could mean an unhappy future for Justi. But the honor of the family meant something.

The next day was warm enough for a ride, so Justi escorted Clara and Alicia into Stowmarket and patiently waited with the horses at the various shops, wondering if this would be the last time she would do this. Clara seemed more in spirits so Justi didn't mind the wasted morning so much. But after lunch Clara waylaid her on her way to the woods, somewhat to Justi's annoyance.

"May I come with you?"

"Not in those clothes. You'll ruin them!" Justi felt guilty when she saw Clara's face fall. "Well, go change. I'll wait for you."

Twenty minutes was the fastest Clara ever changed, and she did keep up with Justi, who consciously slowed her pace a little. Justi took her to the deep woods where the ferns were just uncoiling their green fronds, the trees were coming into leaf, and the wildflowers were beginning to show here and there."

"It's so lovely here I don't want to go back." Clara stooped to gather a bouquet of tiny purple flowers.

"I often feel that way myself."

"I like Homeplace better than Amberly," Clara confided. "It's more wild."

"Yes, especially this part," Justi agreed. "It hasn't changed much in decades. I don't want it to change, ever. Wait until you see it in summer when the trees are in full leaf. The bird songs echo under the oaks like you were in a cathedral."

"I wish I could live here instead of at Amberly," Clara confided.

"Why can't you?"

"Homeplace will belong to you when you come of age . . . and to your wife. I couldn't stay here then."

"I'll never marry."

"Why not?"

"Let's start back. It's getting late." Justi turned to lead the way out of the woods.

"Is it because of your tutor?"

Justi stopped dead in her tracks and whirled on Clara, her face full of shock. "How did you know about him?" Justi whispered.

"Richard told me. I didn't mean to upset you."

"He told you? But why?" Justi turned away to try to get control of herself.

"I made him tell me. I knew there was something different about you."

Justi started walking. It really was time to leave, she thought—early in the morning.

"Justi, wait. Don't leave me." Clara couldn't keep up with Justi's purposeful gait. "I'll get lost."

Justi waited for Clara to catch up.

"It doesn't matter," Clara said, grabbing her arm. "Not to me. I would marry you anyway."

"What?" Justi turned confused eyes on her. "What are you talking about? I can't marry anyone, ever."

"You'll have to. Richard will make you."

"No!" Justi looked horrified.

Feeling herself losing ground, Clara produced her best shot. "Especially if I tell him that we are lovers already."

"You would lie to him just like Gerard?" Justi's hurt was beginning to stir into anger, when suddenly things came into focus for her. "So, that's what you've been up to. You tricked me. You haven't changed at all."

"You have no choice, you know."

"No wonder your husband beat you."

They argued the whole way back, but Justi did not abandon Clara since she knew it would make Richard angry. "To think I ever felt sorry for you," Justi remarked acidly as they passed the bench by the pond.

"I don't need you to feel sorry for me, you nobody. At least I have a position in the world."

"Playing the spoiled beauty may have done very well while you were young. People won't think your caprices so funny now that you are older."

"How dare you!" Clara, raised to the full height of her wrath, hit Justi such a slap that she staggered and fell into the cold waters of the pond. Justi came up coughing and spitting to hear Clara's vicious laughter.

Richard and Harry, just returning to the stables, also heard it, and the shriek she uttered when Justi scrambled up the bank after her. Clara had a good lead by the time Justi started running her down, but Justi was faster, even soaking wet.

Richard grinned at Harry. "The affair progresses."

"How does Justi tolerate her? She must have knocked him in the pond. He's soaked."

Justi caught Clara and not only got her all muddy but started dragging her to the water. Justi had trouble budging Clara while avoiding her flashing nails since Clara outweighed her slightly. Finally, Justi caught Clara around the middle and boosted her over her shoulder like a sack of grain. She staggered to the water under the writhing weight and heaved Clara in.

By the time Richard and Harry arrived, Justi was sitting on the bank, panting and enjoying Clara's efforts to keep her skirts from floating while she made her way to the bank, threatening dire consequences.

"A little rough, aren't you?" Richard admonished.

Justi looked suitably embarrassed and waited, expecting a blast of Richard's famous temper. "At least I refrained from hitting her, which is what she deserved."

"I have no doubt whatsoever that she deserved this," Richard said with a grin. Justi flashed a smile at Richard's surprising grasp of the situation, then frowned immediately when she remembered the cause of the altercation.

Clara's threats and sobbings mingled with Harry's hysterical laughter as he rolled on the bench in helpless mirth.

"Be that as it may, someone must get her out, and since you are already wet ..."

"Are you crazy? She will scratch my eyes out. Let her get herself out." Justi stomped to the house.

Against his better judgment, Richard gave Clara a hand up the muddy bank, and she wreaked an awful revenge on Harry.

"Stop smacking me." Harry shielded his face. "I didn't do it."

Richard knew the pond water had to be cold, but he was sure Clara's wrath would keep her warm enough as she stomped to the house.

"I thought you said the affair was progressing," the disheveled Harry complained to Richard.

"It is, and better than I expected. Do you know anyone else who would have dared to give Clara a dunking?"

"No, come to think of it. I guess Justi's quite a man, after all."

Clara did not appear at dinner that night, and Justi waited all evening to be called to book for her treatment of Clara and for the lies Clara threatened her with. She actually began to pack that night but didn't want to run off without defending herself, even if it meant another session with Richard.

She had just returned from riding with Alicia the next morning when Richard blocked the hallway in front of her and commanded, "Come into the library. I want to talk to you." Justi followed him gloomily, assuming Clara had spread her poison.

Richard sat down behind the desk. He spent too long staring into the fire composing his thoughts. Justi shifted her weight to her other leg and swallowed.

"I've gotten another letter from Dumont," Richard said heavily. "I can't put him off any longer."

"How much does he want this time?"

"A thousand."

"What?" Her eyes grew big. "But I've only got four hundred. Do you think he would be satisfied with that?"

Richard rose and came around the desk.

"He'll never be satisfied. There's only one solution."

Justi looked doubtfully at Richard. "You're not...going to kill him, are you?"

"Actually, that had not occurred to me. Although I admit the suggestion has merit, I think it would be impractical."

"Oh." Justi subsided in relief.

"You're going to be married."

"What?" Justi staggered back, almost falling. Richard gently pushed her into a chair.

"And as soon as possible."

"But I can't, I can't."

"Don't argue that you are too young. You're more responsible than Harry. Besides, it's the only defense against Dumont's tales."

"No, I never could."

"There's Clara or Alicia," Richard went on unheedingly. "I realize Clara is older than you, but you do seem to be the only one who can really handle her. In fact, you have been a good influence on her."

He turned to see Justi resting her head in her hands.

"Alicia, on the other hand, is young and biddable."

Justi stared at him in horror as he puffed off the divergent qualities of the woman and the girl.

A strangled but quite firm "No" finally escaped her.

"What did you say?" Richard pronounced menacingly.

Justi stood up, angry herself. "I can't...I won't marry either of them."

"Perhaps you have feelings for Harry," Richard suggested cruelly.

When it finally dawned on Justi what he meant, she spit out, "You bastard!" and swung at him like a girl, forgetting everything Gerard had taught her.

He caught her wrist easily in an iron grip. "I had to know, Justi."

She struggled to get free. "How dare you compare Clara and Alicia like two pieces of livestock. They should choose their own husbands."

He let her go but stepped out of range.

"Ordinarily I would agree with you, but our need here is extreme. I think it should be Alicia, after all. She will do as she's told."

"Of course she will. She will jump off a cliff, if you tell her to, that's how frightened she is of you."

The truth about himself, delivered squarely between the eyes, as Justi had a knack for doing, inflamed Richard even more.

"You will marry one of them."

"How are you going to manage that? I think the vicar will notice if you are holding a gun to my head, not that it would compel me to such a ruinous act."

"Oh, you'll do it," he warned. He grabbed Justi by the coat collar and wrestled one arm behind her back. "Or you will spend the rest of your minority in your room." He marched a resentful Justi upstairs, past a startled Julia, and locked her in.

Justi's room wasn't nearly big enough for all the pacing the problem at hand required. To tell Richard the truth in his present frame of mind was unthinkable. She really was half-afraid of him when he was in one of his rages. But, according to Harry, Justi had not yet seen Richard really angry.

In spite of the promise she had made to her mother and Sandford, she thought she had better make a run for it. She wrote out her confession and planned to mail it from a safe distance. It wouldn't be fair to make them tell Richard. Her mother would be crushed by Richard, and very likely it would cause a breach between Richard and Sandford. Life was so much simpler before she knew all these people, but also much emptier.

Getting out of her room was no problem. She had, since she was a child, climbed down the ivy growing past her window when she wished to walk about at night. Fortunately, she had been careful that Richard never found this out.

She did forget that the library window was nearly under hers. One would have thought that in the time it took her to write her letter and finish packing the few belongings she had decided to take with her, Richard might have gone up to bed. It was her hard luck that he had chosen to sit in the dark brooding.

With the house in silence the fall of an object as heavy as a valise into the stable yard could not escape Richard's notice. When he went to the window and heard the ivy creaking above him, he whispered "Damn!" and sprinted out of the room and down the hall. He crept out the back door and along the house wall silently. Justi was no more than eight feet off the ground when he whispered fiercely, "Where the hell do you think you are going?"

Justi lurching around to see Richard was too much for the old mortar that the ivy had been feeding on for the better part of two centuries. When he heard the vines give way, Richard stepped underneath as Justi, the mass of ivy and a quantity of stone came down on top of him.

Justi sat up and sneezed.

"Are you hurt?" Richard asked, almost as though they had both fallen over a jump.

"No, are you?"

His only reply was to flip her over and paddle her until he was exhausted and his hand hurt. Harry emerged from the back door with a candle.

"Don't thrash him to death, Richard," Harry complained, pulling Justi up and getting between the two.

"You little coward," Richard accused Justi. "You won't get the chance to run away again."

Believing him, Justi twisted out of Harry's grasp and fled into the dark toward the pond. Richard was after her, stumbling over rocks and roots in the dark, but she was faster and managed to secrete herself below the lip of the bank and still her panting before he came to look over the edge.

"I can't see a thing," Richard complained to Harry. "There are lanterns in the sheep barn. Go get them."

Richard waited by the pond, listening. If they shone the light over the edge at all she would be discovered, yet it was not safe to try to move with Richard so close. When Harry returned with the lanterns Richard and Harry parted after a quick conference and walked, each one, around the pond in a different direction.

Justi picked a moment when Harry's sounds would be louder to Richard than hers, got into the screen of trees and made her way through the swampy area upstream. She stayed well off the normal tracks where they were likely to walk and worked her way up the valley, trying not to rouse the Thompsons' dog. Two hours of careful travel brought her to the oak wood, and she stopped to rest by a log. She could hear someone moving at a distance and relaxed, only to be startled by Richard's voice much closer. He was not shouting, but talking to himself. "Damn you, Justi, why are you doing this? What are you afraid of, boy?"

She would have liked to answer him and truthfully. Instead she lay crouching beside the log. The beating was still ripe in her mind, and she did not think she could take another one. She waited patiently for him to give up the search. She would have to be gone from here well before dawn for they would probably start after her on horseback then. She waited so long listening for no sound other than the crickets and night birds that she fell asleep.

* * *

The noise that awoke her made her start up and bang her head on the log. An "Ouch!" escaped her before she remembered where she was, and an iron hand clamped down on her shoulder.

"Got you!" Richard said victoriously and dragged her to her feet. "How long did you mean to stay out here?"

"I didn't mean to come back," she said woefully.

"But you love this place."

"It's not mine anymore."

"Do you think I mean to wrest it from you? You will have it back when you come into the title."

"I don't want it anymore. It's all ruined now."

"By me, I suppose. Come! We can't stand here talking." He took a grip on her wrist instead of her shoulder, and she knew there would not be another chance to break away from him.

"How did you find me?" she asked as they stumbled along the trail, the lantern clanking at Richard's side.

"I knew where you would be," he said confidently. "I know you pretty well by now."

"You don't know me at all—put the lantern out before you fall and start a fire. It's easier to see without it."

Richard suspected this was a ruse, but did as Justi said and discovered it was indeed easier to see without the glare of the lantern blinding him.

"You must spend a deal of time wandering the woods at night. Ever run into poachers?"

"Now and again."

"What do you say to them?"

"What do you mean? When you encounter someone in the woods with a gun and you have none, you ask him how the hunting is."

"How heroic of you."

"People are poor hereabouts, Richard. A rabbit or a bird might be the only bit of meat a family has for a week."

"Or they may take them into town to sell them."

"To buy bread—why am I even talking to you about this?"

"Why did you run away? It isn't like you."

"I can't live here anymore. I have betrayed you, lied to you from the moment I first knew you, actually from the day I was born."

Richard stumbled but did not fall since he was hanging on to the more surefooted Justi.

"It's your mother you are protecting, isn't it?" he asked.

Justi sighed, thankful that he had at last guessed the truth, then plodded doggedly on. "Yes, but it wasn't her fault. It was Nurse's idea."

"So you are not Lord Mallory after all, are you?"

"No, but I never really wanted to be, especially not after I met you."

"It doesn't matter," he said cheerfully. "I won't tell anyone."

She stopped so abruptly he almost pulled her over. "What? But the title— Homeplace. It's all rightfully yours."

"Thank you very much, but I don't need either one—not enough to create a scandal over it."

"But you cannot be content to let matters stand."

"Why not? If the secret has not come out in all these years it is not likely to."

He pulled on her wrist and she walked reluctantly after him, looking at him as though he had taken leave of his senses.

"But the title—your son should have it and Homeplace."

"I will never marry again. Harry will have Amberly someday, and your son will have Homeplace."

"I can never marry."

"Why not? Is there insanity somewhere in your family?"

"Yes, I think most definitely. How did you guess?" she asked in confusion.

"Your mother must have been desperate when she realized how ill your father was. By what you have said of your grandfather she could only be sure of her place here by presenting him with an heir to replace his son. I would imagine Nurse would have to be in on it, hand and glove as those two are."

"That's right," said Justi, following him past the pond. "But how did you figure it out?"

"I'm not stupid. I remember what you said that night I was drunk. It's nothing you should feel guilty about."

"I can't remember what I said that night. You aren't going to prosecute us then?"

"Don't be absurd!"

"It's still all my fault. Even after Grandfather died, when there was no longer any need for the pretense, I kept it up. Nurse has been dotty for years. Mother would have told you that first day. It was my idea to wait, to see what you were like."

"And what am I like?"

"Confusing. You go into fantastic rages over nothing, then forgive me something like this as though it doesn't matter."

They were approaching the house, but Richard still kept a tight hold on her wrist. Her fingers were numb from the pressure.

"The truth of the matter is I don't care if any Mallory blood runs in your veins or not. I like you for yourself."

Justi digested this slowly. "Wha— What are you talking about?"

"Your mother's infidelity. Frankly I can't find it in my heart to blame her, except perhaps burdening you with the knowledge of your illegitimacy."

It was light enough for him to see the numb shock on her face as she went over their strange conversation in her mind. "But you've got it all wrong."

"Nonsense."

"Let go. I have to leave. There is no way out of this tangle." She struggled to get free of him before he could drag her into the house. Harry was in the hall, but he hardly knew whether to help Justi or Richard. In the end he stood helplessly by as Richard dragged Justi up the stairs.

Julia looked on in despair but said nothing, since Harry had witnessed these scraps before and was able to reassure his mother that this sort of thing went on between Richard and Justi all the time.

Richard dragged her into the empty, unheated north room and, finding the key on the mantel, locked her in. There was no ivy, she reflected, on this part of the house.

Justi made the mistake of flopping down tiredly on the bed, groaned and slid off again. She finally crawled under the covers in her clothes and slept facedown. She wouldn't be able to sit in comfort for a week.

Julia was far from reassured and demanded of Richard what he thought he was doing. Thus attacked for the first time in years, he spoke sharply to her, and earned a rare trimming from his stepmother. But beyond asserting that Justi had been willfully disobedient, Richard would not divulge the cause of the quarrel.

Julia sent Harry to pump Justi later in the morning. She felt it would be undignified to be caught talking through a keyhole. Justi said more than she should have.

"He wants me to offer for Alicia or Clara, and I just can't."

"Of course not," Harry agreed. "They are almost like sisters to you. Don't worry. I'll talk to Mother. She will bring him round."

"Harry, you must not. He wants me to marry so that Gerard won't be able to blackmail us anymore. You can't tell Cousin Julia about Gerard."

"Don't worry. I'll handle it. Justi?"

"What?"

"How long are you in for?"

"Till I'm twenty-five."

"Jesus, he must be really mad."

Evidently Julia's pleas carried no weight with Richard, for no sooner had Firth taken away the breakfast tray than a ladder thumped against the wall below the window. For a mad moment Justi thought Harry was trying to engineer an escape in broad daylight.

She ran to the window and looked out on an altercation in the stable yard. Ned Thompson was there, arms folded on his chest, shaking his head broadly at Richard. She heard Harry say stubbornly, "I won't do it." Jim split and ran when he felt Richard's eye bent on him.

Finally, it was Richard himself who mounted the ladder to nail the shutters securely shut. He paused midway up to allow the ladder time to stop bouncing, took a deep breath and made it to the top. Justi backed away from the pale face at the window. Possibly she alone knew why he was doing this, not just to punish her, but to prevent another escape attempt that could result in a bad fall. Only she knew what it cost him, too.

She went to the other window. Richard moved the ladder himself. Ned and Harry were rewarded by the sight of Richard throwing up his breakfast in the shrubbery. Justi, who almost never cried, even when in pain, cried for Richard and retreated to the other side of the room, praying he wouldn't fall. The second shutter was nailed shut none too steadily, and Justi breathed a sigh of relief as the ladder was removed. He really was a dear, she thought, in spite of his bad temper.

There was nothing to read this time, nothing to do except pace and think. She thought of all the things she and Richard had done together and decided that, no matter what happened, she was glad to have known him. It was important to realize that there were better men than Gerard in the world. That she would ever meet another man such as Richard she did not believe. As well as she knew him, he was still very much a puzzle to her. She would have liked to spend the rest of her life puzzling him out, but this had to end. It was too hard on Richard. There was no longer any reason to keep up the disguise except her dread of him hating her absolutely. Even Richard could never forgive such a betrayal.

Aside from Firth, who brought her food and water, she saw no one. Harry did come to whisper through the door again.

"How is Richard?" Justi asked.

"I have never seen him in such a taking. Even Mother cannot reason with him. He means to keep you in here until you agree to marry."

"She can't want Alicia forced into marriage with me, or even Clara."

"That's the hell of it. Clara appears to be willing. I don't suppose you could—"

"Never, Harry."

"I don't know how we are to get you out, then."

"If only I could write him a—I was forgetting." She went and got the letter from her coat pocket and slid it under the door. "Give that to him. It will explain everything. Then brace yourself for an explosion. We are about to find out if there is an end to his capacity for understanding and forgiveness."

"I expect not, or Clara and I would have exhausted it long since."

Powerful advocates must have been grinding away in her favor, however, because when Richard unlocked and entered the room the letter was unopened in his hand and he looked wretchedly drained. Clearly this stint had been much harder on him than on her.

"Julia has convinced me," he began rather stiffly, "that it is unreasonable to expect you to marry someone you regard in the light of a sister."

Justi remained silent.

"If this is true, why didn't you tell me so?"

Justi tried to meet his tired eyes and looked away again.

"I should tell you that I have decided to take you and Harry up to town for a month or so. You will meet a great many people there. I'm sure I will have no need to blush for your manners. You will make the acquaintance of a great many young ladies your own age. Perhaps you will find one of them to your liking."

Justi stood openmouthed as Richard laid out her future for her. "I shall pay off Dumont, of course, so you will have the whole season to decide. Although we can't hope for a great match for you, you do have your title, after all. There's no telling, really, what may be achieved."

So, this was Richard in defeat, capitulating. She didn't like seeing him this way. She would rather he was raging at her. She especially didn't like that she had brought him to this pass.

Her continued silence unnerved him. He paced about the room. "Think of the fun you and Harry will have, shooting at Manton's, going to plays, and I am not adverse to—"

"Richard." She interrupted the described treat.

"What?"

"I can't go to London," she almost whispered.

"Why not?" he snapped, then brought himself under control with a visible effort.

"Because, if I'm going to make a scandal for you, I had better do it here, not in London, where you know so many people."

"And are you going to make a scandal for me?" He smiled tiredly.

"I should think it's inevitable."

"Why inevitable? You have more sense than Harry and certainly more than Clara."

"Because... You know it's awfully hard to talk to you when you're looming over me like that."

"Very well." Richard seated himself with only the floor between them, for once.

Justi approached to stand before him like a prisoner in the dock. "Don't pay him, Richard. You don't have to. I won't let him ruin you. I care about you too much."

"And I care about you too much. That's the problem. I can almost feel some sympathy for Dumont."

She thought about this for a while before it sank in, then her eyes widened with the realization of what he was saying. "No, don't think that about yourself. It's not true."

"You needn't fear me, child. I will never do anything to you. I have that much control over myself."

"I have to tell you now. I was going to just leave but it's not fair to you."

"Don't say it."

"Richard, I'm not a man," she whispered.

His face, so tired and stern, softened somewhat. "No, of course not. You're a boy still, and what happened with Dumont should not be allowed to ruin your life."

"No, damn it! I'm not a boy, either. I'm a girl." She stamped her foot. "I'm sorry," she added contritely. "I shouldn't be swearing in front of you."

"What did you say?" He was looking rather blank, like he had suffered a loss of hearing or something.

"Of course, I shouldn't be swearing at all."

"No—no, before that." His whisper caught her off guard.

"I'm a girl. Mother lied about me when I was born for fear Grandfather would cast us out." She said it in a rush. "But please don't blame Mother. She thought he was dying. She thought it wouldn't matter. And then we were trapped in the lie."

Richard had opened his mouth but was at a loss for words as the truth began to dawn on him. He was staring at her helplessly and in considerable relief. Justi, who had been anticipating a Last Judgment style of wrath, found Richard's lapse frightening.

"Richard? Are you all right?"

"I don't believe it," he finally managed to utter.

She rolled her eyes in frustration. "Finally I tell you the truth, and you don't believe it."

"But Dumont..."

"I told you he was lying. At least, now you won't have to pay him any more money. Richard, you look awful. Should I send for some wine?"

He mouthed a no and shook his head. When the truth finally sank in it was like a blow between the eyes. This wretched boy had turned his world on end. Yet in his inmost soul this was something he had always known about Justi.

"Well, aren't you angry with me?" Richard's reaction was so at odds with what she had expected that her fears melted away in a lively concern for him. That he had been under a severe strain was obvious, but she now worried that she might have unhinged his reason. "Richard. Richard!"

He wasn't listening. "Why didn't I see it?" he muttered.

"Because nothing would have been more unlikely."

He looked at her again. "The things I've said to you, done to you! Why didn't you tell me before?"

"I was afraid."

"Yes, of course you were." He rose and came toward her. She bit her lip and fell back, half a step only. He untied her hair and let it fall around her face. She looked into his eyes, searching for anger, but saw only sadness and pain. This was much worse.

"Richard, why don't you hit me, or...or something? I can't stand it when you're like this."

He embraced her for a moment only, with a tenderness she had not imagined he possessed. Then he mastered himself and stepped back. "I need... We need to talk to Julia. She will know what to do."

He said this as though they were both in trouble for breaking a vase and he was relying on his stepmother to find a way out of the scrape. He guided Justi into the hall with a gentle hand on her shoulder. She looked at him doubtfully. She was really beginning to fear for his reason.

They found Julia in the sitting room writing a letter. "So, have you two made it up? Come and tell me. Are you going to London?"

"I don't know." Richard handed Julia the letter and sat down weakly.

"Cousin Julia, I'm sorry I lied to you and Richard, well, to everyone." Justi knelt beside Julia's chair.

"What is it, child?" Julia stroked Justi's hair.

"I'm sorry I can't marry Alicia or Clara, but I can't because I'm a girl."

Now Julia looked confused and demanded of Richard, "Is this true?"

He raised his head weakly. "Why would he—she lie about this?"

Julia tore open the letter. The story of Nurse's foolish lie and Justi's strange upbringing brought tears to Julia's eyes. "How like Miriam!" she said finally.

"Cousin Julia, do you think you can forgive me?"

"Yes, of course, except perhaps for what you've done to your hair." She brushed it from Justi's forehead.

"I think I should go away," Justi volunteered, rising, "And then send word back that I'm dead—not from me, of course, from someone else." She paced as she warmed to the tale. "That way, Richard will inherit as he should, and no one will ever know about me. Also Gerard—"

"No!" Richard came out of his stupor and got up. "I won't let you!" This was more like the Richard she knew. "I don't care about a scandal. You'll stay with your family. Julia?" He looked again to his stepmother for support.

"Yes, of course, Richard is right. We must tell everyone the truth."

"I'm afraid," Justi murmured, "I haven't had a vast deal of experience with the truth. Do you think it will serve?"

Chapter Ten

They told Clara and Alicia first. Alicia took the news with wide-eyed acceptance. Clara clapped her hands in delight and exclaimed, "I knew it! I knew there was a reason I couldn't make you fall in love with me."

Richard laughed weakly and Justi smiled ruefully. "You're pretty hard to hold at arm's length, let me tell you."

"And you always could see through what I was planning. I should have guessed you were female just from that."

"Clara, you and Alicia go see if you can find something for Justi to wear," Julia ordered. "I don't want her in those boy's clothes any longer."

Justi looked uncertain about being delivered into the hands of two fashion-conscious young females, but went dazedly out, listening to Clara's plans for her wardrobe in one ear and Alicia's ideas for styling her hair in the other.

"Well, this has been a facer I don't think I'll ever recover from." Richard put down the glass of wine they had finally prevailed on him to take.

"I think you need another drink, and I may join you," Julia sighed.

Harry had bolted from the house after putting the letter in Richard's hands and only just returned at dinnertime, driven home by hunger. He saw the girls in profile going into the dining room. "I say, who is that girl with Clara and Alicia? Do you think I should change my coat?"

Richard smiled devilishly, "You don't recognize her?"

"She looks familiar, but we can't have met, can we?"

"Must be the family resemblance. She's a young relative of ours. Come, I'll introduce you."

Julia was inspecting Justi with approval. The cream dress Clara had chosen from her own wardrobe was very becoming to Justi's dark complexion. Alicia had pulled her hair up and curled the ringlets that hung down in back. It was still short, but passable. Richard was amazed at the transformation. Justi moved a bit uncertainly, as though she was afraid of tripping, but other than that, no one would mistake her for a boy.

"Harry, this is Justine Mallory, your cousin."

Harry smiled charmingly and greeted Justi with the bravado he reserved for females, but when Justi laughed at him he recognized her.

"Oh, famous!" His eyes got big. "What's the joke?"

"No joke." Richard didn't look quite so pale now.

"A play!" Harry guessed. "You're going to do a play."

"No, Harry, I've just finished a play," Justi said. "I'm sorry, Harry. You've been such a good friend to me. I would have told you, if I could. I didn't like lying to any of you." She clenched her hands together in front of her since she didn't have any pockets.

Harry couldn't take it in. He still thought they were all conspiring to trick him. Richard moved around the table, and Justi, not sure of his intentions, took an involuntary step sideways, and looked dumbly for a moment at the chair he had pulled out for her before she sat down.

Julia smiled. "You've a lot to learn, my child."

"Firstly, that gentlemen very seldom strike young ladies," Richard added by way of apology.

"Not unless they especially deserve it," supplied Clara, her grudge against Justi obliterated with the restoration of her ego.

"Well, that will be a welcome change, I suppose." Justi glanced at Harry, who was still gazing at her in rapt amazement. "Stop staring at me, Harry. I can't even eat."

"Well, you were pretty as a boy, but as a girl you're a real stunner."

"I am not!"

"Isn't she, Richard?" Harry appealed for support.

"I wouldn't use that particular term but I think she is quite taking."

Justi scowled. "If you two are going to be making cakes of yourselves like you do over the Allen girls, I'm going right back up to change." Julia subdued this rebellion with a look. "I'm still the same person I was yesterday," Justi appealed to Julia.

"No, oh, no!" Harry said, staring at her with his chin propped in his hand.

Julia looked quellingly at her son. "Harry, you know better than to behave like this."

"Does this mean I can't keep Jasper?" Justi asked to bring Harry to his senses as she innocently buttered a roll.

She looks so impossibly young, Richard thought. He felt guilty every time he looked at her, for all he had put her through, and for frightening her.

"Well, I don't know." Harry turned serious, since he considered himself the shooting expert. "You might ruin him."

She bit her lower lip bravely, but cast her eyes toward Harry so appealingly that he relented. "I suppose I could train him and leave him here for us to hunt with when we are at Homeplace. You could take him for walks. What do you think, Richard?"

Richard tore his gaze away from Justi's totally innocent reaction. It wasn't a trick. It worked because it was genuine. Had she ever looked this way before? He tried to recall and realized he had not paid enough attention to what she was feeling before.

"Yes," he answered, with only the vaguest recollection of what Harry had said. "That sounds like a good plan."

Justi got an odd look on her face when Badger served her. "What's the matter?" Richard asked.

But she didn't answer until Badger had left the room.

"I was thinking, it's going to be hard to explain this to the servants. I mean, you've only known me for a few months, but they have known me all my life as a boy."

"Badger seemed to take it pretty coolly when I told him."

"You mean he wasn't surprised?" Since Badger and the footman had served lunch with stone faces, Justi had no idea how they felt about her transformation. "Oh! I must go see the vicar. I can't let him hear about this from someone else."

"Of course, child." Julia patted her hand. "We'll go this evening. We owe him some explanation for missing church."

Justi had imagined the interview with Vicar Mayfair would be difficult to get through, that he might condemn her, but she should have credited him with more kindness.

He gazed rather myopically at the young vision advancing into his sitting room but recognized the voice at once.

"I'm afraid I have a confession to make, a rather large one."

"My goodness, my goodness," was all he said when she poured out the tale to him. "Extraordinary!" After the initial shock, he became quite thoughtful.

"You know, I think the thing to do is to let me pay some visits this week and break the news for you to the squire and Colonel Allen, at least. Then come to church on Sunday, as always. When news of this gets around, we should have a full house." He rubbed his hands together.

"What will be your sermon? The prodigal son will hardly do," Richard said with a tired smile.

"No, I think rather, 'Let he who is without sin, cast the first stone,' but we'll see. Leave everything up to me."

"But the people in the village won't know," Justi protested.

"They will after Mrs. Harrison goes to visit her sister later this evening."

"Indeed," said Julia.

"Actually it's quite a useful way to spread news about. You would be surprised how these people pitch in to help one another when someone is in trouble. But that's the country for you. I shall make sure, of course, that Mrs. Harrison hears the correct story and that she knows my sympathies are with you, not that anyone in the district would wish you harm."

"There is bound to be talk, though," Richard said with fortitude.

"Oh, yes. I wouldn't think they would talk of anything else for a month."

Justi groaned.

"But after that—" Mayfair held up his hand "—after that, I think they will accept you, and anyone who doesn't, well, that's their loss."

He meditated a few moments, then said, "I think I should give Mrs. Harrison the impression, if you don't mind, Justi, that your grandfather was quite mad and that this was an idiosyncrasy of his. That your mother was helpless to prevent—"

"Vicar Mayfair!" interrupted Julia. "Surely you aren't going to tell an untruth."

"Oh, no, of course not. I shall merely leave her with that impression. She will add to the story herself, as will the next to hear it, and the next."

"Whatever will people be saying about her by next Sunday?" Julia was losing courage.

"I see." Justi brightened. "By the time the gossip has run its course and people come expecting to see me with two heads, it will be anticlimactic to discover that I am merely a girl."

"That's it." The vicar seemed pleased with her astuteness.

"Merely a girl," Richard mused. "Anyone who knew you well would never think that."

Tricked out in Clara's second-best riding habit next morning, Justi was being instructed by Richard in how a lady mounts a horse while Jim stood holding Gray Dawn's bridle in gaping wonder.

"But what if there's no one to give me a leg up?"

"There always will be."

"I mean what if I fall off somewhere?"

"You are not to ride alone from now on, is that understood?" Richard made her try mounting three more times before he was satisfied she knew what to do with her skirts.

"I'm not sure I can stay on sidesaddle."

"Like anything else, it just takes practice."

They cantered up toward the sheep farm. The mare frisked a little at the new arrangement. "You're putting too much weight on the left and throwing her off balance," Richard advised.

Justi tried to rearrange herself. "This is impossible!"

"There's not enough of you, is the problem. Let me shorten your stirrup." She held the heavy skirt aside as he slid the buckle up a notch and pulled the iron into place. He had recovered much of his poise overnight and seemed to be throwing himself into her education with every bit as much vigor as when he thought she was a young man. "Try that."

Justi watched Richard jealously as he mounted Bluedevil. She had given up a lot for him, her whole life, in fact, and there was no turning back. She only hoped it would be worth it.

They trotted up the valley and turned to splash across a shallow ford in the stream. "I suppose I shall need a whip."

"Why?" asked Richard in some surprise. "You never needed a whip to make her mind before."

"I can't give her any signals with my right leg, silly. I need a whip to tell her when I want to turn that way."

"Oh, I never thought of it."

"Being a man, you wouldn't."

"It isn't my fault the custom is for women to ride side-saddle," Richard fumed.

Justi urged Gray Dawn into a canter and tried her over a fence. It would have been scary on a horse she didn't have confidence in, but she thought she could manage most jumps that she would be willing to put the mare over. The only thing that worried her was getting tangled up in a falling horse with the long skirt. A quick dismount was impossible. She now realized that the fall Clara had staged was tricky and could have resulted in a real injury. Being a woman might turn out to be more dangerous than being a man.

It took all of her considerable patience to bear with Richard's criticisms of her horsemanship. He ranted at her until he was hot with frustration, and a lesser spirit than hers would have been in tears. She merely sighed, and said, "I'm sorry."

"What for?"

"I was going to try to get through an entire day without making you angry, and we haven't even made it to lunch." She sounded so woeful, she roused his equally ready compassion.

"You haven't done so very ill, for the first try. I shouldn't expect you to be perfect the first day."

She sent him again that half fearful, half hopeful look that melted his insides. If it had been any other woman, he would have suspected some artifice, but not with Justi. Whatever else she was, she was genuine.

Justi made it a point to seek out old Badger when they returned, to apologize for deceiving him and shocking him.

"Surprised? Not I, m'lady." He put down the tray of dishes he was removing from the breakfast parlor.

"You don't mean you knew?"

"Well, yes, I always suspicioned it. And it had me in a bit of a worry till Mr. Richard—I mean Lord Mallory came on the scene."

"But you wouldn't have given me away."

"After the way you fought to keep this place going? Never!"

"Thank you, Badger. It won't be so bad working for Richard, do you think?"

"No, not since you've shown him the ropes. And it has been lively here these past months." He chuckled warmly.

Justi laughed. "That's putting it mildly." She had picked up her gloves and was on the point of leaving when she turned toward the old retainer. "Badger?"

"Yes, m'lady."

"If I may ask, what was it that gave me away? Surely not my riding or my voice."

"Oh, no. You were far and away too sensible and considerate like for a young lad. And not a bit of trouble ever to anyone, not to mention liking your schoolwork. And so patient with the old lord, too. The thought only had to enter my head that you would have made him a much better granddaughter than an heir, and the mystery was solved for me."

"So, it was my virtues, not my flaws, that tripped me up."

"Yes, m'lady."

"Strange that traits that are approved of, even demanded in a woman, could be thought inappropriate in a young man. I shall remember that."

A shadow crossed Badger's face. "Oh, no. You're not thinking of..."

"No, don't worry. I don't mean to do anything outrageous ever again. Now that I've got a clean conscience I'd like to keep it that way."

* * *

Badger had only to announce to the rest of the staff that he had always known about Justi so that they, so as not to appear dull-witted, each recalled instances that convinced them the young master was a girl. The front presented by the house servants spread to all those employed on Homeplace, and it would have been unwise for anyone to condemn Justi within the hearing of any of her loyal dependents for a masquerade they felt to have been a necessity.

In fact, after Badger's rare visit to the Ram's Head that night, the most popular view, it seemed, for all the Glenncross folk to take, was that they had always known Justi was a girl.

There were few local gentry other than Squire Coates and Colonel Allen. With these two solidly behind her, she might be pointed out in the district but never cut.

It was Dr. Trent who might possibly have suffered the most discomfort from the news. He merely said that it was difficult to tell a person's sex from a swollen knee or a bump on the head. He added the rider that Justi might be a female but, in terms of hard work and abilities, she was more a man than many he could name in the district. This seemed to silence his critics.

Richard had no doubt that, eventually, the story of her strange upbringing would come out in London. In fact, he cautioned her never to deny it but to pass it off as a quirk of her grandfather's that she had been allowed the freedoms of a male in her youth. So long as she behaved circumspectly when in society, he did not fear that her reputation would be regarded as more than flamboyant.

Richard had been perusing a communication from the lawyer when he heard a commotion in the rose garden. He looked out the library window to see Justi beguiling the time before lunch by throwing sticks for Jasper to fetch. A confused lamb went bleating after the dog every time he ran for one, then followed him to Justi. When she finally let Jasper rest, the lamb went back to cropping grass. Other than coming in with consistently grubby hems on her gowns, Justi did not seem to be having much trouble adapting to her new mode.

He opened the window to call to her, "I need to see you in private, now." The stricken look on her face wrung a laugh from him. "No, it's nothing you've done, unless there's something I haven't found out about yet."

Justi shut Jasper and the lamb up in the stable then came up to the house brooding about that wretched translation she had done for Gerard. It had not seemed important at the time she was making a clean breast of things. Now it was beginning to prey on her mind. What if he sent another letter asking her to translate another book?

"I've had some good news from Mr. Baird. He has finally contacted your mother in Scotland, and she writes back that she has no need for her marriage settlement, so the principal is to be assigned to you, under my management, of course. This means you will have an income of your own."

"Does he say how they are?"

"You know Baird. Perhaps you had better write to your mother and inform her that she has a daughter. Good Lord, how will she explain this to Sandy?"

"But she already told him, of course. You don't imagine she would marry him with that on her conscience."

"Sandy knew? And never told me." Richard seemed shocked at this supposed betrayal. "I would have thought he would have had more sense."

"I thought it was kind of him to let me tell you in my own time. He did make me promise to tell you, though."

"Yes, but you were not going to, were you? That night you tried to run away."

"I did write you that letter."

"Coward!" he taunted, half laughing.

"Yes, I thought so myself, at the time. But if you realized how you get when you're angry, you could understand my reluctance to tell you something far worse than anything I had previously done.''

''If I have a temper, it has been well cultivated by my family. Write me a letter, indeed! Did you imagine I wouldn't come after you?''

''I didn't think any further than getting away.''

''Don't ever try anything like that again.''

''Why should I? You are all so kind to me.''

From the sharp stare he directed at her, she took it he thought she was being sarcastic. ''No, I mean it. Everyone treats me far better than I deserve, considering I was trying to rob you.''

She left him again with a lump in his throat and a pounding heart. How could she possess the ability to throw him into physical and mental disorder when no other woman had the slightest effect on him? It wasn't even something she tried to do. Nor was she conscious of bowling him over. He could always conceal his upset with a bluff manner. And he certainly thought he was past the age when he couldn't quell his physical needs.

If the thought of marrying Justi himself had crossed his mind before, he put it from him now. This settlement clinched it. What would people think of him preying on an innocent young girl, someone helplessly in his power, too? She must be married, and soon. He wasn't sure how much longer he could be around her without betraying himself. He reached a decision that stunned the family at lunch that day.

''I think it will be possible for us to go to London this season after all.'' Richard's pronouncement, made coolly enough, caught Julia off guard. Normally he would have discussed such a plan with her ahead of time.

''But I had assumed we are fixed here for some months.''

''Yes, so had I, but I received word from Baird that Justi is to have her mother's portion with its income. No one has let the town house yet this year. I no longer see a reason to delay Alicia's coming-out, especially since she will now have Justi for company."

Alicia looked hopefully at her cousin, whom Richard's announcement had caught with a forkful of food suspended halfway to her mouth. Not trusting herself to swallow, Justi put the fork down and folded her hands in her lap.

"I see, kill two birds with one stone, eh?" Harry took another helping of grilled ham.

"Harry, you know better. That is a very crude way to put it," Julia admonished. "I wish I had more warning, Richard. Really. Arrangements for a London season can hardly be made overnight."

"We shall be here a good month yet. It will take that long to get Justi ready." He looked up to find Justi looking bleakly into her plate. "Well, what's the matter?"

"I can't go to London in a month."

"I agree it isn't much time but I'm sure if everyone helps you can be ready."

Justi stared at him blankly. "No, I mean we won't even have the first cut of hay done by then."

"Justi." Richard sighed.

"I never feel comfortable until we get the first cut dried and stacked. Then we don't have to worry so much if the rest of it gets ruined. Perhaps you had better just leave me here to look after the farm for you."

"Are you implying that Ned Thompson can't manage such a simple thing as making hay?" Richard raised his voice.

"No." She hesitated. "Of course he can handle it."

"Or are you just afraid?"

"What?" Justi whispered.

"Richard, what are you talking about?" Julia intervened.

"Answer me, Justi. Are you afraid to go to London?"

Justi looked surprised but seemed to be giving Richard's question honest consideration. "I don't know. I had not thought about it."

"Your responsibility for Homeplace is at an end. From now on your only occupation is to learn to become a young lady so that you can be respectably married."

Justi hung her head. Richard and Julia read only submission in her manner. Justi could understand that Richard would want her off his hands. She had, after all, been a great deal of trouble to him. But she had hoped, when he took the shocking news of her identity so calmly, that he might actually grow to like her as a woman. He had now made it plain that he considered her an even more irksome charge than before.

Dear Mother,

Since you appear to be fixed in Scotland for a time, I will write to you there. I hope your marriage to Sandford is everything you dreamed it would be. From your letter I can tell that you are happy, and that is what really matters.

In answer to the question I know is in your mind, yes, I did tell Richard. He took it very well, in fact. I had expected him to be extremely angry. You know he has a famous temper. But he seemed almost stunned and he never berated me for it. I think it handsome of him, considering I was trying to steal his inheritance. He doesn't even blame you, so you can come home again with a clear conscience.

The people of Glenncross have accepted me rather well under the circumstances, thanks to the support of Vicar Mayfair. The squire is being very fatherly and Colonel Allen has called to chide me, in a kindly way, of course, for not confiding in him.

I don't know whether to thank you for the dowry or not. Because of my being suddenly so eligible, Richard is taking us up to town this spring instead of waiting until next season. I suspect he would like to get me off his hands as quickly as possible.

So we will be installed in Berkeley Square when you return to England. Julia begs that you two will come and stay with us. Richard will certainly enjoy Sandy's company since we neglect him so much. It seems we do nothing but shop and get measured and look at fashion plates until I see them in my sleep. I had no idea dressing was such hard work.

Everyone has adjusted to my transformation much better than I have. After all, my whole world has changed. I must relearn how to do everything. Dancing is especially hard to manage since I keep wanting to take the wrong part.

It is most irksome to be compelled to ride sidesaddle. I never feel quite safe. And to be constantly chaperoned, even on a walk, sometimes tries my patience to the breaking point.

But I am trying to be good for the sake of Richard and Julia—all of them, really. They could have sent me away. I would have been willing to go. That's what I planned, you know. But they wouldn't hear of it. They have all stuck by me and I do not intend to let them down.

If they think it important to bring me into society, I shall try to do them credit, even though I would much rather be hacking about Homeplace. I think I will have to give up the idea of ever staying here as anything but a guest. Richard has it in his mind, I think, to live here himself, and leave Amberly for Harry's use when he gets married. And, whether Richard marries or not, I couldn't stay here.

There was a time when I thought—well, never mind about that. Richard has made it plain he is not interested in me beyond getting me suitably attached to someone else. He is getting depressingly patriarchal.

We all miss you terribly and can hardly wait to see again. Everyone is well. I hope this letter finds you the same.

Justi

Justi's retraining, begun in a piecemeal fashion by the family, became an organized effort, since they were scheduled to leave by the last week of April. Richard took her riding every morning that was fit, since he didn't trust this critical training to Harry.

In the matter of dance, Richard bowed to Harry's superior knowledge and skill. For a hour or more each day Harry practiced, in turn with Justi and Alicia, all the steps they would need to know, or demonstrated with Clara. Julia played for them and offered her sage criticisms. After she got more practice Justi enjoyed the dancing more than anything to do with being a girl. She would have liked to try it with Richard, but he seemed to be holding himself aloof from the preparations he had set forward.

Julia spent a great deal of time dictating lists of names, titles and relationships to memorize. Justi protested that all this was useless with no faces to go with the names. Julia saw no particular problem in Justi memorizing all about the haute monde first and attaching faces to them later.

They made several trips each week to Newmarket for shopping or fittings. Justi put herself into their hands as far as color and fashion were concerned. Beyond demanding that nothing be too tight to move or breathe in, she allowed them free rein and insisted they use the money from her account to pay what she was sure must be fantastic bills.

"We can do better when we get to London, of course. But we have to start somewhere."

"You don't mean we have to buy more in London! It will be years before I can wear all of this out."

"Justi, one does not wear clothes out. One discards them when they go out of fashion," Clara informed her.

"Seems a damned waste to me."

"Justi, have I Harry or a stableboy to thank for that kind of language?"

"Sorry, Julia. I'll be careful. I promise."

Only in the matter of sewing did Justi ride grub. It seemed such a nonsensical thing to learn, but when she dared say this to Julia, her cousin came as close to losing her temper as possible. Julia took a great deal of pride in her needlework and considered it an essential part of a young lady's upbringing.

Richard only just ducked an embroidery frame when he invaded the sitting room one rainy afternoon. Alicia was looking at Justi with awe.

"Really, Justi!" Julia was shocked. "You are going to have to learn to control yourself. If the thread gets tangled, there are remedies."

Richard returned the offending needlework to its owner with a rueful smile. "I believe you dropped this, Lady Justine." He bowed.

"You are too kind, Lord Mallory." She inclined her head, but ruined the effect by laughing heartily.

"Really, such funning is all very well in the family, but you are going to have to be careful in London," Julia warned.

"You really hate this?" Richard asked seriously as she wrestled with knotted silks.

"I'd rather muck out a stall."

"Justi!"

"Well, it's the truth, and I didn't swear. Seems like I ought to be able to pay someone to do this for me."

"Well, we are running short of time," said Richard, "and I have never been one for lost causes. I think we'd best give up on this skill and just hope no one finds out you can't thread a needle."

"Do you mean it?" Justi asked in delight, those long-suppressed dimples showing.

He laughed at her relief and Julia's outrage. "Come now, let's help her with something she will have to do in public. Do you remember the rules to whist, Justi?"

During their last week at Homeplace the packing began in earnest. Justi complained that they had all run mad and couldn't possibly use half the clothes they were taking with them, but no one paid any heed to her.

Richard was still ferociously protective of her. He still took her riding. He certainly still argued with her and even joked sometimes. But there was no return to the camaraderie they had once shared. He had withdrawn behind the wall he had built between them for whatever reason. He was not cold to her, just disgustingly polite.

She supposed if he wanted her to marry someone else she would try to do so. She had done more difficult things because she considered them her duty. She would miss Homeplace, of course, but she had her memories of it and the confidence that Richard would take care of it. About missing Richard and the rest of them there was nothing she could do. It seemed so unfair to finally have a family and then to have to leave it right away.

"Why so sad?" Richard surprised her sitting by the pond the night before they were to depart.

"I don't know." She looked at him. "I've never been anywhere but here and then Amberly. Is going away always sad?"

"But you'll be coming back."

"Perhaps not. Or, even if I do, it will all be different. Homeplace may not change but I will. I think it's a little like dying."

"It doesn't seem fair to you, does it?"

"Having to be a girl? It is starting from scratch in a good many areas. Nothing I learned before is going to be of much use to me."

"I meant losing Homeplace."

She looked up at him in surprise. "It was never really mine. Perhaps it's not something you can own. It's more like it owns you. I will miss it, though. It would have been good to ride once more up to the oak grove."

"Why?" He pushed himself away from the stand of trees where he had leaned to watch her skate so awfully long ago, and came to stand by the bench.

"To say goodbye. Don't look at me so strangely. Those trees used to be my closest friends." She said it half-jokingly. "That's sad, isn't it?"

He didn't answer for a while. "If I know Julia, she won't be ready to set out much before ten. And Haimes will be following a day behind with the hunters anyway, so we needn't fear to tire them. We'll ride up early tomorrow, just you and me."

"You would do that for me?" She stood up.

"But it's such a small thing."

"No, it's something I need to do. I don't think anyone else would understand that, not anyone who doesn't belong to this place."

They rode out early next day with the mists still rising from the stream and the furrows of the hills. The treetops standing above the soft fog looked like islands in a milky sea.

They said nothing. There was only the soft thud of the horses' hooves, the creak of saddle leather and the jingle of the bits echoing off the tall canopy of leaves. Richard let her ride ahead of him on the trail.

As Gray Dawn waded knee-deep through the ferns, hundreds of tiny white moths flew up around horse and rider in a caressing cloud. The slim figure on the gray horse looked like a being from a fairy tale. She gasped in delight and raised a gloved hand, palm up, like a blessing.

She turned in her saddle and smiled at Richard. His heart gave a jerk. He thought it might be the only moment he would ever see her here where she really belonged. He wanted to keep her here with him, but he did not go to her, and he let the moment pass. She turned away again, not disappointed by him, but puzzled.

He was sometimes so perceptive and gentle, yet afraid to own to these qualities—weaknesses, perhaps he thought them. But his reticence could not ruin her delight in the day.

Richard suddenly knew what he wanted for her. He wanted her to be loved, and that was something he was no good at. That's why he had to find someone else for her, someone who would care for her as she deserved, not rant at her and beat her. He would know the man when he found him. He would know him by the helpless look in his face.

Justi had plenty of time to change while the baggage was being carried out. She packed the riding habit into the last open trunk. When Richard and Harry emerged from the house they found Justi sitting laughing on the front steps. She was watching three ladies and their maids instruct Badger, the footman and two dragooned grooms in how to load the baggage. The postboys who came with the carriages hired to convey the ladies, servants and baggage would have nothing to do with the fray, except to keep their horses steady.

"Is it always like this?" Justi asked in delight.

"I forgot. You never traveled with Julia before. It's practically the only time she loses her reason."

"Look, why are they taking all that stuff off again?"

"To see what's underneath," explained Harry. "Aren't you going to make sure all your trunks are there?"

"I'm staying out of it. If even half my luggage reaches London, I shall have plenty to wear."

"Harry and I will take my curricle with the grays for the first few stages. That way Haimes can pick the grays up tomorrow and bring them along with the hunters."

"Now I know why you were so accommodating as to leave us a chaise all to ourselves. No doubt they will discover their nightclothes are at the bottom of the pile and we shall have to go through all this again."

Richard laughed and waved as he went to check his team, but he did not actually leave until he had handed the ladies in and secured the door. Even at that, he had Harry keep a watch back for the first few miles to make sure Julia didn't turn around for something she imagined she forgot.

By the time they reached the inn Richard had designated as their stop for a late luncheon, Justi was more aggravated than amused by her traveling companions. She was the first to join Richard and Harry in the private parlor hired for their use. She discovered these two had consumed a considerable amount of a fine local ale while waiting for them. Yet Richard said, "You made good time."

"Only because I wouldn't let them stop." She flung down her hat.

"What did I tell you, Harry?"

"All right. I owe you a crown."

Justi ignored the bet. "I can certainly see why you refuse to travel with them. Alicia, poor thing, is queasy most of the way, Julia gets the headache, and Clara is so bored she gets on everyone's nerves. They missed all the scenery."

"How did you keep them going?"

"By pointing out that the more often we stopped, the longer the trip would take."

Harry poured a small glass of ale and handed it to Justi. "Don't give her that!" Richard recovered the glass.

"She drank it before."

"Not anymore, you young fool. I think you've had too much yourself. Call the waiter and ask for some lemonade."

"I didn't like it above half anyway," Justi confessed.

"Remember that inn we stopped at near Farnwell? I didn't think I could get so castaway on ale."

Since Justi had been recalling that night in January, it irked her to have Harry bring it up.

"I say, that must have presented quite a problem for you, having to share a room with me," Harry teased.

"Harry," Richard said warningly, for he could see the flash in Justi's eyes.

"At least it solved one for you," she retorted.

"What's that?"

"You finally got to sleep with a woman."

Richard choked on his drink and Harry yelled "Justi!" and nearly clouted her before he remembered she was a girl.

"That's enough, both of you."

"You're worse than Clara. You think you can say anything and get away with it now."

"I'm sorry, Harry, but you did have it coming," she said in her defense.

"No one knows anything about that," Richard warned, "and if you say anything, Harry, I'll skin you alive."

"No one knows about what?" Julia asked Richard as she entered the parlor.

The three jerked guiltily and looked so uniformly at a loss that Julia laughed.

"Richard has a surprise for you when we get to London," Justi recovered to say. "So please don't spoil it by plaguing him about it."

"What surprise?" he whispered fiercely in her ear as the girls came in.

"Trying to think of one should keep you occupied the rest of the trip."

Even Justi grew restless at being shut up so long during the afternoon. Julia recommended she study her lists of names. Still complaining that this was useless without knowing which people went with which names, she asked Clara to describe them to her.

Clara's verbal sketches, which usually dwelt on some absurdity, and her summations of peoples' characters laced with quite shocking bits of gossip, had Justi in hysterics. Although Julia remonstrated with Clara for giving Justi such a bad impression of the ton, Justi noticed that she never denied any of the stories so drolly told.

Alicia was exhausted by the time they reached Halstead and Julia also lay down to rest, so that only Clara and Justi appreciated the hot dinner Richard had laid out before them almost as soon as they alighted.

* * *

Justi woke often during the night whenever some vehicle came into the yard, or even passed on the road, but she seldom slept the night through, anyway, unless she was worn to the bone. So she awoke at her usual early hour and went into the parlor.

When Richard entered, she was sitting on the window seat with one leg curled under her, watching the comings and goings in the yard. She hopped down as soon he opened the door but not before she read reproof in his eyes. He wasn't even that much older than her but, of late, he had been acting almost fatherly. She hated it because that wasn't at all the way she felt about him.

"At least I didn't go out for a walk alone, which is what I originally thought of doing."

"Am I supposed to be delighted at the prospect of all the imprudent things you have so thoughtfully refrained from doing? And why haven't you ordered tea? I know you like it early."

She shrugged. If Richard was going to be cranky over such minor things it was better to let it run its course. She had to bite her lip sometimes, though, not to laugh at the lengths to which his fault-finding was carried. Since Richard wrongly interpreted this as her effort not to cry, it always put an end to his criticisms much faster than Justi arguing with him.

"Did you sleep well?"

"Well enough. It's amazing how much traffic there is even in the middle of the night. Will it be this noisy in London?"

"Not in Berkeley Square." Richard began to talk of London and the plays and balls he and Harry would escort them to. By the time a bearish Harry joined them, his humor was restored enough to rate Harry on the size of his hangover.

"I'd like to make an early start. We aren't more than three hours from home."

"If Alicia is still asleep, I'd rather not wake her, poor thing. But I do see why you push the journey along so. The less time spent on the road, the better."

"You don't think it would help to drive slower, like Julia says?"

"No, I think it's the moving scenery that makes her queasy, not the rocking."

"Clara says she could be better, if she put her mind to it," Harry volunteered, though he looked none too well himself.

"How can you say that? Of course she can't help it. And she makes herself worse by worrying about holding us up."

"Well, I certainly have never spoken harshly to her on that account."

Justi's lips twitched. "No matter how much you have wanted to."

Richard looked up from his breakfast rather conscience-stricken. "You say she fears me."

Justi hesitated. "I did say that once, didn't I?"

"I swear I've never given her cause."

"For someone as shy as Alicia, just hearing you rant at the rest of us insures her obedience. I don't know what she would do if you raised your voice to her."

"What am I supposed to do?" Richard did raise his voice, and Harry winced. "Let the rest of you get away with murder, so as not to upset Alicia?"

Justi laughed. "Now that would be dull."

"You, on the other hand, I believe, are not afraid of me at all."

Justi looked innocently up from her tea. "Surely there is no need. You did say you don't beat young ladies."

"In your case I may make an exception."

With so many hours to spend together in the curricle, Richard had a chance to ask Harry about something that had been puzzling him.

"Dumont was lying. He had to be. I won't believe he actually made love to Justi. If he had she would have told me."

Harry roused himself from a near doze. "Yes, Gerard was lying."

"Then why did Justi let me force that false confession out of her?"

"Oh, that was my idea," Harry said brightly, not realizing he might be treading on dangerous ground.

"Your idea! Here, you drive for a while. Let me get this straight. You told her to confess to some particularly damaging acts, even though you were convinced of her innocence."

Harry took the reins. "Yes, and it worked, too. Once she confessed, you immediately forgave her, and we had her sprung in an hour."

"The two of you planned that?"

"Wasn't it great! It took Justi hours to get her story right."

Richard was almost too stunned to be angry. "You know, I used to imagine that I was in control. I can see now it was no such thing."

"Richard, what's the matter? We aren't tricking you most of the time. I swear."

"It's not that. You believed Justi, even before you knew she was a girl. I didn't believe her, and I'm not sure why."

Harry drove on in silence for a time, then quite unexpectedly handed the ribbons to Richard.

"What's the matter? Can't think and drive at the same time?"

Harry scowled at him. "I think we are just different. I mean, I accept people at face value. I believed Justi because I just naturally think the best of people."

"I am witness to how often that gets you into trouble."

Harry looked at him with knit brows. "And you always think the worst of everyone."

"That's not true!"

"Well, maybe not Julia and Alicia, but everyone else, especially people you don't know well, or someone you take an instant dislike to."

"I suppose I did think Justi a sullen, pampered brat when I first encountered her."

"Perhaps that's why you disbelieved her. Richard, will I get that way when I'm your age? Suspicious of everyone?"

"If you've had as many traps set for you as I have, perhaps."

The second day was harder on Alicia, but Justi decided to push on without stopping, for fear that she wouldn't get Alicia back in the carriage again.

Richard must have been watching for them. When they reached Berkeley Square, he came out himself to carry Alicia up to her room.

To Justi, the Mallory town house looked more like a Greek or Roman temple than a residence. It was a half story up off the street, with a columned front portico and another on the side street. The entrance hall was grand, and Justi peeked in one door to see a vast ballroom that ran the length of the house with windows opening onto the side portico. She really wondered how she could live in a place that was all stone and glass with no trees about. It was more like a palace than a home.

It was apparent that someone had ordered a fire kindled and Alicia's bed warmed. The way Julia and Clara looked at each other, Justi realized that this much consideration for someone else's comfort must be a new start for Richard. He could be so sweet when he really concentrated. Of course, it wouldn't last. That's what made it so charming.

Chapter Eleven

The others traded news of the journey over a cold luncheon, also thoughtfully prepared. Then Julia and Clara went to rest and supervise the unpacking, respectively. Justi wanted a walk more than anything after being cooped up for so long in the carriage, so Richard commanded the yawning Harry to take her to the nearby park for a stroll, while he repaired to one of his clubs to puff off their presence in town.

Hyde Park was only a ten-minute walk away, and Justi was surprised and delighted to find such a huge block of gardens and trees right in the middle of London. The lake and the flower gardens were more than she hoped for. She thought she could truly take an interest in flowers, now that she had the time, but all appeals to Harry for the names of the different varieties were fruitless.

"Perhaps you want to go home and rest, Harry. You're looking a bit wretched again."

"Oh, I shan't be sick on you if that's what you're worrying about. My God! Look! There's Graham." Harry bounded away to accost a young man wearing a striking blue coat and walking a long-haired lapdog.

Amidst the handshaking and more exuberant greetings between young cronies parted for half a year, Graham let go the dog lead, and the moplike creature would have made good its escape had Justi not stepped on the end of the leash.

"Sorry, pup, but you could get run over. Come here." By tickling the creature's chin and scratching its ears, once she found them, Justi was well on the way to being fast friends with the dog before Harry was nudged by his acquaintance into a remembrance of his manners.

"My cousin, Lady Justine Mallory. This is Graham Fairchild. We were at school together."

"I didn't think you were Harry's sister," Graham said.

Graham made an exaggerated bow, risking the crushing of his shirt points and momentarily blocking Justi's fascinated gaze upon his paisley waistcoat. She blinked and reprimanded herself for staring by the time Graham invited her to take another turn around the circular walk. He handed the leash to Harry and took Justi's arm so adroitly that she couldn't quite figure out what happened for a minute. She suppressed a laugh and had the satisfaction of finding out from her new acquaintance the names of some of the plantings.

Harry walked abreast of them on Graham's other side, dragging the reluctant Fiona in his wake. Justi heard several school reminiscences she was sure Richard would have frowned upon, but laughed along with the friends. Graham promised to call the next morning with his mother, *sans* dog, and acquaint them with the latest gossip of the town.

Harry brought Justi back by way of the stables since he was sure she would want to check out these accommodations, and she requested that they sit for a while in the small square of grass separating the stables from the house. There was only one bench backed up against the row of hedges that blocked a view from the street. It all seemed quite fortresslike to Justi.

"Graham's mother keeps him pretty much on a short lead, like the dog. So he has to dance attendance on her or she will cut his allowance."

"But he's a grown man. Why doesn't he just work for a living?"

Harry stared at her in disbelief. "It isn't fashionable to work. You're supposed to live on your income, although almost everyone I know lives beyond it."

Justi still looked confused. Having been used to earning money, and spending it as she liked, the idea of living off someone else seemed uncomfortable. She especially didn't see how a man could bear it.

"That's exactly it. Nothing to do but hang out for a rich wife."

She almost thought Harry wasn't joking. "But, Harry, what's the difference if you are living off your mother or your wife? You still lack independence."

"That's where a fellow has to watch the marriage settlements to make sure he gets control."

"And what about the unfortunate bride?"

"Why, what else has she to do?"

"I mean, how does she feel being married for her money?"

"Ten to one she knows nothing about the money end of it."

"How unfair!" But she couldn't sway Harry to see the pointlessness of such a way of life.

Harry looked speculatively at her. "I don't suppose you would like to marry Graham? He's not a bad sort, really."

"Harry, I hardly know him!"

"Just asking."

"Well, please don't plant that thought in his head. I can think of nothing I would like less than having someone plan to live off my income. I almost wish I didn't have one. Then I could depend on no one having ulterior motives."

Richard strolled out of the house toward them, attracted by the familiar sounds of argument between the two. They seemed more like brother and sister than Harry and Alicia did.

"I thought you might like to see your room and rest a bit before it's time to change for dinner. And Harry had better have a nap if he plans to go out raking tonight."

* * *

The room he led her to was bigger than her bedroom at Homeplace, and had yellow wallpaper with pink rosebuds. She ran to the window and looked out over the little garden and the top of the stable.

"Oh, thank you, Richard."

"I thought you might sleep better here than if you were over the main street. And this is Emily, one of the housemaids, but she can do for you while you are here." Emily dropped a curtsy. "You are not to go out without her or some other escort. Do you understand?"

"Yes, of course, but I hope you like to walk, Emily, for I do, and there is so much to see."

"What do you mean?" Richard looked taken off balance.

"Why, museums, galleries, Saint Paul's."

"Oh, you can take a hackney to go touring. Just don't leave the house unless you tell someone you are going."

"I'll remember."

He left them alone to get acquainted as Emily unpacked Justi's new wardrobe. He omitted to tell Justi that Emily had been given pretty strict instructions about where Justi was allowed to go and had his leave to prevent possible indiscretions by threatening to snitch.

To Emily, Justi seemed so docile and agreeable that she breathed a sigh of relief. She had thought she was being given the charge of a temperamental beauty of wayward disposition. She now saw that Richard's care for Justi sprang from his fear that her ignorance would get her into trouble. The young Lady Justine was, by report, just come from the country, and had never been to town before.

Clara voiced the opinion at dinner that Justi should have a French maid to put her in fashion.

"But I like Emily. Besides, I wouldn't want a maid who knows more about fashions and hairstyles than I do. She would be running my life."

"We shall stay home tomorrow morning if Lydia Fairchild means to call. I don't want to miss her," Julia planned. "Then we'll go shopping in the afternoon."

Justi turned to look at her, round-eyed. "Shopping? What could we possibly need?"

"Well, we won't know until we go shopping, will we?" Julia reasoned. Justi looked to Richard for clarification, but he merely shrugged helplessly and recommended, "Do as Julia says. She won't steer you wrong."

The horses arrived that day, but Richard commanded they have a day's rest before being ridden, so Justi occupied the next morning with walking about the neighborhood in Emily's company. They were out at such an early hour, though, that they encountered no one except tradesmen and servants.

After breakfast, Richard left the house. Harry had not appeared yet. The women retired to the morning room to work at various sewing tasks, except Justi, who used the time to practice on the pianoforte in the adjoining drawing room. She was at this when the somber butler announced the Fairchilds. She stopped playing and rose, but the formidable dame who greeted Julia affectionately waved her cane and said, "Continue child, continue."

They seated themselves in the drawing room as Justi played to the end of the piece, and looked round to see if more was expected. Evidently, Mrs. Fairchild was satisfied, because she beckoned. "Well, you are not as pretty as your mother was at your age."

Justi laughed. She didn't know if the stout old woman sought to discompose her or not, but she did not rise to the bait. "No, I will never be as pretty as Mother at any age. Have you seen her since she remarried? She looks like a girl again."

"No, I have not!" Mrs. Fairchild uttered this as though she had been personally affronted. "A very hurly-burly affair. They were no sooner married, she and Sandford, than they were off to Scotland. When do they mean to return?"

"We had thought they would be back for the season," Julia said uncertainly. "But by her last letter, they seem to be inclined to linger a little longer, so we really have no idea."

"It's all of a piece. Neither one of them has any decision. I do not approve of marriage between people of the same age."

Justi was so much intrigued by this utterance that she sought enlightenment. "You think the man should always be older, then?"

"Yes, of course. How else would the wife know how to go on?"

Justi could have said many things, such as pointing out that her mother had been married before, but Julia was forever glad that the child had the sense to smile sweetly and refrain from being drawn into useless argument. Julia had no idea that, compared to Basil Mallory, Mrs. Fairchild, as an irritant, was a mere novice. Harry stumbled in then to create a diversion. After greeting their guests he took a bored-looking Graham out to see the horses.

"If your father had lived, things would have been different."

Justi jerked. "My father?"

"Yes, he wouldn't have kept your mother buried in the country like your grandfather did. You would have been to town long before now."

"Well, I'm here now," Justi said inadequately.

"It was no love match, but they were perfect for one another. Basil arranged it all."

"You knew Grandfather?"

"Oh, yes, he was held to be a handsome man in his day. Too bad he was so stubborn. Everything had always to be his way. He must have been hard to live with."

"For Mother, yes. But, of course, I always studied to please him," Justi said demurely.

"Then did just as you liked the minute his backed was turned, eh?"

Justi laughed in surprised delight. "You are very perceptive, ma'am." She began to revise her opinion of the guest.

Graham and Harry burst into the room. "Did you really ride that big black, Justi?"

"Well, yes, before I met Richard. But Bluedevil was really too big for me. Richard looks much better on him."

"How did you manage him?"

"I'm not sure I really did. Perhaps I was just lucky he didn't throw me."

"Harry says you used to dress as a boy, and ride astride."

"Harry!" Julia saw disaster yawning at her feet.

Justi feigned embarrassment. "Yes, I had to. You see, Grandfather became quite odd in later years. He wanted an heir so badly, he must have pretended I was a boy. Eventually he really believed it."

"And I suppose that fool Miriam let this go on."

"She had no choice. She was completely in his power. And she was, I think, more than a little afraid of him."

"He must have been insane."

"Oh, do you really think so? It didn't seem so odd to me. But I didn't know any better."

"There, there, child. Don't take on so. No one can hold your upbringing against you. Not if you behave yourself now."

"Julia has been so patient with me. There is no way to thank her for all she has done."

"And she has nothing to blush for in either you or Alicia. You may come to visit me and play for me tomorrow."

"Yes, I would like that."

When the Fairchilds had left, Harry made himself scarce, and Julia reclined on the sofa with the beginnings of a headache.

"To think it had to be Harry who let it out. I had hoped we could get through most of the season without anyone knowing."

"I'm sorry, Julia. I did the best I could."

"Perhaps it's better that everyone knows about Justi from the beginning," offered Alicia. "That way it could never be thought that we were trying to deceive them."

"She may be right," Clara added. "Besides, this will make Justi more interesting."

"One should not strive to be interesting," Julia said.

"Do you think she will tell anyone?" asked Justi.

"My child. She will tell everyone." Julia sat up again. "But there's no help for it now. At least she seemed to be pleased with you."

"She's very strange, but I can't help liking her," Justi confessed.

Richard took the news well. He brought his fist down on the luncheon table and made the plates jump. "Just where is Harry?"

"He hasn't come back yet," Julia said.

"If it had not been Harry, sooner or later I would have said something odd, and they would have known, anyway."

"No doubt, but you might not have blurted it out to one of the worst gossips in London."

"I knew it was a mistake to come," Justi said to her plate.

"Nonsense," pronounced Richard. "I just wish people could have gotten to know you before you became a curiosity. Now, stop pouting, and eat your lunch."

"Is that what I was doing?" She looked at him in surprise.

"Yes, not intentionally, of course, as Clara would do. But you are becoming more female all the time."

"That doesn't sound like a compliment."

"It wasn't meant as one."

Justi laughed. "You aren't going to beat Harry, are you?"

"If I thought it would do any good..." Richard looked at her sharply. "You know where he is, don't you?"

"Yes, he's hiding out in the stable, and I imagine he's pretty hungry by now."

Richard threw down his napkin and got up.

"If I can forgive him, don't you think you can? I care more about Harry than any of these people in London." Real concern showed in Justi's face. She knew enough about Richard's wrath not to want anyone else to have to face it.

"Comber!" Richard bellowed. The butler appeared in the room as if by magic. "Please send someone out to the stable," Richard said formally. "Inform my brother that we are holding lunch for him."

Some minutes later Harry peeked uncertainly around the doorframe and then slid into his seat. Richard stared hard at him, but said nothing.

Justi smiled. "Actually I'm rather glad it's out in the open. Now we can all be comfortable again."

"I think we should all treat it like a very good joke," said Clara. "If everyone sees that we take it lightly, they may also."

"It seems a good plan," said Julia.

"Especially since we have no choice." Richard's growl arrested Harry's assault on the platter of roast chicken.

"So that's all settled." Harry turned his attention to his meal and Richard shook his head.

They ventured out shopping that afternoon, and although Julia and Clara encountered many female acquaintances, no one remarked particularly about Justi, except to say they had known her mother or to trade commonplaces. Julia was beginning to hope they might ride out the thing unscathed.

Richard had promised to take them to a play that evening and Justi sought him out to ask what it was about.

"Oh, hello," she said, entering the study, "Richard not here?"

"No, I'm Braden, his secretary." The pleasant young man rose from his account books to shake her hand. "You must be Lady Justine."

"Yes," she said, laughing, "but it still sounds a little strange to me. Please call me Justi."

"I'm afraid I owe you an apology."

"Already? But we only just met."

"You see—" he cast his eyes down guiltily "—I'm the one who hired Dumont."

"Oh, but I don't blame you for that, and I'm sure Richard does not. We were all mistaken in Gerard, even my mother. Besides, I could be said to have brought my troubles on myself, and it has all turned out for the best."

"Yes, I could hardly believe—what I mean is, you don't look at all like a boy."

"Why, thank you." Justi laughed at Braden's embarrassment. "But I do have rather a low voice for a girl, don't you think?"

"Yes, I suppose."

"And, if you closed your eyes, you could imagine I was a boy?"

"I don't know."

"I always practiced to keep my voice low, never to squeak or shriek. Now I can't talk any other way. I have gotten used to doing everything differently, except that. I just can't seem to change it."

"Oh, I don't think you should. I like your voice."

"I wish Richard didn't mind it so. You see, if he closes his eyes he can imagine I'm still a boy and it disturbs him."

Braden was struggling with the notion of his employer being disturbed by this child. "I expect he will get used to it in time."

"I haven't much time," Justi confessed sadly. "He has only brought me up to town to marry me off. I suppose I have been a trial to him, but I never meant to be. Why does he do that, take on other people's problems so eagerly?"

"He always has been responsible, since I have known him. Perhaps he just likes you."

"If only that were it," Justi said woefully. "I expect I had better go and change. It's wearisome to have to spend so much time dressing and undressing."

"What's the matter, Braden? Why are you brooding?" Richard asked when he came into the study.

"I was just talking to Lady Justine."

"Oh, no, what has she said now?"

"It's not that, although she is direct," Braden assured him.

"Delicately put. If only I could impress on Justi the need for delicacy—why the dinner table is not a good place to discuss lambing, for instance."

"She's actually quite an amazing girl, to have coped with Dumont, if he is anything like you say he is."

"Yes, she is amazing. Do you like her?"

"Yes, I genuinely do," said Braden, resuming his writing.

"Would you like to marry her?"

"What?" asked Braden, nearly turning over the inkpot.

"I had much rather think of her with you than anyone else."

"No! I mean no disrespect, but I'm pretty sure I would not be equal to the task."

"Well, I suppose I will find someone," Richard said as he went through the letters Braden had prepared.

Braden looked at Richard a little strangely, wondering if his employer had any idea how Lady Justine felt about him.

Richard unscrupulously canceled Harry's plans so that he could also act as escort. It was important that everyone knew there had been an addition to the family, for if Justi wasn't invited to parties, they would not be able to take her about.

Justi, Alicia and Clara sat in the front row of the box, and although she felt a little on display, she became so fascinated observing other people, she soon lost her shyness.

Several gentlemen called at the box during intermission—friends of Richard or Harry, she supposed, since she didn't recognize any of the names. She must remember to ask them each for a list of people she might encounter. She didn't realize that these envoys were there to ascertain her identity, connections, position in the family and possible suitability, and pass this information on to the inquisitive in the audience.

"How do you like it so far?" Richard asked as the curtain was about to rise again.

"Well, the hero is a bit stupid, but I suppose the plot wouldn't work at all if he could figure it out."

"I wasn't asking for a literary criticism. I merely meant, how do you like being out?"

"Oh, am I?"

"You seem to have taken well enough. At least you are not overly shy, like Alicia, or overly bold, like Clara."

"Ha, another false compliment. I hope I cannot be accused of being overly proper."

"I just meant that I find myself worrying less about what you may say than I feared."

"If only you knew the number of things I think of, and discard without saying, you would not be so complacent."

Richard laughed. He seemed to be pleased with her for no particular reason she could discover, but it was such a comfortable feeling, she vowed to do nothing to disturb his good humor.

The ladies paid their call on Mrs. Fairchild the next morning. Fiona greeted Justi with approval, rather than the sharp yapping that usually got her dismissed from the morning room. By scratching her ears in just the right way, Justi settled the lapdog comfortably for the visit and won another nod of approval from the woman who could make or break her.

Justi, in fact, seemed to be unconscious of the dangerous waters into which she sailed, and her vulnerability was somehow appealing even to such a hardened gossip. During the recital in which the girls performed in turn, Mrs. Fairchild wrested the whole tale from Julia. She was much more inclined than the Mallorys to condemn Miriam for letting things come to such a pass, and told several incidents that foreshadowed Basil Mallory's unfortunate, but, one felt, inexorable, insanity.

"He fought a duel over a horse?" Justi had never heard this one.

"Yes, someone insulted the breeding of an animal he had sold so he called the fellow out. Wounded him, too, as I recall."

Justi's eyes grew big, but she said nothing, not being sure what her response should be. She did store these tidbits away to tell Harry later.

"You say she has a thousand a year? That's not vast, but she is a taking girl. I'm sure you shall achieve something suitable for her."

Mrs. Fairchild's habit of discussing people as though they couldn't hear her had put even her contemporaries to the blush, but it only made Justi laugh. When they were taking their leave, Justi asked quite spontaneously when she could call again, since she considered Mrs. Fairchild a wealth of information about the town. Justi never did anything by halves; if she had to get to know these people, she may as well make a start.

Mrs. Fairchild, who actually seldom entertained formally, would be pleased to receive them at a tea for a few friends on Friday, if the girls would play for her again. Her aged butler gave a start, for it was the first he had heard of this entertainment.

* * *

Harry took Justi out riding early next day to Hyde Park, where a good gallop could be had. Neither one paid much attention to the time, so they were terribly late for breakfast, and Justi had still to change from her habit. They all stared rather consciously at her as she entered the breakfast parlor, so she checked over her dress to see if her maid had forgotten to do up anything.

"Aren't you going to open your letter?" asked Alicia.

"Oh, is there a letter from Mother? No," she said in disappointment as she scanned the enclosed card, "it's an invitation from a Lady Edderly. Do you know her?"

"Yes, we have all been invited to her ball," Julia said.

"I suppose—" Harry yawned "—you'll expect me to turn out for this thing."

"If you haven't that much consideration for your cousin, I should think you would want to go for your sister's sake," Richard commanded.

"Yes, please, Harry," Alicia begged. "I can face it so much better if you are with me and perhaps dance the first dance with me." Even Harry could not resist the helpless appeal of her limpid blue eyes.

"Yes, of course, I'll go," Harry conceded.

Richard looked suspiciously at Alicia, but there was no artifice there, either. Like Justi, her appeal was in her lack of design.

Friday afternoon Richard encountered Julia writing notes in the salon and thought to ask how the tea had gone.

"A complete success. Lydia asked just the right women. And they were all pleased with Justi and Alicia. Clara begged off so I thought it best to not bore her. She has been so good lately. I sent the girls upstairs to rest, since we are apt to be out late at Edderly's tonight."

"You convinced Justi to take a nap?"

"Well, I left her lying down on her bed, but I rather think she has a book secreted under the pillow."

"No doubt." Richard laughed.

"Richard, I think since Lydia has decided to help us, we can pull this off. So fortunate that Fiona likes Justi, too."

"Fiona? I don't recall a Fiona."

"Mrs. Fairchild's lapdog. She simply dotes on Justi."

"Good Lord, are you telling me Justi's future may depend on being in the good graces of a lapdog?"

"No, of course not, but it certainly helps. Richard, do you realize how impossible this would have been if Justi were not so quick and biddable? What is it?"

"She does seem different, somehow. I almost think I don't know her anymore. The old Justi would never have submitted to some of the restrictions we have placed on her now. Or he—she would have found a way around them. To tell you the truth, I rather miss that mischievous boy I used to abuse so outrageously."

"She's growing up, Richard. It would have happened anyway. Only, if you had not rescued her, she would have been very confused and unhappy."

"You think she will be happy with this sort of life?"

"Yes. Why not?"

"Whoever she marries had best own a farm somewhere. Nothing else will satisfy her, I'm afraid."

"I shall keep that in mind. It's good we are bringing the girls out together. Alicia attracts enough attention so that people are diverted from thinking about Justi's upbringing."

"Perhaps you had better rest for a while, yourself."

"Yes, I'm going up now."

Justi was the first one dressed that evening. Once Julia had told her what would look best, a cream gown, not too low cut, with a string of pearls, she never thought of changing her mind. Clara and Alicia, on the other hand, had their maids running back and forth, and had each been through several changes of clothing and hairstyle.

Justi slipped into Alicia's room to find her almost in tears. "Whatever is the matter?"

"Everyone is cross with me, or perhaps I am cross. I actually shouted at my maid, she was so stupid."

"You're just nervous, I think. You should be looking forward to this."

"I'm so glad I haven't got to go through this alone."

"You talk about it as though it will be an ordeal. I'm sure we won't be the only girls at their first ball tonight."

"I never thought of that." Alicia dried her tears. "Could you do my hair up like yours?"

"I'm the one who should be worried. I do seem to fall into the most awful scrapes without meaning to. If I accidentally do something dreadful, they won't shun the rest of you, will they?"

"I don't know." Alicia was diverted from her own fears. "What might you do?"

"I have no idea. That's my problem. I've only been at this such a short while. It will be wonderful if there aren't dozens of things Richard and Julia have forgotten to warn me about."

"I can't see that you are worse off than I am. At least you don't blush all the time for no reason."

"Oh, there's a trick to that. Just take a deep breath and pretend you are suspended above a level plain that goes on and on. Everything is perfectly flat and simple. You can see everything clearly. You know exactly what to do and you are in complete control."

"That won't work with someone staring at you."

"Oh, best of all then. You are above them, remember, but your head is up so you can see everything, so you have to look down on them, like this."

Justi demonstrated with her chin up and her eyes half-veiled by her lashes. "Try it. Perfect. Now, remember, you can see everything about them, but you are a complete mystery, which you are. No one knows anything about you."

"But there's nothing to know about me."

"Yes, but they don't know that. So you smile, just a little, with the corners of your mouth, like this, as though you
know something amusing about them that you may or may
not tell, you haven't decided yet. Now practice on me and
stop laughing. This will work, really, and remember to
breathe."

"Have you actually done this?"

"Many times, and remember, I actually had something to
hide."

"How's this?"

"Perfect. You don't look frightened at all. Now to try it
on someone else."

An opportunity arose as they descended the stairs to dinner. Harry and Richard were in the hall.

"I say!" Harry exclaimed, rather dumbstruck, when
Alicia looked at him. "You look so...well, I don't know."

Alicia turned and winked at Justi. Richard's brows shot
together in an attempt to define the difference in his young
sister.

"What are you smiling about, Alicia?"

"Why, I'm just happy, that's all."

He felt more than a little old, seeing her looking so grown-
up.

"Perhaps it's the new hairstyle," Justi suggested from
behind him. "Don't you think it makes her look older?"

"That must be it." Richard's brow cleared, but he turned
to find the same look of amused speculation on Justi's face,
and it bowled him out. "And why are you smiling?"

"I must be happy, too."

"You are sharing some joke. Out with it."

They laughed together but never revealed the secret.

They were all announced in due course by title and name,
Justi following Richard as Lady Justine Mallory. Those who
didn't know they were distant cousins might have assumed
they were married. She enjoyed this fantasy so much she

would have been reluctant to correct such a misconception. Everyone turned to stare at her as she knew they would. She smiled that sweet, knowing smile and walked over to Richard.

He took her hand and asked, "What were you thinking about when you smiled so devilishly just then?"

"I think I had better not tell you."

"You may as well. I'll get it out of you. You know I will."

"It's just that when they all looked up at me like that with their faces so concerned, they reminded me of a flock of sheep encountering an unknown."

Richard started to chuckle, and his amusement with Justi did not go unobserved.

"Then when they all started talking to each other again, the picture was complete. The insecure ones always run bleating to the older sheep for reassurance."

"Do you realize you have just called the cream of London society a flock of sheep?"

"Well, when you look at how they ape each other and start silly scares and rumors, I really think it's the sheep who suffer by comparison."

"Stop! I'll never be able to look at them again with a straight face."

"Sorry, Richard. I'm sure once I get to know them better I shall like them more than my sheep."

Still laughing, he led her over to meet some of the matrons who had been speculating on her ability to amuse and captivate such a bulwark of restraint as Richard Mallory. The word was that he sought a husband for her. Perhaps, once he had his sister and his cousin off his hands, he would give some thought to his own marriage. Richard would not have been laughing if he had known the fresh hopes he awakened in maternal breasts that night.

Justi and Alicia danced every dance with someone different, many of them rather shy young men, whom Justi took such pains to put at their ease that she forgot to be nervous. Alicia, though still shy, did not blush unduly, and after the first dance was so enjoying herself that she couldn't believe she had never wanted to come to London.

Graham Fairchild was one of the applicants for Justi's hand, and she chided herself for wondering if Harry had told him about her income.

"Wasn't it rather awful having to play a boy all those years?" he asked curiously.

"Actually, I consider myself to be quite lucky to have grown up with so much freedom. Looking back, there isn't much I would change about my life."

"But wasn't it sometimes . . . awkward?"

"It has, from time to time, been rather amusing, and occasionally exciting."

"I thought you were going to say frightening."

"It's the same thing, isn't it?"

"You are the most unaccountable girl. Harry says you even got to see a mill."

"Oh, I hated that, and I was truly scared when I saw Harry go down, but he thought it was a piece of the greatest adventure, probably the highlight of his stay at Homeplace. Even Richard enjoyed himself, and he is usually so staid."

"I wouldn't take you to a mill," Graham said protectively.

"Well, of course, no one would now." She found herself out of patience with his stupidity, but laughed. She decided then that Graham was definitely not husband material.

Clara was in high force, and by the end of the evening had rebuilt her court of admirers from two years ago, adding several younger men who thought themselves singled out by her attentions. She treated them all abominably, making promises only to break them and be forgiven.

"How do you get away with it?" Justi asked on the way home.

"But they ask for it. They like to be treated cruelly."

"Well, I could never do that," Alicia asserted. "Promise a dance to someone, then go off with someone else."

"It's a game, child. Everyone plays it."

"Have a care you don't overplay it, Clara," warned Julia. "Men have been known to grow bored with such tricks. Or don't you wish to marry again?"

"I think it suits me to be a widow."

"You mean you think you can get away with more," Alicia suggested.

"Besides, I wouldn't care to marry any of the men I've met so far this year."

"That's because they are all very attentive," Justi said. Clara looked at her inquiringly. "We shall have to find one that is indifferent to you, and if I advise him to throw you into an ornamental pond, the match will be made."

They all laughed. "That is one story you had better not tell anyone. It would require a deal more explaining than any of us could handle," Clara said.

Richard and Harry had sent them home and gone on themselves to a gaming house as a reward for spending such a dull, albeit successful, evening. The vast store of young men sent to solicit dances with Justi and Alicia had been marshaled up by Harry, and Richard had not been lax in finding more eligible, if somewhat older, partners for them.

The two men did not return until nearly dawn, so that Justi would either have to ride with a groom or wait for one of them to wake up. Richard had said she might ride with Haimes for escort, if she behaved herself, so she sent for her horse to be saddled and requested him to ride with her to the park. She asked if Richard had been exercising Bluedevil enough.

Haimes braced himself suspiciously. "Now you know you are not to ride that horse, m'lady."

"Of course not. He belongs to Richard now. I merely wondered if he was kicking down his stall."

"Lord Mallory usually rides in the afternoon."

They were enjoying a canter along the tame yet inviting tracks of Hyde Park. The early sun was still drawing the night mists from the grass when a Hussar officer of ramrod bearing appeared from the mist like a ghost rising up on a battlefield.

Justi recognized him as someone she had met the previous evening and was proud to be able to put a name to the stern face.

"Lady Justine, you are up early."

"Captain Maitland, good morning. If this were the country you would not think so. Everyone misses the best part of the day here in London. And the horses like it so much better when it is cool out."

"You put your mount's comfort before your own."

Justi had the sense to realize this bluff utterance was not a reproof, but a compliment. "Because it pleases me to do so."

"Do you ride here every morning?"

"Every morning that the weather is decent."

"Perhaps we shall meet again." As they got to the edge of the park, he sketched a salute and turned off in the opposite direction.

They did, in fact, meet and ride together often. Justi saw no reason to avoid him. He was quite interesting when she could draw him out. But he seemed to discuss military matters with reluctance. So she talked to him of Homeplace and they compared notes on farming.

For his part, Maitland found her unaffected and eager to learn, plus her horsemanship impressed him. She was neither flamboyant nor overly cautious. She rode with a confidence that was pleasing.

If it irked Justi a little that Maitland should appoint himself her guardian for this portion of the day, she was too considerate to show it. Try as she would, she could not picture him as a husband, at least not hers, for if he had a sense of humor she had as yet failed to discover it.

* * *

Julia wondered one morning when she found Justi quite alone in the breakfast parlor that the girl could dance half the night, go to bed for a few hours, then get up and ride at eight.

"The truth is I never did sleep much more than five or six hours unless I was sick. And I do catch an hour's sleep before dinner now."

"I fear the pace is beginning to tell on Alicia, and we still have half the season to go."

"Perhaps we should stay home a few nights."

"But how can we? There are so many invitations, sometimes two or three a night. And then there is our ball to plan at the end of June."

"Our ball?"

"Yes. Richard's surprise is really for all of us. We are to have a masquerade ball here. I can't remember having one since I was a girl. I planned it for later in the season, so that I could get a date that isn't already taken. Also, people need time to decide on a costume. Will you help me with the invitations?"

"Yes, of course. What do you go as?"

"I don't know yet. Richard says you may go as any female you like."

"Well, really now, how stupid does he think I am? Only an idiot would dress up in boy's clothes when we have been at such pains to put that out of people's minds."

"Don't take on so. I'm sure he meant well."

"But I haven't done anything outrageous for such a long time, I would have thought he would begin to trust me by now."

"Of course he does. He just doesn't want anything to go wrong. He's under a strain, you know."

"Is it money?" Justi looked conscience-stricken.

"No, not that precisely, but the decisions he has to make soon regarding you and Alicia will affect you for the rest of your lives. If he makes a mistake now, he would never forgive himself."

"Must Alicia marry this year? She is still so persuadable, I'm afraid she will agree with whatever Richard advises and not speak her mind."

"I would like her to be married so that Richard can get on with his own life."

"Has he said anything about that? I mean, I have seen him with a great many women and he treats them all, whether dowager or maiden, with the same cool civility. He doesn't appear to care for any of them very much."

"Perhaps he has not had time to think about it yet," Julia said, all the time wondering how long it would take Richard to get over his first marriage.

"I am trying to be very practical about myself. I know that there is no point in my waiting. My feelings are not likely to change."

"And of course you want to be married."

"Why, no, I never planned on it at all."

"What?"

"I mean before, when I was a boy. I knew I could never marry or even have a lover. I accepted that, the way I had to accept everything about my life. When I weighed it out, Homeplace seemed worth the sacrifice."

This aspect of Justi's former life had never occurred to Julia, and she was almost overcome. "Such a decision for you to make all on your own."

"Not a decision as much as a realization."

"But that's all behind you now."

Justi truly did put her mind to choosing a husband, but since she compared everyone to Richard, it was not surprising that she found them all rather bland fare. No one had his provoking combination of thoughtfulness and mulishness.

Richard looked, too, but no one seemed to fall head over heels in love with Justi, not after she laughed at them and told them not to waste their silly compliments on her. She didn't play the game by the rules. In fact, she didn't play at all. She almost seemed to prevent anyone from becoming seriously attached to her, though the younger men valued her opinions on horses, and that she could listen to their jokes without blushing.

Most of the offers he got for her hand were from men older than himself, which was embarrassing enough. They wanted a steady wife, someone to stay home and watch over the estate while they went off hunting, racing or what all. It wasn't the future he would have chosen for her, but he couldn't deny it was one to which she was well suited. But the thought of condemning her to a life without love was almost more than he could stand. There was time yet, he assured himself. Nothing had to be decided right away.

Alicia, on the other hand, was breaking hearts by the score without even trying. She had only to walk into a room for Richard to observe a new conquest falling at her feet. Far from being jealous, Justi was amused at Alicia's spectacular success.

Clara made light of Alicia's conquests, claiming that it was nothing to her coming-out some years before. Since both Justi and Alicia ingenuously believed her, there was no real jealousy among them. And they discussed the points of the men they had met rather ruthlessly in private.

Richard still found it his duty to escort them to many functions. Although he spent most of his time in the card room, he was there if Julia needed his assistance. He didn't realize it at first, but one very dull night at Almack's it occurred to him that Clara and Justi protected Alicia against undesirable company better than he did.

Clara systematically captivated and drew off the worst of the rakes, since she felt she could handle them. Justi managed to fascinate the less eligible of the suitors, those over thirty, those with too little fortune, soldiers and second sons. She had a knack for finding out rather quickly what interested them, and seemed to be able to hold them as long as she liked.

Justi was startled to see Richard leaning against a pillar in the ballroom chuckling.

"What's so funny? You have to tell me."

"Does young Mr. Bevers have no idea he has been culled from the flock of eligible suitors?"

A delightful laugh escaped Justi. "No, of course not, none of them do. But are we so obvious?"

"Only to me, but then I know you."

"Well, Alicia is too polite to get rid of them."

"Thank God you and Clara lack her sensibilities. So you still think of them as sheep."

"I suppose not. Sheep are creatures of little intelligence and vast imagination. That's why they are so easily terrified."

"Don't say it." He laughed.

"What? That these men lack imagination?"

"Is there no limit to what you will come up with?"

"Only to you. I begin to think you are the only intelligent man in London. It quite gives me a contempt for the rest of them."

"Seriously, wouldn't you like to be in charge in your household?"

"I suppose it would be better than being at someone's mercy."

"I have a feeling your husband will be destined to be outjockeyed by you at every turn."

"That sounds awfully dull, somehow."

Justi was invited everywhere, and Mrs. Fairchild took a delight in watching her protégée enliven the London scene. She had not gone about so much in years. Her son was forced to escort her to the balls and parties, but since he left her as soon as they entered to amuse himself with the other gentlemen, his lot could not be thought to be a hard one. She was ensconced on a sofa watching the dancing at the

Marchonds' party. Lord Marchond had asked if it was true Justi was raised as a boy.

"A fluke of her grandfather's. He was quite mad, you know." She directed this at the dignified graybeard peering at Justi through his quizzing glass. She seemed to think this excused such extraordinary behavior. "It hasn't done her any harm that I can see, except that she is more plainspoken than most girls her age. She is not a beauty, of course, but is quite charming in her own way. She is lively and witty without being malicious."

Lord Marchond looked slightly askance at Mrs. Fairchild, whose razor tongue was not always known for its justice.

"Have you spoken to her yet? Justi, come here, child."

As Justi became acquainted with her host, the dignified black-browed Baron Waltham made his usual late entrance with his little dowd of a wife, who almost shrank from him. Justi thought there must be a story here and vowed to ask Mrs. Fairchild how the odd pair had come together.

"What do you think of them?"

Justi replied innocently to Mrs. Fairchild, "Why, I do not know them. What should I think of them?"

"That they are well suited," Mrs. Fairchild baited her. Lord Marchond coughed to cover a bark of laughter.

This was so clearly not true that Justi, in good conscience, could not agree. She also knew Mrs. Fairchild was toying with her.

"In what way are they remarkable, ma'am? The world is full of men and the women they married when they were young."

Mrs. Fairchild tore off into such a roar of laughter, and Lord Marchond with her, that Justi had a chance to curtsy and make good her escape. She rather thought she was quoting someone when she said it, but could not remember who. At any rate, that comment would be all over by morning. She really must be more restrained.

* * *

Having once bent her mind to the task of becoming a lady, Justi worked at it as tenaciously as at any of her farm tasks, but it did not seem to her an easy target to hit or even see.

Men seemed most amused with her when she said things neither Julia nor Richard would approve. She was careful not to lose her head and let high spirits goad her into an unbecoming freedom of behavior. Her frank speech might add spice to a conversation, but only if she did not overdo it.

She determined that the best she could do would be to learn as much as she could while in London so as to have that to fall back on if conversation lagged. She and Emily, and often Alicia, spent several afternoons a week visiting galleries, cathedrals and other improving places.

Justi liked looking at paintings well enough but was not overly fond of monumental architecture. She could not make out what held up Westminster Abbey. She understood Homeplace as a building, and knew all too well its failings. She had confidence in Amberly and Mallory House as being safe, although she could never like all those columns on the London house, but she never felt quite safe in cathedrals. Not comprehending what made them stand, she had no confidence in them not falling. Even Alicia laughed at this nonsense.

"Churches are built by men and men are fallible," Justi asserted.

Alicia stared at her as though this was an entirely new thought.

Several hours after one of these expeditions Richard called her into the study with an amused look on his face.

"What is it?" she asked, smiling when she realized he was not angry.

Those dimples almost made him forget what he was going to chide her about.

"Your maid, Emily, has finally found the courage to divulge where you took her."

"Today, you mean?"

"Yes, I fear she was quite scandalized."

"By Saint Margaret's, the lending library or the Royal Academy?" Justi inquired patiently.

"Actually the Royal Academy."

"Oh, the nudes. I thought I heard her gasp once or twice. But really it was not all that interesting."

"No?" Richard asked, arching an eyebrow.

"We all vastly preferred the Society for Painters of Watercolors—that is mostly scenery, you know."

"Then I can rely on you not offending her sensibilities again?" Richard asked with a smirk.

"I shall not, of course, but if you laughed at her it is very much too bad of you."

"I would never do such a thing."

"You had best not, for Alicia and I both like Emily. She holds such sensible views on things—well, usually sensible. You do realize how much she disapproves of this house?"

"Really?" queried Richard, getting on his high ropes. "I assure you I have never done—"

"I said the house, not you, silly. Now that we have shown her all those classical paintings she realizes Mallory House is not a converted church as she had supposed—"

Richard guffawed.

"—but may have been a pagan temple of some sort. She even speaks of human sacrifice as being a possibility here in the dim past."

"And did you inform her that the house is scarcely fifty years old?"

"Alicia filled her in on the house's noble history. I must say I cannot myself forgive your father for cutting down a row of trees to add those classical porticoes, though it must have looked quite blocklike before."

"There used to be quite a large garden until I added the stable block," Richard teased.

"If you mean to taunt me, I personally find the stables one of the more attractive features of Mallory House."

"You would," Richard observed.

"Horses must be kept somewhere."

"Did you convince Emily we are neither pagans nor cannibals?"

"I think Alicia finally assuaged her fears. By the way, how did she manage to describe my fall from grace?"

"With a great deal of reluctance, but she did see it as her duty. I must admit at first I thought she meant you had been scrutinizing real people without any clothes, though I hardly saw how that could be possible even for you."

Justi burst into delicious laughter. "She did not tell you they were in paintings?"

"Now who is making game of her?"

"No, not of Emily. I'm picturing your face until you realized what she meant."

"Get out now, baggage, until you learn some respect."

When Richard was like that, playful and amusing, Justi held out some hope that he might take an interest in her as a lifelong companion. But it never lasted. The next time he saw her he might be curt, as though he had to make up for his woeful lapse. On one of their cultural expeditions from which Emily had been carefully excluded Justi asked Alicia, "What was Evelyn like?"

Alicia wrinkled her pretty brow. "She seemed nice enough."

"Seemed nice?"

"Yes, I suppose I should not say so and I was only eleven at the time, but I remember it so well."

"What?"

"Evelyn's sister was staying with us. They were wandering around the garden talking. They didn't realize I went out there to sew. Evelyn complained so bitterly of Mother taking over and running the house—and it was not true. The servants only came to Mother for instructions because Evelyn couldn't be bothered with such matters."

"You would think she would be glad of Julia's help and advice."

"I could never quite like Evelyn after that, especially because she was always so sweet to Mother to her face."

"You never told Julia?"

"I could not. It would only have hurt her. But I think Richard must have heard such things from Evelyn."

"How terrible for him."

"I think it was the unhappiest time of Richard's life. I have always been a little in awe of Richard but I felt so sorry for him then. I wish I could have done something."

"When she died ..."

"He was angry for a long time, not with us, but he still cut up stiff over the smallest thing. Even Mother could scarcely talk to him."

"Almost as though he was angry with himself," Justi mused.

"He is so much better now, Justi. I am not afraid to talk to him anymore. Why, he's almost human."

"I'm not sure he would consider that a high tribute."

"You know what I mean."

"Yes, I think I know."

They returned late from shopping the next day and Richard met them in the hall. "What the devil have you been up to?" Richard demanded, looking at Justi's stained gloves and grubby skirt. "We are due at the Trilbys' for tea in half an hour."

"Tea? You don't even like tea," Justi said.

"Never mind that. You're filthy. What happened to you?"

Alicia and Emily stood their ground behind Justi in case she needed help with her story.

"There was a colt over his traces in Oxford Street and I was able to hold his head until we could get him untangled."

"He calmed down straight away for Justi," Alicia contributed. Since she was as pristine as when she had left the house, Richard's wrathful gaze merely passed over her.

"We couldn't just walk away and let the poor beast cast himself in the street," Justi said in her own defence.

"Was there no groom?" Richard demanded.

"Yes, with a great bite out of his hand," Emily contributed. "That's really why we stopped, sir. Someone had to bandage his hand. The driver was no use."

"I'm glad to see Alicia had no part in this escapade."

"She stopped the traffic for us," Justi said.

"What?"

"She's quite good at it," Emily said helpfully.

Justi was beginning to chuckle. "Inside of five minutes we had no end of help straightening out the harness. No one would drive over Alicia."

"I have no doubt—now go change your clothes on the instant," he said, and all three girls ran up the stairs.

When Justi came down a scant fifteen minutes later, thanks to the help of both Emily and Alicia, Richard eyed her critically.

"Why are we two going to tea together?" she asked as he hurried her down the steps to the waiting curricle.

"Because we two have been invited."

Since he lectured her the whole way there on her behavior and proper topics of conversation she assumed he considered Lord Trilby a hot prospect and vowed not to embarrass Richard no matter how boring Trilby was.

"I wish I was pretty like Alicia or Evelyn," Justi said, looking unhappily at her brown hands and putting on her gloves.

"Evelyn who?" Richard asked.

"Evelyn, your wife." Justi looked at him in surprise.

"Who told you about Evelyn?"

"Clara showed me her picture at Amberly."

"Oh." He had to search his memory to call up the image of his dead wife. "I suppose she was pretty. It's hard to remember after all this time, but that's not important."

"It's not?" Justi thought he really ought to be able to remember someone he had loved.

"No. What you say, how you conduct yourself, is very much more important than how you look."

The Trilbys consisted only of Lady Agnes and her son, Jasper Trilby. Richard thought Justi's dimpled smile upon being introduced had less to do with her pleasure at the meeting than the unfortunate match of names with her hound.

Trilby was as subdued as his mother was talkative. Justi suspected she might be a contemporary of her grandfather's and mentioned him.

"Don't speak of that man to me."

"He's dead now," Justi supplied cheerfully.

"No. Really! I remember when he started a brawl in the Duchess of Belfour's card room." Justi led Lady Trilby from one reminiscence to another as she sipped her tea and laughed, ignoring for the most part Richard's disapproving looks. Under the effects of her third cream cake Lady Trilby went on to relate a particularly scandalous tale of Basil Mallory's seduction of the wife of a peer and how he had to leap half-dressed from her bedroom window as the husband came in the door.

Thereafter Justi had only to say, "Grandfather says," to have her assertion boldly contradicted by Lady Trilby, whether it was about the proper method of weaning a calf or bolusing a sick horse. Lady Trilby was a storehouse of home remedies, and Justi even made a mental note of a few of her recipes to test later. They could have gone on comparing medicinal notes for hours, but when they got to discussing prolapses Richard judged it was time to leave.

* * *

Julia heard Justi and Richard returning, for they were arguing the whole way up the front steps, and she came out of the drawing room to try to mediate.

"Really, your behavior was unforgivable," Richard asserted.

"I thought I did pretty well against such a dragon. I did not make her truly angry and I even got a grudging laugh from her."

"I am not talking about how you handled his mother. You scarcely even spoke to Trilby."

"Well, he scarcely spoke to me," Justi said hotly.

Julia wrung her hands since the quarrel in the front hall had already attracted Comber and a footman.

"He is not very outgoing," Richard defended.

"And I know why. If you want that marriage for me it is her I will have to charm, not Trilby. He will do as she tells him."

Julia moaned and covered her face.

"That's not true."

"Don't be so blind, Richard." Justi impatiently tore off her gloves.

Richard blinked. "If he is considerate of his mother—"

"She terrifies him and she doesn't like him for it. Well, she does not terrify me, not after dealing with both you and Grandfather."

"I am not like your grandfather!" Richard shouted since Justi had begun to tramp up the stairs to place herself beyond earshot.

"No, you are much louder," she said over her shoulder. "We had best forget the whole affair. How long would Trilby last with his mother running his household and me running everything else?"

"My God! You've divided it up between you."

"I'm only saying how it would end up," she leaned over the banister to tell him.

"You will marry him if I say so." Richard actually shook his fist at her.

"If I marry him it would be for his mother's sake, not his." Justi's firm voice carried down to him and the assembled servants quite well. "I almost feel sorry for Trilby." She disappeared then.

"So do I," shouted Richard before Julia could tug him into the drawing room.

"You were a little hard on her, weren't you?" Julia asked as Richard poured himself a brandy and downed it.

"She won't break."

"No, unlike Evelyn, she won't break." Julia seated herself primly.

"What is that supposed to mean?" Richard asked as he filled his glass.

"Only that Justi is not too delicate to be a mother. You would have no worries on that score."

"What?" sputtered Richard.

"You are making such a piece of work over marrying her off, when the answer is obvious—marry her yourself."

"Do you think I want to put up with her tricks the rest of my life?"

"It would not be a dull life, at any rate," Julia observed calmly.

"Besides, I could not take advantage of her like that. She trusts me."

"She more than trusts you. She would do anything to please you, including, unfortunately, marrying someone else."

"Justi cannot possibly love me after the way I have treated her."

"Haven't you seen the way she looks at you? Or are you as blind as she suggests?"

"I've seen it." Richard slumped into a chair. "I cannot marry her."

"Why not?"

"The same reason I should not marry at all," he said tiredly. "My abominable temper. No one should be subjected to it for a lifetime."

"I think no one would if you did marry," Julia stated. Richard frowned at her.

"I mean I think marriage is what you need . . . physically as well as—"

"I know what you mean, madam," he said with a snarl.

"And it's not as though Justi would mind an occasional little flare-up."

"No, she is used to them by now."

"Exactly," Julia said as she left him to change for dinner.

It wasn't many days after that, when Justi was returning from a ride with Harry and some friends, that Richard decided to sound her out on the subject of her suitors.

"Could I see you for a few minutes?" he said from the study doorway. "Don't look so. You haven't done anything."

She sat down and laid her whip and hat on the table. He thought she looked very fetching in her new red habit.

"I have had an offer for you I wanted to discuss, several, in fact. Teasdale came only today . . ."

"Teasdale? But he's so old."

"Young Rushley has also spoken . . ."

"Too young."

He began to pace but still had his temper well under control. "Captain Maitland, of course, is . . ."

"Too stiff."

"Haversham."

"Too short."

"Let me guess, Marsh is too tall. I think I see a pattern here. What about Mr. Darnley?"

"Too—I don't believe I know a Darnley."

"You don't." He leaned over the back of her chair. "I just made him up."

"Too ephemeral, then."

"Justi, stop it," he said in exasperation. "There is also Trilby."

"So, his mother brought him up to scratch. I thought so."

"There's a lot to be said for Trilby."

"Such as?"

"At least he would not beat you."

"No, I suppose not," Justi said sadly.

"You have to choose someone."

"Because you won't stand this nonsense for another year?" She looked at him bleakly.

"It's not that. What is likely to change in a year? The same men will be here, a few younger ones perhaps. But you've made it plain you don't want a young husband."

"I suppose you are right." She wasn't playful anymore, but sadly serious. "What should I do?"

Richard couldn't bring himself to name a man. None of them was right for her. "Is there no one you can like?"

"Yes, but he does not think of me in that way." She looked at him, biting her lip.

"Who is he? Do I know him?"

"Yes, but I had better say no more."

"He's not ineligible? Married?"

"No, he is perfect, but I think he has no thought even to marry, and if he did, it certainly wouldn't be me."

Reaching the end of his rope, Richard advanced on her. "Either quit breaking your heart over this fellow or make a push to get his attention, for God's sake."

Justi blinked. "Is that allowed?"

"Of course, so long as you don't make a fool of yourself."

"I had not thought of it. But I suppose it is sound advice." She rose to leave, feeling in better spirits than she had for some time. Richard wasn't going to force her to marry someone she could not like. And there was still a chance she might win him.

Richard could almost see Justi's fertile mind coming alive with ideas. He knew a moment of misgiving about what his intrepid cousin might invent in the way of mantraps. He only hoped they would not be too outrageous. He even felt a vague sympathy for the unknown fellow to be the object of this campaign. He was not conceited enough to imagine it was himself.

Chapter Twelve

"So, it's true, Rabbit," a voice Justi dreaded said from behind her.

She raised her chin, took a deep breath and coolly asked, "What's true?" She took another sip of her champagne as she turned to confront her enemy. "Gerard." She feigned polite surprise. "I didn't know you were in London."

"We hardly travel in the same circles, do we, Lady Justine?"

"I wonder that you are here tonight, then." Her graceful arm swept to indicate the crowded ballroom.

"I came in through the back door. I had to see you. I can't believe you mean to pass yourself off as an eligible young lady."

She laughed knowingly, as Clara had taught her. The most dangerous mistake she could make would be to show her fear of him. "That's not very complimentary. Do I still look like the boy you taught a year ago?"

"Not at all." He stepped back to survey the primrose silk gown, the upswept hair adorned by a single rose and the sparkling eyes regarding him through half-closed lashes. "I wouldn't have recognized you, except for your voice. You are, in fact, lovely, quite lovely."

She nodded a polite thank-you, but she had heard such compliments before.

"If only I'd known you were so lovely." He took her hand and kissed it. She did not flinch. "I don't think I would have given you up quite so readily."

She slid her hand away. "What else could you have done?" She asked as though she was merely curious.

"Finished my seduction of you, of course." His voice was as caressing as a snake. "If I had done so, your guardian would have had to let us marry."

"Do you really think so?" She drained her glass and set it down. Where was her plaguey court when she needed them?

"You do find me attractive," he whispered.

She regarded him speculatively, the fair face where too much drink was already leaving its telltale marks. "Well, perhaps...your accent. But recollect I have seen you at your worst."

"You drove me to it."

She laughed. "Thwarted love? Come now."

"It is lucky I didn't go ahead and spread that tale I threatened Mallory with."

"Yes, you would have looked a proper fool."

"Now I could tell a quite different story." He came close beside her to speak into her ear. She fingered the necklace at her throat, absently, it seemed. "A story of our love and the cruelty of the man who tore me from you."

"Well, yes, I suppose you could." She looked at him sideways. "But do you really think you should? At best, they will believe me that there was nothing between us, which coincidentally is the truth. At worst, they might think that you raped an innocent girl. That would not look well for you."

"I do not think your so estimable guardian will take the chance."

"What did he pay you the first time?"

"You mean besides my paltry salary? Two hundred."

Justi raised one eyebrow.

"I shall ask for more this time."

"He won't pay you again."

"He was quite reasonable last time."

"Yes, but that's when he believed you." She tapped his arm with her folded fan. "Since then he has spoken of rending you limb from limb if he gets his hands on you."

"We'll see."

She met his challenging look with a confidence she didn't feel.

"There you are, Justi. I'm supposed to take you down to supper, remember?" Harry approached from the crowd.

"Harry, let me introduce to you an old acquaintance, Gerard Dumont. Harry Mallory."

"How do you—Gerard?" Harry withdrew the automatically extended hand. "You're not that tutor?"

"Yes, the same." Gerard looked on his guard.

"Well, of all the nerve."

"Adieu, Lady Justine, Monsieur Mallory." Gerard bowed circumspectly and left.

"Harry, I was never more glad to see you than just now."

"I should think so. Perhaps I should have called him out. What do you think?"

"I'm not properly acquainted with those rules, but I think that would have been wrong unless he offered me some insult."

"Never tell me he sought you out to apologize."

"No, to gloat, I suppose."

"Well, I'm telling Richard."

"Please don't. He has so much on his mind. I hate to bother him with this. Ten to one we shall never see the fellow again."

Justi filed Gerard's new threat away at the back of her mind. She had more important matters to deal with. If she could win Richard, nothing Gerard said would matter.

Justi covertly watched Richard with other women. She could content herself with one thing. If he seemed indifferent to her, he was completely impervious to them. He might flatter and charm them, but not the most dashing of the beauties he encountered made the slightest dent in his composure.

"He flirts well, doesn't he?" Mrs. Fairchild said at her shoulder.

"Is that a talent to be admired? It seems such a pointless game. He says things he does not mean to women he scarcely knows for no particular reason. A conversation about the weather would have more value. They deny his compliments and call him a rogue, and make simpering fools of themselves."

"Forgive him. He must be light on his feet now. Since he has a title, he is more at peril than ever."

"I had not realized. I did that to him." Justi was resting on a small sofa with her new intimate while Harry went to fetch lemonade. Harry scarcely left her alone at dances now. It was a little irksome and was causing some talk but it was sweet of him to worry so much for her.

"How long have you been in love with him?"

Justi jumped, and turned from watching Richard lead another through the steps of a dance she longed to perform with him. "Am I so obvious?"

"You are certainly jealous, and you haven't answered my question," Mrs. Fairchild continued.

"I suppose I started to like him when he took care of me. I hurt my leg falling off a carriage. We have had many fights since then. But when did I love him first? I think when he hurt his back and was so helpless. His pride was hurt, too, and I had to be so careful not to wound him further, yet manage to keep him from getting up."

"You sound almost as though you were married already."

"That is how I think of him, and from time to time I almost thought he cared in that way, too. But he has been at great pains to marry me to someone else, so his regard must be otherwise.

"He is a great fool if he does not marry you, and so I shall tell him."

Justi laughed. "I would do much to win him, but no one tells Richard what to do. It merely sets his back up."

"What are you going to do, then?"

"Take his advice. Try to get his attention."

If Mrs. Fairchild had known Justi better, such a statement might have worried her. Instead, she settled back to watch a green girl try to win a man they had stopped taking bets on.

As the season advanced, plans went forward for the masked ball. Alicia chose to dress as Shakespeare's heroine, Juliet. Clara would be Madame de Pompadour. Richard raised an eyebrow but said nothing. Julia said she would merely wear a domino over her gown, and Richard was condemned for a spoilsport when he said his only disguise would be a mask.

He vetoed Saint Joan for Justi, but she was not set on this choice since it might be a bore to spend the whole evening in doublet and armor. She did say something also about Sappho that sent him off to the library. He returned some hours later and mouthed one word, no. Justi merely shrugged. She was sitting at the desk in the drawing room writing out the invitations.

"You have met a lot of men since you came here. Is there not one who interests you?"

"These people, the vicar would say they are like the lilies of the field. They toil not, neither do they spin. Is their only purpose sport, gossip and intrigue?"

Richard thought for a minute. "I am one of them."

"No, not anymore. That's why you must understand that I could never be like that, not only that. Not when I've known a life with so much more substance."

"Before I met you, my life made sense to me," Richard said. "I thought I was making a good job of it, managing my family and the estate. You made me see how shallow our way of life is."

She looked at him in sympathy and understanding. "I'm sorry, Richard, but look what you did to me. I was happy at Homeplace, at least I thought I was. You gave me a family and made me realize how empty my life had been. Now you tell me I have to leave it, and I feel lonely already."

"To marry, to start a family of your own."

"To go away with a stranger."

"Would you really rather not have known?"

"No matter how much I regret anything, I would never wish not to have known you, all of you. This has been the best year of my life." She hesitated a little before asking, "What about you?"

"Yes, I'd rather know the worst, always, even about myself," Richard concluded.

"I find that a little hard to believe," she said, laughing, "having seen you in more than one of your rages."

"I didn't say I wouldn't be angry. I just said I'd rather know the truth."

"Next time I have bad news for you, perhaps I'll write you a letter."

"Coward."

"I'm a woman now. No one expects me to be brave."

"Harry's right. You are as unscrupulous as Clara."

To Justi's surprise, Richard appeared dressed for riding as she finished her early tea the next morning.

"Didn't you go out last night?"

"No, I thought I had better rest up for the ball. Julia is sure to think of a dozen last-minute jobs for me. But she's not up yet, so let us enjoy a good ride."

Justi rather liked trotting through the empty streets to the park. It gave her a feeling of getting a jump on the day. Bluedevil made it a little more exciting than usual by pretending to spook at a carrier's cart, and then a cat shooting across the street, but he quickly settled under Richard's iron grip. They had a good gallop then, if a short one, and walked the horses for a while on the trails, not saying anything.

The last time they had ridden alone together was their last morning at Homeplace, the ride that was a goodbye present from Richard. She shuddered to think she might never go back there again. Justi stole a look at his face. It was more tired now. His eyes were troubled. She began to wonder if this ride was by way of being another farewell and was about to ask him what was wrong when she heard hoofbeats overtaking them.

A little "Damn!" escaped her, and she looked anxiously at Richard. He seemed merely puzzled, not censorious.

"Captain Maitland," she said. "Good morning."

"Good morning, Justine. You are out early, Lord Mallory."

"For once."

"Yes, this town life is debilitating. If it were not for my duties I would never come near London."

Twenty minutes spent in conversation with the captain served to set the crease between Richard's brows into what Justi imagined was a nagging headache. Maitland frequently had that effect on her.

"Tired?" Richard asked her finally.

"Yes, yes, I think I am tired," she agreed eagerly.

"I don't know how you manage it, Justine, to dance till all hours and still be about so early," said Maitland.

"No doubt the resilience of youth," observed Richard.

"Tomorrow, then?"

"Perhaps," Justi said.

"Is he on his way to a parade?" Richard asked when Maitland had left them at the park entrance.

"No, I don't think so. He always dresses like that."

"How do you stand that fellow?" Richard complained.

"I used to think my patience nearly infinite. It's surprising how often he uses it up."

"I had no idea . . . Justine."

She sneered at him. "What's even more shocking is that he's the best of the lot."

Richard eyed her in disbelief.

They returned to find Miriam and Sandford waiting with the family in the breakfast parlor. Miriam looked confusedly at the fashionable young lady who embraced and kissed her. Sandford shyly accepted a kiss on the cheek. His expression of wonder was even more diverting than the look on his face the day he'd discovered her identity.

"I can't believe it," Miriam said, at last.

"They have done wonders, don't you think?" Justi executed a turn for them. "But I didn't even know you were coming. I was worried you would miss our masquerade."

"There was one thing I couldn't miss."

Justi looked confused.

"Your birthday, silly."

"I forgot," she said, laughing.

After they had eaten and Justi had opened her presents, Richard looked thoughtful and drew a rather crumpled letter from his pocket.

"Baird sent this down for you. He said you were to have it on your eighteenth birthday."

"Why, this is Grandfather's hand." She opened it and read quickly down the page.

"Mother! He knew! Perhaps not the whole time, but before he died, he knew I wasn't his heir. That's why he sent for Baird and changed his will. He says he knows he can rely on me to do the right thing."

Justi thrust the letter at her mother.

"That explains the rather strange wording of the will," Richard said. "The entailed part of the estate was left to Lord Mallory, the stud farm and library to Justi Mallory."

"Well, if that isn't the outside of enough," blurted Miriam, "to come back from the grave to deal us such a blow."

Even Justi had never seen Miriam incensed before and began to laugh. "It's all right, Mother."

"When I think of the shifts we were put to in order to conceal your identity. Never was there a more provoking man, living or dead!"

"You will be happy to know we are revenged on him, Mother. We gave it out that I was raised as a boy because of his eccentricity. Everyone in London thinks he died raving mad."

"Depend upon it. He would only think that a very good joke."

"I begin to think," said Richard, "that I missed something by not calling on Great-Uncle while he was alive."

"Oh, you would never have gotten along," Justi said. "You're too much alike." He threw her a severe look, entirely worthy of the old earl.

As they were removing to the morning room, still laughing over the letter, Richard summoned Justi to the study. "I need to talk to you for a moment."

After she sat down he put some accounts into her hands. "Although I am still legally responsible for your affairs for the time being, I see no reason you should not manage your own income. Since your mother has asked that you go to stay with them for a time, there is no real need for you to marry this year if you do not wish it." He paced to the window.

She looked at him, dumbfounded. "I'm not to go to Amberly, then?" she asked sadly.

"Why, yes, of course, for Christmas we will all gather there. I imagine you will be staying in Sandford's house, though."

She looked at her lap and fought back tears. "And after that?"

He looked at her and said carelessly, "I believe your mother has some idea of taking you to Europe if this war ever ends. No doubt you will make quite a hit there with your knowledge of languages."

"But I don't want to go to Europe."

"You didn't want to come to London, but you seem to manage to amuse yourself here."

"I thought that's what you wanted. I would as soon be at Homeplace."

"We both know that is not possible. You may visit it with your mother if you want to check up on my management of the stud farm, or when you are married," he said almost bitterly.

"You're cutting me loose. Why?"

"Isn't that what you wanted?" He turned to look out the window.

"Yes— No— I mean..." She bit her lip. "It's all a bit sudden. I want to thank you for everything you've done, or tried to do."

"No matter. You have been by far the least worrisome of my charges. Now I imagine your mother is waiting to talk to you." He left the study abruptly.

Braden came in to find Justi still sitting on the small sofa, staring into the empty grate.

"Anything the matter, Justi?"

"Why, no, I suppose not."

"It's just...Richard looked so awful when he passed me."

"Did he? We were not fighting, for once, if that's what you mean. Perhaps we need to. It does seem to clear the air."

As she went up the grand stairs that had once seemed so foreign to her, Justi wondered why Richard looked awful.

It was his decision to set her free, unless Sandford had something to do with it. Why would he look awful over that? She would have thought he would be glad to get rid of her. Unless perhaps he would miss her, too. Was it just possible that under his so tightly controlled exterior Richard cared more than he let her know?

The receiving line at the Mallory town house that night was a study in diversity. Alicia looked charming with her long gold hair unbound except for a demure cap, and the high-waisted deep blue velvet gown truly became her. Clara was magnificent, and because of the height of her white powdered wig, towered over all of them, but she confessed to Justi that it was rather hot.

Justi was wearing a long, loose, creamy Greek chiton, bound at the waist with gold rope. Gold sandals adorned her feet, and ribbands of gold wound through her upswept hair. She looked like she had stepped off an ancient vase. When she stood with one foot slightly forward, her bare toes peeked out from under the robe, her bent knee showed sharply through the filmy fabric, and her thigh muscle was well-defined. For once, the firm muscles of her arms were not disguised with a shawl or gloves, but adorned with gold arm bands.

Richard wondered that Justi could so easily don a costume from another century and feel at home in it until he remembered that she had undergone an even more startling transformation. Stepping from boots and pantaloons into muslin gowns with the small puffed sleeves that were in vogue must have been even more unnerving.

"That Greek thing Justi is wearing is much too revealing," Richard whispered to Julia.

"You said she might be a goddess for all you cared. You should have asked to see the costume beforehand. It's been ready for weeks."

"All her other choices seemed so much worse." Suddenly it occurred to him that if the costume had been ready for weeks, he had been very subtly manipulated. Justi had never intended to come as any of those other outrageous people she had suggested. Richard laughed in spite of himself, then became rather sad.

Where had she learned such subterfuge? He could remember a time when that innocent look was genuine, when she was no more aware of her effect than a child. He couldn't help but feel that he was responsible for killing something very precious in her. To think that it would have happened sooner or later was no comfort to him.

Watching her dance now reminded him of that day he watched her ice-skating in January when she first aroused his longing. He realized with a start that he had not managed to cure himself of his desire for her. If anything, it had gotten worse. It was as well she was going away. Seeing her in anyone's arms but Harry's brought him to a cold sweat.

Harry had borrowed a guardsman's uniform from one of his friends at the last minute, and was feeling rather dashing.

"I rather like this. What do you think, Richard? Maybe I should enlist."

"God save us! Are you mad?"

"Lord, Richard. You used to be able to take a joke."

"Where's Justi?" Richard glanced around in a panic. "She was dancing with some Spanish fellow I didn't know."

"Calm down. I'll look for her."

Gerard had no sooner grabbed Justi's arm and led her into a dance than she guessed who was behind the crimson mask.

"Do you have any idea how hard it is to get near you?"

"How could I? I quite thought you had left town. Really, Gerard. Don Juan? Is that how you see yourself?"

"I suppose you are something Greek."

"Don't you recognize Athena, the goddess of wisdom? I wanted to come as Diana, but Harry wouldn't hear of it since I am such a deplorable shot."

"I have thought of nothing but you since we last met."

"Really? I haven't thought of you at all."

"Let me tell you something that will keep me in your thoughts. *La Petite Innocent!*"

"What?" She was glad of her mask, but knew it had not covered the shock in her voice.

"Come. We cannot talk here."

He led her out of the ballroom, down the hall toward the back of the house and opened a door at random. The morning room was lit but not occupied. He pulled her in and said, "I did quite well off that book you translated, *La Petite Innocent.* I have another for you to do."

"Are you mad? I won't. You can't make me work for you anymore."

"You had better stay on good terms with me, for it is me you will have in the end."

"Certainly not."

"Then I will ruin you. I have only to reveal the identity of the translator."

"Who would believe you?"

"As you said yourself once, it doesn't matter so much what the truth is. What matters is what people are willing to believe. And I think they will be willing to believe you translated it. Someone is sure to ask Meecham, and he will tell them. Then you will be ruined. You will have to come with me."

Justi was thinking furiously. She could not agree to do as Gerard demanded, deceive Richard again. She realized he not only meant to blackmail her for the rest of her life, but actually make off with her.

"Is it agreed? Once the tale is set about, no man of breeding will ever marry you."

Justi's face lit up. "But that is exactly what I want," she said on impulse.

"What?"

"If no one else will marry me, then Richard will feel he has to. It's perfect. I could not have planned it better myself. When will you set it about?" she asked eagerly.

"Now see here—"

The door jerked open. "There you are," Harry said with relief. "Richard was worried . . ." Harry saw the Spaniard's hand instinctively flinch toward his sword hilt.

"Don't tell me," said Harry, drawing his saber, "Gerard."

"Harry, no!"

Justi jumped as the blades clashed together. Gerard employed the same tactics on Harry as he had on her, attempting to back Harry into furniture and trip him up. Unfortunately, Gerard had not been drinking, and it soon became apparent that he was more than a match for Harry.

Justi looked around for some weapon she could use as Harry toppled another chair and Gerard pierced the cushion with his rapier. Had she been a normal girl she might have run into the hall to cry for help. As it was she could only think that she must do something to keep Harry from being killed. She moved to the small table by the sofa.

Richard entered to find Harry on the floor disarmed, Don Juan pointing his sword at him and Justi inserting her hand into a vase, to swing it hard against the back of the victor's head.

"Crude, but effective," was Richard's judgment as the masked swordsman crumbled onto the carpet.

Justi started guiltily. "He's drunk. Where are those footmen when you actually need them?" she asked, flushing.

"Come out of this mess. We'll call them. Harry? Are you all right?"

"Go. I'll clean up in here," Harry offered valiantly as he struggled to his feet.

"That was one of Julia's favorite vases," Richard reprimanded Justi as he steered her out of the room.

"Don't you think she would rather have her son unscathed?"

Richard ordered two footmen from the front of the hall to help Harry evict the unwanted guest, and he didn't seem the least bit curious about the man's identity.

"Surely, he wouldn't have wounded Harry."

"I never trust anyone who's had too much."

Richard took her to the salon set up with refreshments and handed her a glass of wine. "No, I know you don't like it, but drink it anyway."

She sipped the claret slowly.

"So, you had a close call. How did he get you to go with him?"

"I thought it would be better than making a scene." She looked innocently up at him over the brim of the glass.

"A scene! As opposed to a duel fought in the morning room with pottery shards all over the carpet. I suppose I should be thankful there wasn't bloodshed, as well."

Justi laughed weakly. "I had not thought of it like that."

"I have a feeling my life will become quite dull once you go out of it."

She looked at him as openly and invitingly as she could, but he only turned quite cold again.

"By the by, I don't want to see that dress on you again."

Try as she might Justi could not twist his statement to mean that he wanted to see her out of it. "Why ever not? It is not low cut."

"It reveals your arms too much."

"I did have a few qualms about that, but the arm bands disguise my muscles."

"It's the fabric," he complained. "I can see every move you make in it."

"That is true of half of the women in the room. Why are you so conscious of it with me?"

"Because I am responsible for you," Richard blustered.

"You do want to get rid of me?" Justi countered.

"Yes— No! Not like this."

"You are sure you cannot stomach Maitland?" She was toying with her wineglass now.

"Never!"

"I cannot manage any of the rest of them." She sighed with a pout, setting the glass on a table.

"What game are you playing?" Richard demanded in a whisper.

"Game?"

"You have learned far too many female tricks since I brought you up to town."

"But isn't that what you wanted? It is my only occupation now—being a woman. I may as well be good at it."

"But you don't like it," Richard probed.

"No," Justi said truthfully and looked him in the eye. "It is a game, as you say, but one where people get hurt. I don't like it."

Richard was spellbound. The face that looked at him was neither female nor male, but Justi, some unique creation who could bounce between the two sexes in a reality of her own making. Yet she was real enough to touch, and he almost, in his trancelike state, did so. But he caught himself.

"Let us leave off this game," Justi begged, "and speak frankly for once. Do you care for me at all?"

"Of course I care about you," Richard said with a dry mouth.

"That's not what I meant and you know it." She stamped her small foot. "Do you love me the way you loved Evelyn?"

"No!" he said as though to push the repellent thought from him.

Justi gave a small gasp. "I see," she said bravely, when she was able to speak. Her face looked empty, as though this was the answer she had feared.

"I never loved Evelyn," Richard groaned.

Justi's face lit as she turned this around in her mind. Richard thought she had never been so beautiful.

"But I cannot marry you," he sighed.

"Why not?" she demanded. "If you never loved her you cannot still be grieving, except for your son."

"I am no good with children. I fear I might hurt them. Witness what I did to you."

"I think you would make an excellent father—but not to me."

Richard stood speechless so long Justi asked, "What are you thinking? I never know. You are as much a mystery to me as the first day I met you."

"I was thinking of my father and how he used to beat me."

"Why? You have scarcely ever spoken of him."

"Because I am very much like him. I hate myself for it, but I cannot help it."

Suddenly his face went hard again. It was like a door shutting Justi on the outside. "A very good ruse, child," Richard said with a cold smile. "You almost had me."

"What?" she gasped.

"It's really the only way you can get Homeplace back. I almost forgot that."

It took a moment for the injustice of this to dawn on her. Then her dark brows drew together, and a look of the most elemental fury came over her face. She called him something extremely vile in gutter German and walked away from him looking very like an enraged goddess.

Richard breathed a sigh of relief that she had not used her fists on him.

Justi went riding as usual the next morning with Haimes in attendance. Captain Maitland had obviously been waiting at the entrance to Hyde Park.

"You should not have kept your horse standing for me, sir."

"There are times when these beasts can wait on our comfort, my dear. I am being sent with my regiment to Spain," he said abruptly, as they began to trot down the ride.

"And you want my answer," she guessed sadly, "to know if I will be coming with you or not."

"Certainly not! A war train is no place for a woman, even such a capable one as you. But I do wish to marry you and install you at Haverstock before I leave."

"You make me sound like a piece of furniture, sir," she said unhappily.

"You are not like these other misses, to demand fancy words from a soldier like me. We have spoken bluntly enough to each other for me to know you bear the same contempt for this life that I do."

"I have a very great regard for you, sir. If it were not for the existence of someone I dearly love, I would be honored to accept your offer, but I would insist on going with you to Spain."

"And I would insist that you remain in England."

"I think we know each other well enough to know we are each unmovable on some matters. Our married life would consist of many more battles than this war you are engaged in, each of us insisting on doing as we thought best and torturing the other. It will not do, sir."

"But you have always seemed so sensible to me." He slowed his mount to a walk.

"I have perhaps misled you by always being on my best behavior with you. If you knew me better you would never consider me a suitable wife."

"I wish you would reconsider your position."

"I have spent many sleepless nights considering my position and I have decided that if I cannot marry the man I love I will not marry at all. I may be miserable myself, but that is no excuse for me to ruin someone else's life, particularly someone I regard so highly.''

"I suppose there is no more to be said then," said Maitland stoically. "I won't see you again before I go.''

"You will be careful, won't you?" Justi asked, dropping her formal tone.

"Careful?" he asked with a wry smile. "My dear, you are talking to a veteran.'' He cantered off with a wave.

She could never decide from this last speech if he meant he was always careful, or if he meant it was a stupid question—that there was no possibility he could be such a thing as careful. She had never understood soldiers. But that was no surprise. She did not understand Richard.

Perhaps war did something to them. If Richard had gone off to Spain she would gladly have gone with him. The only thing that made London bearable at all was his presence. Even Homeplace without Richard would not be home anymore. The thought that in future she might not get to see him more than once or twice a year left her so desolate she cut her ride short and went back to the house.

After she had changed Justi went to the drawing room feeling very depressed and sat down at the piano. If there were no callers, like today, she would play while Julia and Alicia sewed in the morning room.

"Justi, not this morning, I think," Julia whispered from the doorway.

"Aren't you well, Julia?" Justi asked, following her into the morning room.

"No, dear, it's Richard. There was a terrible scene this morning. That Frenchman came. What is his name? The one who tutored you.''

"Gerard came here?" Justi went pale.

"It was amazing," said Clara. "I've heard of someone being thrown out of a house, but this is the first time I actually saw it done. So nice having Richard mad at someone other than one of us for a change."

"I believe you're enjoying it, Clara," Alicia accused.

"How could I not? Do you suppose Richard will ever tell us what it's all about?"

"Anyone with ears, including the servants, knows he came here for money. I don't know how I shall face them." Julia sat down again and covered her eyes.

"Did Richard send for me?" Justi whispered.

"No," said Alicia, her eyes big with concern. "He just shut himself up in the study and won't talk to anyone. He sent Braden to work in the breakfast parlor."

"Perhaps I should try to talk to him," Justi offered, although she was far from feeling courageous enough to do so.

"Oh, please keep out of his way," Julia begged. "I've had more than I can take for one day without having to listen to him thunder at you."

No one but Clara had much appetite for lunch, even though Richard did not join them. Harry must have had the good sense to dine at his club. After Clara asked her for the third time if she didn't know what was going on, Justi asked to be excused.

She spent the afternoon in her room, pacing and waiting for the inevitable summons. She now wished she had gone to see Richard immediately. Anything would have been preferable to the waiting. Much better, of course, to have told him about the book months ago, but somehow it seemed so much worse than anything else she had done. And it was nice to have him pleased with her for a change. Much better still not to have translated the damn thing in the first place, but that was beyond help, and all for the sake of a hundred pounds, which probably did not last Gerard a month.

She would surely have to leave this time. No one could
forgive such a deception, not even Richard. Tomorrow
morning, very early, before her normal riding time, she
would steal out the back door and be on her way to the coast
before anyone woke up. Where she would sail off to really
depended on what ship was in the harbor. She did not particularly care. Nor did she take into account that England
was at war with half of Europe and that the situation
changed from day to day. She did not even know what
countries would be safe to go to at that moment.

She called her maid to go with her to the bank, where she
drew some money for "shopping," then sent Emily on a
fictional errand while she ascertained from the hackney
driver when she could catch a mail coach for Portsmouth.

She planned to take nothing with her. She could obtain
clothes later. If only one of Harry's suits fit her, she would
be all right. She intended to resume her old identity, not to
throw off pursuit, but merely because she thought it safer to
travel that way. After this, she did not expect anyone to
come after her.

Richard's nonappearance at dinner was ominous. The
butler's attempt to interrupt Richard earned him a cursing.
Harry had returned, finally, and tried to joke everyone out
of the dismals throughout what seemed an interminable
meal. Justi had no heart to join the theater party that night
and insisted they go without her. Much as they hated to de-
sert her, the offer of a short escape from the tension in the
house could not be passed up. Harry escorted the rest of the
ladies to the waiting carriage, and Justi climbed the stairs to
her self-imposed exile.

She paced until she was tired out, then threw herself down
on the bed. She slept awhile, then woke to hear Julia's voice
in the hall. Emily came in to turn down her bed, but the
footman appeared to request her presence in the study "at
her convenience." Justi went down immediately. The butler opened the door for her but was his usual expressionless

self. She wondered how servants managed not to laugh at the predicaments their households got into.

"Sit down. This won't take long, but I wanted to catch you before you went to bed."

"I didn't go to the play tonight."

"Oh, I didn't know." Richard's eyes looked very tired, but he seemed to be in control of himself. "I wanted to prepare you for a rumor you might hear." He walked to the desk and dropped a thin, red-bound volume in front of her.

Her eyes flew to his face. He didn't know.

"I've read it, or most of it. It is a particularly gruesome example of this latest trend in pornography. Dumont intends to tell everyone you translated it. Of course, that's impossible. He must have done it himself. But if the idea was put about, it might be believed. It is unlikely that anyone who knows you well will give credence to the rumor, but there is bound to be talk, perhaps even a scandal." He paused and sat down.

For a moment, Justi teetered on the brink of not telling him. The woman she was becoming would have lied to him, she found to her surprise. It was that part of her that was still childlike that encouraged her to play fair for once.

"Justi, I have decided Dumont must be stopped. I'm sorry, I wanted you to have...so much. Time, for one thing, to decide what you wanted, to find someone. My advice to you now is to marry as quickly as possible."

"Richard, I can't," she whispered. Any thoughts of winning him were far from her mind now. She sought only to hurt him as little as possible. He had not believed Gerard this time. He had put his faith in her. Now it was time for her to crush it. Anything but the truth would be a betrayal, and the truth would drive a wedge between them forever.

"You can try to brave it out. You might even carry it off. I am no judge, anymore." He leaned back tiredly in the chair behind the desk.

"I can't marry anyone, because it's true, what he said."
She looked at him, wide-eyed but tearless.

"What?" Richard asked absently.

"I did translate the book." Once she said it she ignored
the growing look of horror on his face and stumbled on. "I
did it to keep him from blackmailing you. I didn't know it
wouldn't work. I never meant to hurt you."

He rose, looming over her, his face white with fury. "You
stooped to this after I forbade you to do such work again?"

"Yes, I could not see any way out of it," she answered
desperately.

He raised his hand, and she steeled herself for the blow,
but he remembered in time. "You! Get out of my sight!"

She would rather he had hit her. It wouldn't have hurt as
much. She stumbled from the room and numbly went to
bed, but sleep was far away, by a day, at least, and many
miles.

Chapter Thirteen

"What the devil?" Harry said, stumbling into his room in the dark, somewhat the worse for drink. "Justi! What are you doing in my clothes?"

"I have to leave, Harry. I've done it for good now. Richard will never forgive me."

"Now, now, sit down." He tripped and sat down on the bed. "You always say that, and he always forgives you."

"Not this time. He's found out about that book I translated."

"What book?"

"I forgot. I didn't tell you. Gerard sent me a book and demanded that I translate it for him."

"Really, when did you do that?"

"Harry, be quiet. You'll wake someone. I worked on it at night."

"What's it about?"

"You know those books I was translating from French."

Harry whistled. "What's it called?"

"Harry, stop it."

"No wonder he cut up so stiff."

"Harry, I really hurt him. I've seen Richard angry before, but this was different. He was speechless."

"Surely he'll get over it."

"Not this time. He'll never forgive me. He told me to get out of the house." She rose to leave. "I'll send your clothes back. I've got plenty of money. You've been a good friend to me, Harry." She hugged him. "I'll never forget you."

"No point in saying goodbye. I'm coming with you."

"Harry, you can't. Richard will be mad at you, too, then."

"He won't know where I've gone. Where are you headed, anyway?"

"Portsmouth, for now. I don't know yet where I'll go. It depends what ship I can get."

"I'll come as far as the coast, then." Harry had some idea of talking Justi out of her flight. If not, he should be able to stop her in the port. He was pretty sure she had not thought to apply for a passport.

"Harry, you can't just go jauntering off with no word to your mother."

"I'll leave her a note. I'll say I've gone to the races with Graham for a few days. Aren't you going to leave Richard a letter?"

"I think I've written far too much already. Besides, there's nothing left to say."

"Then pack me a clean shirt and neck cloth while I write this." Harry scrawled the note quickly, but it said nothing about Graham and managed to mention Portsmouth quite prominently. The sky was beginning to gray when they crept down the stairs and made good their escape toward the stables. Justi hesitated, then turned toward the building where they could hear the horses thumping quietly in their stalls.

"Fine. You don't even write your mother, and you have to stop to say goodbye to your horse," he whispered fiercely.

She shrugged and pushed the door open, and was immediately grabbed by two strong pairs of arms. She used fists, elbows and boot heels to some effect against her attackers, but didn't think to scream before she was knocked unconscious by a blow to the chin. Harry would have been of more use sober, but that would not have helped against the third assailant who caught him from behind with a cudgel.

"I thought you said we was after a girl, Dumont."

"This one, fools. Tie and gag her, then put her in the carriage, quickly."

"What about him?"

"Leave him. Mallory wouldn't pay anything to keep her name clean," he said to the unconscious Harry, as he dropped a screw of paper beside him, "let's see if he'll pay to get her back alive."

Justi did not come fully awake instantly. As she struggled to open her eyes, she noticed her hands felt numb and the sheet must be caught in her mouth. What's worse, everything seemed to be rocking precariously. She really began to wonder if she was drunk. Then an ugly laugh came from nearby, and in her struggle to get up she fell off the seat. Gerard undid the gag, picked her up and sat her on the seat.

"Do you know where you are?"

"What?" Her mouth was dried out.

"You're with me."

"Gerard? I can't remember."

"By now your estimable guardian should be scurrying about rounding up my money."

"What are you talking about? Why would he give you money now?"

"I'm holding you for ransom, you little fool."

"You wh—" She laughed hysterically, feigning an amusement she didn't really feel.

"What is so funny?" Gerard asked suspiciously.

"Your timing. That might have worked up until yesterday. He'll never pay you now. You see, I told him the truth this time, that I did translate the book."

"I don't believe you," Gerard said with a shrug.

Justi pushed herself straighter on the seat and tried to ease the pressure of the rope on her wrists. At least her feet were not tied. There might be some chance of escape.

"He was madder than I've ever seen him. I thought he was going to kill me. He gave me twenty-four hours to pack and leave."

Gerard looked at her doubtfully.

"Why else would I be dressed like this and sneaking out before dawn? He's not going to pay for a piece of trash he said he never wanted to see again."

Gerard was appalled. Things were not going at all as he had planned. "We'll see."

"Where are we going?" she asked him. Not, "Where are you taking me?"

"Dover, and it's only thanks to me that you are making the trip alive. My hirelings would have found it much easier to kill you." If he thought to make her cringe, or to regain control of the situation himself, he was out.

"That would be unwise. You could never then return to England."

"If he pays what I've asked, I won't need to."

"Perhaps I'll come with you. I was headed for France, anyway," she lied.

"No— I mean, I've no intention of dragging a lot of extra baggage with me. Besides, the money will last twice as long if I haven't you in tow."

"Why, Gerard, you're finally learning economy. I'm proud of you." She settled herself in the corner of the carriage with the apparent intention of going to sleep.

"If he doesn't pay, I'll simply marry you. I believe you have an income."

"Oh, enough for me." She yawned. "I'm afraid you would consider it paltry."

"But he will give it to you."

"You're off there. He's under no obligation to do so. It is his to use as he pleases, and if anything happens to me, he gets the capital and the income. Now that I think of it, he may not mind if you do kill me. He has only to go to the law and tell them who signed the note—you did leave him a ransom note, didn't you?''

"Yes—no, he won't call in the law." Things were moving too fast for Gerard. He truly regretted taking the gag off his now unwanted prisoner.

"In his present mood, nothing is more likely."

"I don't believe it."

"Recollect I know him better than you. Money means a great deal to him. Wasn't he willing to sell me to the highest bidder this season, a gamble he lost on?''

Since Gerard had no trouble attributing his own morals and motives to others, he was shaken, and beginning to regret the expense of his hirelings and even the chaise and pair that carried them. In fact, if his scheme did not work, he couldn't pay the ruffians their share, and he might fare worse at their hands than Justi.

"He'll pay. He has to. He may even come to get you. You had better hope so. I don't know how else you will get back.''

"The only reason Richard will come after us is if you've hurt Harry, and then it will only be to twist your head off.''

She really had no idea how badly Harry was hurt, and apparently neither did Gerard, since he lapsed into a brown study over the possibility of being pursued by Richard. She could not count on Harry being in any fit state to come after her. Then it crossed her mind that they might have killed him and it would be all her fault. She worried over Harry's fate so much, she began to wonder if she cared whether she escaped or not. She didn't think she could evade Gerard and whoever was driving, at least not with her hands tied.

But since Richard certainly wouldn't care what happened to her, she would have to make a push to help herself. That's how it was before he came along. She had always managed to take care of herself. How she came to depend upon him so much, she would never understand. Never again. He had made it plain she was on her own. But this thought made her so sad, she shivered a little, and shrank back into the corner of the chaise.

Since Justi was in the habit of riding early, Haimes made it a practice to go to the stable first thing in case her mare was called for. When he came across the unconscious Harry, he merely thought him to be sleeping off an excess of drink. It wasn't until Harry came to and remembered what had happened that Haimes could be induced to attend to the lump on the back of Harry's head. That's when Harry found the note and, headache or not, bolted for the house. He unceremoniously shook Richard awake and thrust the paper under his nose.

"What the devil?" When Richard could see properly he observed that Harry had a smear of blood on his face and split knuckles.

"Richard, he's taken Justi. We have to go after her now."

"Who's taken her? What are you talking about?"

"Gerard. Read it, for God's sake."

"How did this happen?" Richard began putting on the clothes Harry was flinging at him as he digested the contents of the note.

"She was running away again, and...and I decided to go with her to take care of her. Don't look at me like that. I thought I could talk her out of it."

"Not likely, once she's made her mind up. But why was she leaving?"

"You told her to, she said. Don't you ever listen to yourself in one of your tirades? Pretty convincing!"

"Oh, Lord." The memory of their last interview came back like the aftertaste of sour wine. "I didn't mean it. Why didn't you come and tell me, instead of abetting her?"

"Rat on her, with her looking like she had not a friend in the world, and trying to be so brave about it? Why didn't you marry her? Then none of this would have happened."

"But she can't love me." Richard paused before sliding on his breeches.

"Of course she does, even I know that." Harry unearthed a pair of pistols from Richard's bureau. "If you were not so stubborn you would marry her and make us all happy."

"I can't take advantage of her like that. I am old enough to be her father."

"Only if you were fathering babes when you were eleven or twelve. Will you get dressed, Richard? There's no time to lose. I was knocked out for nearly an hour."

"At least we know where they are headed—Dover." Richard flung the note into a corner and finished dressing by guess. "Harry, are you all right to drive?"

"Yes, of course." Harry looked up from loading the pair of pistols.

"I'll order the grays put to. I'll ride on ahead on Bluedevil. You follow with the curricle, fast as you safely can, do you understand?"

"Yes. Richard?"

"What?"

"You don't think he'll hurt her, do you?"

"Depends if he's drunk. Then he might do anything." Richard grimly took the pistols Harry handed him and stowed them in his pockets. They both made for the stable.

Justi awoke with a jerk when the coach stopped. Gerard's hand dashed to his pocket, and he drew out a pistol.

"Not one word," he commanded, pointing it at her.

"Don't be an idiot," she whispered. "If you fire that pistol in here it will attract a lot more attention than me shouting."

As the truth of this dawned on him, he moved over to her seat, and she wished she had not said anything. He put his hand around the back of her neck with his thumb under her chin, forcing her head up. He stared intently at her while the hostlers changed the horses. She hoped she didn't tremble in his grasp as she remembered all the evils of her captivity in the armory. She must have moved a little for he pressed her head back even farther. She was sure he could feel not only her breathing, but her pounding pulse.

Justi closed her eyes to shut out his face and wondered just how serious he was. Gerard might be stupid enough to manipulate to some extent, but she had no doubt he would hurt her without compunction if her escape failed. She couldn't believe she had fallen asleep with him a few feet away. However much she threw him off balance with her verbal fencing, he was still incredibly dangerous.

When the team had been changed and they lurched forward again, he took his hand away but remained beside her. She was feeling light-headed and weak. She slid as far into the corner as she could and pretended to resume her interrupted nap.

She had, for the tenth time, devised a plan only to discard it for lack of information. Even if she could manage to evade Gerard at the next stop, she didn't know if the driver was armed. Her guess was that the man was, and would not hesitate to shoot her. They would have to put up some place in Dover. Maybe some opportunity would come to her then.

"Halt!" a gruff voice shouted beside the road. This was followed by a shot, a yelp from the driver's seat, and the jerky stopping of the chaise.

"Halt, I say."

Justi recognized the harsh but beloved voice, and her heart gave a leap of joy. Not only wasn't she alone in this, but Richard still cared enough to come after her.

"Everybody out! Now!"

"Damnation!" Gerard cocked his pistol and thrust it in his pocket. "Stay here and keep quiet," he whispered to Justi. He jumped to the ground and slammed the carriage door shut. Justi could barely see him through the slit of the blind, facing the blowing great black horse with his hand in his pocket. "I have little money," he complained, beginning to withdraw his hand.

If Richard's pistol was covering the men on the box, and Harry wasn't out there backing him up, he could be in trouble. Justi slid off the seat, managed to turn the door handle and lunged out at Gerard's back. His gun went off harmlessly in his coat and they both landed on the road in a heap.

"Don't move," Richard warned the hirelings as he slid off Bluedevil and pulled off his mask. Gerard struggled up first, but Richard knocked him off his feet with one backhanded blow.

"Are you hurt?" he asked, as he slid a knife from his boot and cut her bonds, still keeping one eye on his prisoners.

"No." She shook her head, the dark hair falling over her eyes.

"Good, shoot if they so much as move." She took the pistol from him, and for the first time was glad that she had some idea how to handle it.

Gerard was struggling up again, a mistake on his part. Richard systematically proceeded to give him such a brutal beating that even Justi, who had ample reason to hate the man, cried, "Enough. Don't kill him, Richard. He isn't worth it."

"Get on Bluedevil," Richard commanded her, taking the pistol.

Justi mounted the still heavily breathing horse and slid behind the saddle so Richard could get on. She held Richard tightly around the waist as they cantered back the way they had come.

Richard halted the blowing animal as soon as they were out of sight of the chaise, and slid off. "I've ridden him nearly to death."

"Let's walk him. I'm tired of riding," Justi said, sliding off into Richard's arms. "You came."

"Of all the damn fool starts! Did you imagine I wouldn't come after you?"

"I wouldn't have blamed you if you had not. Oh, Harry—is he hurt badly?"

"No, in fact, he should be on his way now with my curricle. At least one of you knows how to take orders."

"Most likely he just didn't want to pass up a chance to drive your grays."

She surprised a bark of laughter out of him. They walked on in silence for a minute.

"Richard, do you hate me?" she whispered.

"I'm responsible for you. It's my job to pull you out of these stupid scrapes. I could wish you didn't fall into quite so many of them."

"But do you hate me?"

"Never!" He embraced her then, by way of convincing her, and kissed her in a way that had nothing to do with being her guardian.

They were both nearly knocked down by Bluedevil trying to scratch his sweaty brow on their shoulders. They laughed, and scratched and praised the heroic animal.

"I should have known you translated that god-awful book."

"Oh—how?" She looked at him in that innocent way he imagined she would always have.

"Dumont would have been far too lazy."

"I'm sorry, Richard. After all your work, I've spoiled everything."

"Yes, I'm afraid you're ruined. It's broad daylight."

"Oh, I don't care for that."

"That's the problem. You really don't care, do you?"

"Only because it matters to you. That's why I did all of this, to make you happy, but nothing ever turns out right for me, even though I always mean well."

"There's only one thing to be done."

She stopped walking and turned to face him, ready to accept exile to the smallest island in the North Sea.

"If I let you marry any of the men who have offered for you, there would be one scandal after another. And I know your mother and Sandy couldn't keep you in line. I shall have to marry you myself."

"Richard, do you mean it?" She flung herself on him just as Harry drove up.

"It's the only way I can see to keep you out of trouble. But I am still afraid I might hurt you in one of my rages."

"Nonsense! You have not murdered me as yet. We surely can have nothing left to fight over."

"So, you've finally made it up?" Harry laughed, reining in the team.

"Decide to push them on one more stage, eh?" Richard asked as he disentangled himself from Justi.

"Well—yes," Harry said doubtfully.

"Quite right."

"Harry, Richard is going to marry me."

"Well, it's about time. I am the first to wish you happy."

"I'm afraid I can't afford to take you anyplace exotic for a honeymoon, at least not for a while."

"You know where I want to go."

"Yes, Homeplace."

"Oh, there's one thing," interposed Harry.

"What?" asked Richard, looking up from his betrothed.

"Do I still get to come for the shooting in the fall?"

Richard threw his whip at Harry's head. "Yes, provided you walk Bluedevil back while I drive Justi. We'll rest at Maidstone. It's only a few miles."

"Richard, you're going to let Harry ride Bluedevil?"

"He's too tired to kill the boy today, and so am I."

Epilogue

Richard awoke with Justi's warm flesh against his chest. She still had that look, in sleep, of total innocence after all she had been through. He didn't move, but watched her sleep. He wanted to be with her every minute. It physically hurt if she was out of his sight for too long. He was sure the first few intense months of their marriage had amused and intrigued all the servants. Quite unfashionably, he and Justi shared a bedroom and stayed together the night through, when they slept. Firth and Emily quickly got used to the notion of not coming into the bedroom until someone had rung for them.

Justi woke up, as always, with a look of disbelief and wonder as though she feared it had all been a dream. She kissed him, then slid down under the covers to arouse him. She crawled on top of him and rode him until they were both panting with relief and delight.

The first time he had felt her strong internal muscles squeezing him, he had been amazed. No other woman had ever aroused him to that extent, and certainly none had ever so satisfied him before. She also made love with candor and a sense of fun he had never experienced. He felt vulnerable when they had finished, with every nerve jangling at the slightest touch of her hair or breasts. But Justi played fair and didn't torture him unduly in getting out of bed.

After she washed up and crawled back under the covers, she pressed herself against his back to warm him. He used to think she was running a fever, as she seemed to always be hotter than him. She laid her arm along his thigh and breathed a sigh of contentment as she rested her cheek against his shoulder blade. She seemed to need these last few minutes close to him each morning to reaffirm their bond.

Eventually, they dragged themselves from bed, put on their robes and rang for hot water. Temporarily, Justi used her old room as a dressing room. Richard had half a mind to add a passage, but this was the end of the house where he wanted to add a new wing, so they would have to open the end of the hall. He was taking great care with the design of their sleeping apartment in the new wing, and the nursery.

The first floor would house a large salon, which could be used as a ballroom, and a larger dining room. The ground floor would be given over to a much-needed new kitchen. He showed Justi his plans after breakfast, and she poured over his first rough sketches with excitement.

"Once we move into the new wing," he pointed out, "we can close off the northwest rooms and have the chimney rebuilt."

"Can we have a circular drive like at Amberly?"

"Yes, if you like."

"Homeplace will look so much more inviting. And windows—tall windows."

"As many as you like," he said, folding her in his arms.

As they rode into Brinley, Richard said, "We may not be able to start the new wing for a year or two, yet."

"I don't care how long it takes. In fact, I don't want much company for a while."

"We'll have Harry with us in the fall."

"Just the three of us. It will be like old times."

"Well, not quite the same. Harry had better be able to entertain himself. The one thing I was thinking of doing next year was going to Ireland for a new stud. We can keep the best of the mares out of Darvin and start a line with the new stud."

"Without having to buy more mares. Why didn't I think of that?"

"Because you couldn't afford even the stud, and neither can we right now. At present, about all we can do is have the ivy pulled down and the stones repointed."

"A good start. We wouldn't want the children climbing out the windows." This vague reference to children brought a sharp look from him. He was pretty sure she was pregnant, but wondered why she had not said anything yet. She certainly knew all there was to know about such things.

They collected the post when they were in Brinley and rode back by way of the oak wood. As always, this spot, more than any other on Homeplace, brought a peace to Justi that Richard now shared. They dismounted and walked through the mature ferns to one of the fallen oaks.

"I was thinking of having Gray Dawn bred."

"What brought this on?"

"Well, I won't be riding her much for a while. It will give her something to do while I am pregnant and nursing."

"You wretch." He spun her around to face him and hugged her to him. "What a way to tell me."

"I could have written you a letter."

He kissed her unmercifully and sat her down on a bed of ferns against a giant log. They opened their letters. Justi had not read far before she groaned, "Oh, no. Julia says Clara has run off to marry Sir Emery Poole. She washes her hands of her."

"Really?" Richard scarcely looked up.

"Really. Is that all you have to say?"

"What do you want me to say? It's not as though she needs my consent."

"Nothing, of course, but I can remember a time when you would have ordered the horses put to and driven off to try to scotch the scandal."

"You know, sometimes I think, if I had interfered less with Clara and Harry, they might have been more responsible, like you. Listen to this. Harry is still coming in October, but not until he has seen to the training of his new hunter, the repairs to the stable and the dredging of the lake. Does that sound like our Harry?"

"Not much. Are you sure he isn't funning?"

"I don't think so. His letters aren't full of questions anymore, so much as information about Amberly. I really grow quite optimistic about him," Richard said, folding the letter and relaxing against the tree.

"You grow complacent. You haven't had a harsh word for anyone since we got married."

He slid down and rested his head in her lap. "That's because everything is perfect now, each and every day. We shall have more days together than we can count, and they can all be as wonderful as this one."

She brushed his hair with her fingers. "Sleep if you can for a while. I have worn you out." She guarded his rest like the lady fair of some weary knight who had, at last, finished his quest.

* * * * *

Harlequin Historicals®

COMING NEXT MONTH

#227 MARIAH'S PRIZE—Miranda Jarrett
In this installment of the *Sparhawk* series, a desperate Mariah West
convinces jaded Gabriel Sparhawk to captain her sloop, never guessing
at his ulterior motives.

#228 THE HIGHLANDER—Ruth Langan
Scottish chieftain Dillon Campbell abducted Lady Leonora Wilton as an
act of revenge against the English. But one look into Leonora's eyes and
it became an act of love.

#229 SIMON'S LADY—Julie Tetel
The marriage between Simon de Beresford and Lady Gwyneth had been
arranged to quell a Saxon uprising, yet the Saxon bride has much more
than *peace* on her mind.

#230 SWEET SONG OF LOVE—Merline Lovelace
When knight Richard Fitzhugh was called to battle, he left behind a meek
child bride given to him by the king. So who was the curvaceous beauty
who now greeted him as *husband*?

AVAILABLE NOW:

#223 UNICORN BRIDE
Claire Delacroix

#225 TIMELESS
DeLoras Scott

#224 A WARRIOR'S WAY
Margaret Moore

#226 HOMEPLACE
Laurel Ames

Fifty red-blooded, white-hot, true-blue hunks
from every State in the Union!

Look for MEN MADE IN AMERICA! Written by some of
our most popular authors, these stories feature fifty of the
strongest, sexiest men, each from a different state in the
union!

Two titles available every month at your favorite retail
outlet.

In July, look for:

ROCKY ROAD by Anne Stuart (Maine)
THE LOVE THING by Dixie Browning (Maryland)

In August, look for:

PROS AND CONS by Bethany Campbell (Massachusetts)
TO TAME A WOLF by Anne McAllister (Michigan)

You won't be able to resist MEN MADE IN AMERICA!

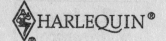

HARLEQUIN®

Weddings, Inc.

Harlequin Books requests the pleasure of your company this June in Eternity, Massachusetts, for WEDDINGS, INC.

For generations, couples have been coming to Eternity, Massachusetts, to exchange wedding vows. Legend has it that those married in Eternity's chapel are destined for a lifetime of happiness. And the residents are more than willing to give the legend a hand.

Beginning in June, you can experience the legend of Eternity. Watch for one title per month, across all of the Harlequin series.

HARLEQUIN BOOKS... NOT THE SAME OLD STORY!

DESTINY'S WOMEN

Sexy, adventurous historical romance at its best!

May 1994
ALENA #220. A veteran Roman commander battles to
subdue the proud, defiant queen he takes to wife.

July 1994
SWEET SONG OF LOVE #230. Medieval is the tale of an
arranged marriage that flourishes despite all odds.

September 1994
SIREN'S CALL #236. The story of a dashing Greek sea captain
and the stubborn Spartan woman he carries off.

Three exciting stories from Merline Lovelace, a fresh new
voice in Historical Romance.

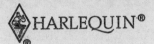

HARLEQUIN®

COMING SOON TO
A STORE NEAR YOU...

CHANCE
OF A LIFETIME

By *New York Times* Bestselling Author

This July, look for CHANCE OF A LIFETIME
by popular author
JAYNE ANN KRENTZ.

After Abraham Chance had wrongly implicated her sister in
an embezzlement scam, Rachel Wilder decided to do her
own sleuthing, posing as his housekeeper. Not only was
Chance onto her deception, he was uncovering a
passion in her even more consuming
than revenge....

Watch for CHANCE OF A LIFETIME, available in July
wherever Harlequin books are sold.

HARLEQUIN®

Don't miss these Harlequin favorites by some of our most
distinguished authors!
And now, you can receive a discount by ordering two or more titles!

HT #25551	THE OTHER WOMAN by Candace Schuler	$2.99 ☐
HT #25539	FOOLS RUSH IN by Vicki Lewis Thompson	$2.99 ☐
HP #11550	THE GOLDEN GREEK by Sally Wentworth	$2.89 ☐
HP #11603	PAST ALL REASON by Kay Thorpe	$2.99 ☐
HR #03228	MEANT FOR EACH OTHER by Rebecca Winters	$2.89 ☐
HR #03268	THE BAD PENNY by Susan Fox	$2.99 ☐
HS #70532	TOUCH THE DAWN by Karen Young	$3.39 ☐
HS #70540	FOR THE LOVE OF IVY by Barbara Kaye	$3.39 ☐
HI #22177	MINDGAME by Laura Pender	$2.79 ☐
HI #22214	TO DIE FOR by M.J. Rodgers	$2.89 ☐
HAR #16421	HAPPY NEW YEAR, DARLING by Margaret St. George	$3.29 ☐
HAR #16507	THE UNEXPECTED GROOM by Muriel Jensen	$3.50 ☐
HH #28774	SPINDRIFT by Miranda Jarrett	$3.99 ☐
HH #28782	SWEET SENSATIONS by Julie Tetel	$3.99 ☐

Harlequin Promotional Titles

#83259	UNTAMED MAVERICK HEARTS	$4.99 ☐
	(Short-story collection featuring Heather Graham Pozzessere,	
	Patricia Potter, Joan Johnston)	

(limited quantities available on certain titles)

	AMOUNT	$
DEDUCT:	**10% DISCOUNT FOR 2+ BOOKS**	$
	POSTAGE & HANDLING	$
	($1.00 for one book, 50¢ for each additional)	
	APPLICABLE TAXES*	$ _____
	TOTAL PAYABLE	$ _____
	(check or money order—please do not send cash)	

To order, complete this form and send it, along with a check or money order for the
total above, payable to Harlequin Books, to: **In the U.S.:** 3010 Walden Avenue,
P.O. Box 9047, Buffalo, NY 14269-9047; **In Canada:** P.O. Box 613, Fort Erie, Ontario,
L2A 5X3.

Name: _____

Address: _____ City: _____

State/Prov.: _____ Zip/Postal Code: _____

*New York residents remit applicable sales taxes.
 Canadian residents remit applicable GST and provincial taxes.

HBACK-AJ